Love & a Gangsta

A NOVEL BY
ERICK S GRAY

WHERE
HIP HOP
LITERATURE
BEGINS...

© 2009 Augustus Publishing, Inc.
ISBN: 978-0-9792816-4-8

Novel by Erick S Gray
Edited by Anthony Whyte
Creative Direction & Design by Jason Claiborne
Photography By Sanyi Gomez

Augustus Publishing paperback July 2009
www.augustuspublishing.com

Acknowledgements

I endured some trials and tribulations that made me bend, but not break, that made me bruised, but not broken, that made me frown, but with faith, I always come around. And without a strong mind, and strong support from some outstanding people in my life (They know who they are) Thank you.

First off, I got to thank the Lord my personal savior for all that he has done for me. I know that without Him that I am nothing and I give all glory to Him.

But I have to thank all my readers, fans, family, and my fellow authors who supported me all these years. Those that know me know that I've been through some hard times—
The road would have been much unsteady and challenging. I stumbled a few times, but always caught my grip and stood tall and say to myself no rest till I reach my success.

It doesn't get easier, we only get stronger.

I would love to have y'all comment me on my book, so get at me by email *grayspencer2000@yahoo.com*

Is it truly better to be feared than loved...?

Good judgment comes from experience.
A lot of that comes from bad judgment...

Prologue 2002

Soul reclined on the tattered green couch with Alexis crushed against him. Clad in a black thong and skimpy white shirt, her curvaceous figure was barely covered. Soul was staring at Alexis's D size jugs but his mind was on America, who had been his wifey for five years. Their relationship was supposed to be going strong. Soul quickly glanced at his Rolex, five in the morning. He was tired but knew he had to finish packing up the work that was on the coffee table in front of him. Two keys of uncut cocaine, three keys of Ecstasy, and a loaded .9mm were on the cluttered table in front of Soul.

It had been Soul's world since he sold his first vial of crack when he was ten, and got his first piece of ass when he was eleven. Hustling had been all he knew and loved. America was the only other love. *Another half-hour and I'll get back to work*, Soul thought, closing his eyes. It was five-thirty. Alexis was nestled against him and suddenly he felt her tugging at his zipper.

"You don't get enough?" he asked.

"Go ahead and sleep. Let me do me, baby," Alexis replied, tugging at his thick piece of meat while stroking him hard again.

Soul didn't resist. He positioned his hands behind his head and allowed Alexis to pull his dick and watched as she began sucking it. With her moistened lips wrapped tightly around his member, she took him deep down her throat.

"Hmm, hmm… Damn shit… Oh… Goddamn!"

He grabbed her thick weave and pushed her face further down on his lap. In a few minutes, Soul was in bliss and ready to explode. Suddenly loud knocking on the door interrupted her head game.

Soul reacted quickly, pushing Alexis to the carpet. Frantically pulling up his jeans, he quickly began packing up the work.

Bang — Bang — Bang.

"Police, open up now!"

The apartment door had heavy-duty security. The reinforced steel doors would give Soul time before the police barged in. Alexis helped him snatched up the drugs off the table and ran for the bathroom. They started flushing the works.

The banging against the door could be heard above the flushing of the toilet. Three keys washed away into the sink and bathtub. Alexis watched sweating, her fingers covered with residue. Soul in a flash tore open the bag of pills and tossed it down the drain.

Soul dashed to recover the gun still on the table. It was too late. Police pounded the door in and had already rushed in with their guns drawn. The small living room became even tinier with strange faces, flashing badges, papers and a sea of blue vests with NYPD markings.

"Get down! Get the fuck down, now!" One of the men in blue ordered.

Swarming Soul, they forced him to the floor. Restraining him with his arms behind, he was handcuffed forcefully and led out. They dragged Alexis, kicking and screaming from the bathroom.

Within minutes, both Alexis and Soul were in police custody. They watched as police ransacked the apartment. The only thing left for them to seize was the loaded 9mm and the ecstasy Alexis wasn't able to flush.

A beady-eyed sergeant looked at Soul, "You going to jail now, muthafucka! You fuck with us, we fuck with you… Get this nigger out of my sight and book him for gun possession and drugs."

It was a sticky situation and Soul sighed. Watching the cops hauled Alexis butt-ass naked out the door, Soul knew he had fucked up. They shackled him in iron bracelets and led him away. Soul was busy thinking how he was going to explain it all to America.

1

Life is not always a matter
of holding good cards.

But sometimes playing a
poor hand well...

America
2006 Jamaica, Queens

Finally the day I thought about for four long years was here. In the shower, the water cascading off my brown skin, thinking about his touch made my nipples swell in anticipation. I remember his hands caressing me night after night. My thoughts left my thighs shaking in excitement

I wanted to be oh so fresh for him. I kept myself pure for years just because I love him. My girlfriends thought that I was crazy, going without dick for so long. When you're strongly in love with a man why fuck another. I was longing for only one to be inside me. The thought of him coming back to me soon was sexual satisfying. Don't get me wrong, I love sex, but if it wasn't with Omar, then I was cool and did without until he returned.

Omar captured my heart the very first time we met. He was from the streets, but had a strong aura and I accepted him. Soon afterwards, he took my virginity and I wanted to have his babies.

On the streets, he was known as Soul. He rapped, played the piano, and the guitar. His musical gifts were phenomenal and he was a great dancer. Soul played basketball like he belonged in the pros. Most of all, he was a gentlemen. Despite his street reputation, my baby knew how to take care of me inside and outside the bedroom.

Omar wasn't perfect. Like every other man on this planet, he had flaws. The streets possessed him, and sometimes hustling and hanging with his homeboys got in the way of his talents.

Soul was a crack dealer. He got into too many fights. He drank too much. A rumor was floating around the hood that he was cheating on me. I looked beyond his bad qualities and wanted us to be together forever. Soul was my first, and I wanted him to be my last.

I met him when I was fifteen and he was seventeen. Back then he'd hangout with his boys in front of the bodega on the corner of Supthin and South Road. Soul was hustling and getting into trouble like all the youths on the corner.

He was cute and his style was different from his peers. They wore their pants low and sagging off their butts, but Omar rocked khakis and wore his jeans with a belt. They sported Timberlands, but you would catch my baby in Gucci loafers or soft bottom shoes, sometimes he would wear a suit and wing tips. While his friends wore cornrows, Omar took a trip to the barbershop once a week and kept his low shadow in style. His boys wore jewelry like they took advice from Mr. T. Omar sported a thin gold chain and a small cross his mother had given him.

One cool summer day, Omar bumped into me as I was coming out of the bodega carrying groceries for my aunt. We locked eyes briefly. I remained silent and walked passed the same group of boys who lingered in front of the store on the daily. I was walking down the block and heard someone running behind me. Startled, I spun around and saw Omar jogging up to me.

"Hey hold up, youngin'."

"Youngin'?" I snapped. "Please, you're barely older than me."

"Yo, let me carry that for you," he chuckled.

"Why?" I answered reluctantly.

"It would be the polite thing to do. Besides, you're too small to be carrying that huge bag."

"I was doing fine for half a block without your help. Does it look like I'm struggling?"

"Yo, you got some mouth. How old are you?" He smiled.

"Old enough."

"You feisty, girl. I like that," he countered.

"Whateva!" I said, walking away.

Omar was persistent. He then said, "Being a man, I'm not going to let you carry these bags to your crib by yourself. My mama raised me better than that."

"Oh, she did, huh? And did she teach you about harassment too?"

"Harassment? Yo, why you coming at me like that, shorty? I'm just tryin' to help you?"

I stared at him with a grim look.

"You don't trust me, huh? I look like a guy who's gonna take your bag, huh?" He asked with the warmest smile. It spread from ear to ear and

ERICK S GRAY

was contagious.

"See, there's that smile I was lookin' for."

"Oh just shut up about it," I joked.

He took the bags from me and we walked side by side to my home. I was attracted to the swagger of this lanky six-foot frame cut with six-pack abs and nice arms. He wore denim shorts, wife-beater, sporting new red and white Jordan's.

"So what's your name, beautiful?"

His onyx eyes went around my curves. He licked his full lips. I paused not wanting to tell him. My mother, before she passed away, named me *America*. It sounded patriotic, but I dreaded the first day of school when the teachers would do roll call. They would reach America and I saw the perplexed look on their faces. It was as if they weren't reading it right.

"America…?" Teachers used to ask incredulously.

All the kids would laugh. The first week of school, my name would be the butt of everyone's joke. That was the only thing they could joke about with me because I was cute, and popular with the boys and some of the girls liked me.

"My name's America, okay?"

I was waiting for him to laugh. Surprisingly, he didn't.

"I like that, America… God bless America," he said.

I smiled.

Omar stayed awhile when we got to my crib, and I took the groceries to my aunt. We talked for hours that day and many more. Soon, we became inseparable. He became my heart. We spent days together, talking, laughing, and falling in love with each other.

My thoughts were with him everyday of his incarceration. I visited him often trying to keep his mind at ease and reminded him what he had waiting for him when he got out. I couldn't wait to nestle in his arms again. Part of me was missing every day without him. I yearned for his touch, and to feel his breath against mines. I hungered for our bodies to be entwined, and for him to devour me. My pussy throbbed uncontrollably, and my panties were saturated with escaping juices thinking of him.

I was trying to cool off in the shower, but it got no better. I was

13

so fucking horny there was an ache in my body that refused to leave. It got intense because in less than twenty-four hours my baby will be loving every curve, shape and inch of me until my pussy put him to sleep.

Four years of waiting, and being faithful to my boo. I sighed ready to explode. This scene had repeated so many times, I lost count of how many times I masturbated alone in the dark with the toys I had purchased over the years. Visions of Omar grinding and gyrating between my legs kept rewinding in my mind. Many nights I had stayed up sleepless, thinking of Omar, a pillow between my thighs while fondling my tits.

There were many nights of long cold showers. Being horny and alone without my man around was a most unbearable situation. I'd pour my pain into songs and poems, many days and evenings. The words were so emotional, repeating them filled me with sadness and became unbearable.

I smiled removing the showerhead and putting one leg up on the porcelain tub. Then I positioned the spurting water next to my animated kitty-cat, setting the speed just right as the water rushed against my pulsating pussy. Moans escaped my lips and I moved my free hand in between my thighs, masturbating my clit. Moving my fingertips faster in a circular motion, I was losing control. The spurting water against my over-excited pussy lips did the trick.

"Ah, hmm… Hmm. Ooh yeah! Oh God, I missed you so much, dear Omar," I cried, having an explosive orgasm.

Thoughts of my man making love to me were embedded in my mind. His dick prints were etched on my vagina walls and made me feel like he was inside. But tonight there'd be no further need for pretension. My man finally will be home after four long years of keeping his pussy pure and tight. I peed while my lips purred.

2

The biggest troublemaker you'll ever face.
Watches you from the mirror every morning...

Omar

Pussy was the only thing on my mind. True story. Four years of not getting any, and I was thirsty for my boo-boo. My sexual desires got even stronger within the week of my release. I thought about my girl everyday, all day. She was the first and last thing on my mind when I woke up and went to sleep at nights. She was the only reason why I survived in here for the last four years.

America came to see my like twice a month, and I loved her for that. The trip upstate was about seven hours to Franklin Correctional facility in Malone, New York. Sometimes she did the drive alone, or took the greyhound to come see me. America always came to see me looking her finest. I really hated to see her leave.

Her visiting me was a gift and a curse. Seeing my woman looking so fine and sexy was a true gift. I couldn't do nothing but give her a hug, a kiss, and hold hands across the table. My dick was so hard, it felt like it wanted to escape from my pants and rip into her warm flesh. But there was no excessive display of affection during visits, my curse for being here.

Pictures of America, her songs, and letters plastered my cell wall. Guards and cellmates envied me because I got at least three letters every week. Sometimes a poem or a song came from America. Every night before lights out, I read the soothing words she had written, fantasizing about warm days and long nights with her.

I would stare at a picture of the two of us together taken at Coney Island in the spring of '98, against the background of a painting of Jay Z holding up cash. We were young and looked cozy like we had no care. I was hugged up on her and both our smiles were ear to ear. The picture cost me five bucks but being locked up, it proved to be worth even more. It was the best of the good times. I was eighteen back then.

I remembered her attitude being a little rude when we first met. I thought she was cute. She was wearing lose fitted gray sweats, white T's and her feet looked small in a pair of white and blue Adidas. Her hair was in two long pigtails. The scent she had on made my heart do sprints. I saw her coming out of the store and couldn't let her just walk by me and not attempt to kick it to a girl so beautiful. America was trying to be reluctant, trying to spit fire as if she wasn't interested.

Up in my bunk, I continued peering at her photos. My abdominal muscle tightened as I reminisced over the first time we had sex. She was a virgin. I had been with lots of girls, but was intimate from the start. When it came to America, like she said, I made love to her. Before that I was just fucking girls.

America was different. My uncle, Ray gave me the keys to his basement apartment. Uncle Ray was a hustler like me and was always telling me how America was too fine a woman to ever let go.

"Boy, you treat her like the wonderful woman she is, and she'll treat you like the king you are. Always respect each other."

Uncle Ray was seventeen years my senior and he knew a lot about life. He was in and out of jail since I was in diapers. He had mad respect on the streets.

I brought America to my uncle's crib on a Friday night. She was the most nervous fifteen-year old I'd ever seen. We had been together for six weeks, and this sexual yearning I had for her was suffocating me.

She was wearing a denim skirt and pink halter. Her hair was in two long pigtails. My uncle's comfortable, one-bedroom bachelor's pad, with big screen television, and a great stereo system, made a good impression. She became less tense once she realized we would be alone. Besides a leather couch, and his bedroom set, he had no furniture since he was hardly home.

Uncle Ray had a king size bed in the bedroom. A mirror and drawers stood above a burgundy area rug with gold trim was spread out on the parquet floor. My uncle wasn't much of a decorator, but his place was nice enough to make America fill comfortable in.

I led America to the bedroom. She quietly followed. Then she touched me, stared at me with her soft brown eyes and smiled. She knew what time it was. I had made it all clear. I never wanted to mislead her in anything.

"Are you nervous?"

"A little," she giggled.

Her soft touch had me hard. I caressed her gently when we were near the bed. She felt relaxed in my arms. But I wanted to make sure she was ready for what was about to happen.

"Are you sure you're ready, America?"

Her eyes took on an aura of innocence, telling me that I'd have to lead and she'd follow me into our first sexual episode. I wouldn't have it any other way. It was a honor to be her first, but what I hoped for was to be her last. She smiled faintly and nodded.

America sat next to me on the bed. I moved slowly, but lust wanted me to tear off her clothes, skip foreplay and fuck the shit out of her. Slow down my beating heart, she was different and I had to take my time.

I moved my hand up and down her smooth open thigh. My dick pulsated in my pants. I pressed my lips against hers and kissed her good. Our tongues tangled, wrestling as our breathing became one. I moved my hand further up her skirt until I felt the wetness of her panties. She flinched but didn't pull away.

She stared at me for a moment. I was wondering what was on her mind. She remained silent and I prayed that she wanted to continue. My dick was harder than the man of steel and if I couldn't get pussy, then I'd be in for a very bad night. Fortunately, she wanted to continue. America positioned herself on her back and braved a smile.

"I want you to be my first, Omar. I love you and I trust you," she softly whispered.

I pulled up her skirt, and removed her panties unhurriedly. She reclined with her head amongst the plush pillows on the bed. Her breath became louder her round breast smiled at me while her curly pussy hairs, barely covered moistened lips. They seemed clamped together tightly like a bank vault after closing. I definitely knew she was pure now.

I moved my lips closer to her honey brown skin, kissing her gently starting with her belly button. She moaned a little. My hands slid up her chest, she cupped her hands over mine, and pressed them to her breasts. Her tits tasted like soft fruits.

Spreading her legs wider, I began kissing her inner thighs. Her breathing turned into moaning when my tongue and lips neared her pussy.

I don't normally be eating out pussy, but I was willing to go all the way with her. She trusted me and was giving me something she couldn't take back.

I gradually opened up the lips between her young thighs with my tongue and mouth. With my head nestled between her warm thighs my tongue began piercing into her, and she released enough juices for me to drink.

"Ooh… Ah… Ooh yes this feels real good oh… Oh yes!"

America gripped my head and held it in place. With her thighs clamped around my ears, she dug her nails into my shoulders and screamed, "Jesus Christ…Oh God yes!"

I looked up and smiled when I saw her beautiful eyes rolled back in her head. I smiled when all I saw was pure ivory. My dick never felt so hard I thought it was about to rip through my boxers. America looked like she was still in la-la land after my licking. I stood up dropped my jeans, soon afterwards my boxers fell. I stared at America in all her glory and held my big black dick.

America's eyes were wide when she saw my erection ready for action. She was beautiful, and untouched. And my dick was extra fucking hard with just that thought alone.

"You got condoms right?"

"Yeah."

I went into my pants pocket on the floor and removed a box of Magnums. I hastily tore the box open, removing a condom and ripped it open. Then I rolled the condom back on my thickness, and climbed atop positioning myself between her inviting thighs. She was tight I tried to slide right into her, but it wasn't happening. America gasped and grabbed my shoulders. I held my weight off of her, and continued to ease inches of myself into her. It was pleasurable but it was work.

"Ouch ugh… Oh shit! Omar slower… Oh baby, baby please, it's too big!"

Her eyes were tightly shut while her nails dug into my shoulders. I pushed a few more inches into her, slowly opening her bit by bit. I could feel her juices all over me. It took an hour of slow pushing before finally getting into my rhythm. A few more minutes and her hot, tight love-box caused an immense explosion like I never felt before. We didn't have sex for another two months after the first time. America proved to be worth the wait.

Lying in my bunk staring at her photo thinking about the first time we had sex got me hard. My hand was in my pants holding my thick, pulsating dick. I was slowly jerking-off and staring at America's picture.

"You 'bout to see home soon, and be in some pussy again, and you in here beatin' off. Go head wit' that, Soul," my cellmate, Rahmel interjected.

"Yo, this shit feel like a fucking dream, son. I can't believe a nigga's 'bout to go home," I said.

"Soul, you gettin' your freedom again, and your woman stayed by your side and held you down for four years. You're a blessed man. What's the first thing you gonna do when you get out?"

"Shit, I'm gonna take my woman and fuck her till my dick can't work anymore. And then I'm gonna wake up and do it all over again. I gotta make up for long lost time."

Rahmel laughed.

"You think I'm joking. I'm backed up. Shit, I'm 'bout to put in some work."

Rahmel took a seat on the bottom of my cot. He hunched over with his elbows pressed against his knees, fingers clasped together, and looked at me with some importance deep in his gaze.

"You got a second chance at life. Soul, I envy you, man. I got another five years behind these walls. Been denied parole three times because of violence in my past. The system doesn't think I'm ready to be released early, ain't that some shit… white man judging my rehabilitation, like he God and shit. Being in here, they take everything from you. Shit, Soul, I miss the touch, the smell, the feel, and even the taste of a woman. My wife died when I was five years in this hellhole, they wouldn't even let me attend her damn funeral. They said I was a threat to society. Now my daughter's gone, her grandmother had some nerve, moving my little girl to Texas. How she gonna take the only thing a man has left, and move her a thousand miles away. I know I've told you this before, but I feel you need to hear it again, Soul."

"I guess I can take you one more night, Rah."

"In here you got nothing, but out there, you got everything to look forward to. I spent fifteen years trying to be a father to my daughter behind these walls… Impossible. I missed my daughter's first steps, her first words, and her first day of school, cause I'm contained miles away from her like some fuckin' animal allowing for our children to make the same mistake we made."

"I hear you Rah."

"Do right by America, Soul. And don't come back to this place. You got many talents, take advantage of them. And you're fortunate to have a love one waiting for you behind these walls. Don't make her do time with you ever again. She doesn't deserve it. Every strong black woman deserves her man by her side, not on the inside. It'll be hard Soul, but don't be discouraged. You're gonna have some challenges come your way… Challenges make life interesting. Overcoming them makes life meaningful. Take that with you when you leave this place and please stop jerking off now."

I nodded. Rahmel got so deep that when he talked to you, you just shut up and listen. An O.G from South Jamaica, Rahmel was in his mid thirties, and well respected wherever he went. He used to kick knowledge to his little brother, Omega and me, history, current events, politics, and science. I mean shit that you thought he didn't know anything about he would lecture it to us once in a while. But when beef came around, you saw a different side of him then. It was the side of him that got him locked up.

Back in the fall of 1990 Rahmel caught two bodies on Guy R. Brewer and South Road. One was a cop. I was ten when he was sentenced. In the beginning, Omega took it hard we both looked up to Rahmel. He used to call me his little brother and always treated me like family.

"Soul spit a lil' sump'n for me, since this being your last night in here," he said.

"No doubt, what you wanna hear?"

"Sump'n to keep me up," he smiled.

"Yo, yo, yo, as I sit alone and try to keep my head above the sky, insecurity got my mind blackened like a soulless child. I do my best to keep my head above the rest, when I feel too stressed, I break down and cry like the rest. Sometimes I feel my life is lost, everything I achieve comes wit' a cost. Wanna ball my fist and come storming out with full force, show the world that I'm much more than a ghetto ugly child. Got a few friends that I trust, while the rest I give dap to and keep tabs on the most. Determination in these eyes you see, bleed, seek richness and greatness with every breath that I breathe. My life was ignorant in my past, sex, drugs, and uneducated, I see why the white man laugh. My heart dies every time I get disrespected by my own kind, wish it was peace back on the block, when these fools' attitude is misery and just don't give a fuck, make this buck and shoot everything up! I wish the Lord's hands could come down and wash me from all my sins, but I feel the power of the devil sometimes possessing me within. Telling me it feels good son, damn, kill them niggas and hit them tight skins again. It's outrageous how some of us became so weak within!"

"Yeah, preach young blood, preach on. Follow your heart, believe in yourself and Him and the Lord will lead you from there," Rahmel said giving me dap. "Look out for my brother, Omega once you get home."

"True indecd, Rah. I'll make good on my word."

3

Strong people surmount obstacles,
struggle against adversity and survive...

America

I glanced at the time for the umpteenth time in one hour. The seven-hour trip to Malone, New York was tiresome, but I didn't do it alone. My girl, Joanna made the trip with me, sharing driving chores. Around three in the morning, we left Queens to get to Franklin Correctional facility by ten.

I was a kid on Christmas Eve waiting for Omar to walk out the gates and in my arms. My body was flooded with anxiety and excitement all at once. All I could think about was, finally loving my man the way I wanted to without any restrictions. I tried to remain composed in the passenger seat.

My short denim skirt and tight blouse felt constricting. Every breath I took caused my chest to rise in desire, accentuating my firm breasts. I was comfortable in open toe sandals. Manicure, pedicure and hair were in place. I showered in Eternity, by Calvin Klein, the fragrance that Omar loved.

"Shit, I don't know how you lasted girl, four years without any dick. Shit if he was my man, and he was locked up like that, he better know that I'm renting this pussy out to the next until he's out. A woman need maintenance, I just couldn't be doing the Virgin Mary thing like you did," Joanna said jokingly but was actually serious.

"That's the reason you don't have a man," I snapped back. "Guys love a woman that's loyal."

"Yeah, but behind your back he fuckin' that bitch, this bitch, the bitch that works in K-mart, even the handicap bitch down the street. But you slip up one time and he gonna wanna start actin' all crazy. Niggas ain't shit. They dish it out, but when it's payback time, they start actin' like you just killed their mama, cuz you get caught cheating once."

"Omar is for real, he always was and will always be," I assured her. "He'd be stupid to fuck up what took ten years to build."

"Just be careful. You're definitely coming up with that music, girlfriend. You got some good fucking pipes that'll give Mariah a run for her money. If you don't do sump'n with it and blow, I'm gonna smack the taste out your mouth my damn self. Just because your man is getting out today, doesn't mean you should stop what you've been working on these past four years."

I smiled. "Thanks for the support; I didn't know you care like that."

"America, you know we go way back. I gotta stay looking out for you girlfriend. 'Specially as much as bitches be hating on us because we the shit. You're the only bitch from 'round the way that can keep up with my fine ass when it comes to style and pizzazz."

"I agree. You're keeping up with me," I joked.

"Don't get it twisted, I'm Beyonce and you're Kelly. Okay…?"

"Whatever!"

"But on the real…I don't wanna see you get hurt, and I know you're all horny and hot after being backed up. Before you wipe the cobwebs from your pussy and give him some, you better have him do a HIV test," she suggested.

"What?"

"He's been locked up for four years without any pussy. You used to tell me that his dick stayed up more than the American flag."

"Unless he was with some female in there, he's good. Omar ain't no faggot," I spat.

"Shoot, you don't know what went on with him behind those walls. Yeah, he can start out good but you've heard the stories. Niggas switching up while they inside, he probably slipped and fell into something, and never stopped falling," she proclaimed.

"Omar ain't no homo-thug, okay Joanna?"

"You never know he could have the monster."

"If you wanna stay my girl, please don't go there," I warned.

"The monster knows no boundaries and I'm saying—"

"Joanna…!" I shouted cutting her off. "Do not go there," I said firmly.

Joanna knew Omar better. And I truly felt appalled that she tried to imply he couldn't wait for me.

"I'm sorry," Joanna said.

"We've been best friends since the ninth grade, Joanna. I know you are just looking out. So it's already forgotten."

Joanna was biracial and tan skinned. Her hips were thick with a curvy figure, and blessed with a phat booty. She was so beautiful that she caught a couple of print gigs in magazines. She had mad respect, because of her father, Montana. He was a notorious drug kingpin who had Merrick Blvd and Baisley locked down back in the eighties and early nineties. Her father was Dominican, her mother Italian.

"America, you're kinda quiet, you okay?"

"I'm fine."

"You're still not mad, right?"

"No, I understood where you were coming from. But to set it straight, I trust Omar, and I know he ain't like that," I stated, looking her square in her eyes.

"I know, but you hear stories," she said.

A loud beeping and humming sound disturbed me, as I was about to reply. I noticed the tall steel reinforced gate of the prison sliding back.

"Oh thank you God," I shouted. "I think he's coming out now."

I saw Omar walking out the prison, a smile on his face. He was dressed in some worn out looking gray sweats, a plain green T-shirt, and had a small bag in his hand.

"That's him, my baby!"

I made a quick exit out the car and ran towards him like I had no sense. He dropped the bag he had in his hand and opened his arms to greet me.

I leaped into his arms, straddling him as he held me in his grip and close to him. I immediately started kissing him, shoving my tongue in his mouth, not giving him a chance to say one word to me. I felt his warm breath in my mouth, and his hands clutching my ass, with my legs wrapped tightly around him.

Tears of joy flooded and he let me go, looking me up and down. I flung my arms around my man and stared into his handsome face.

"I missed you, baby," I exclaimed, hugging him tighter.

"I missed you too," he answered in a soft deep voice.

I couldn't let go. We held each like this without interference. It felt like I was dreaming.

"I appreciate you driving way out here," he said.

"Baby, I wanted to see you the minute you stepped out of that place. Look at you," I said, eyeing his gear. "They couldn't give you something better to put on, this ain't you?"

"I know," he said.

"I got you," I said.

I embraced him passionately and gave him a deep rooted kiss again. I didn't want to let this man go. I felt this sudden bulge in his sweats rub up against me. I had him hard.

"I know, true indeed," he said smiling.

"Don't worry, baby, I'm definitely gonna take care of that once we get back home," I said squeezing his hard on gently.

I missed his dick so much, that I wanted to fuck him right there in front of the jail.

Beep! Beep! Beep!

I heard the horn, and then Joanna shouting, "Would y'all two hurry up! It ain't like Queens is right around the corner from this fucking place."

"I see you brought this bitch with you, huh."

"Yeah, I had to, it's a long drive."

"Indeed, it's cool. I'm glad to see another familiar face," he smiled.

We walked back to the car with me in his arms, looking like a teenage couple again. I couldn't wait to melt in his grip and pour myself all over him.

"Hey Joanna, I see you still loud and ghetto," Omar said, as he hopped into the backseat of my sliver Acura Legend.

"You ain't drop the soap in there, did you, Omar?" Joanna countered back with her smart mouth.

"You still got jokes, huh bitch?" Omar snapped back.

"But who's been the bitch for the past four years, huh? How did Bubba treat his number one ho?"

"Fuck you!" Omar replied jokingly.

He and Joanna always had jokes on each other. They had that love hate thing going on.

"You know we missed you around the way," Joanna said.

"Yeah, true indeed, I definitely missed y'all," he said.

I turned around in my seat, and couldn't stop staring at him. It was like seeing him for the first time. Omar smiled back at me. His eyes were speaking to me and his body language was secretly seducing me.

"I love you," he smiled.

"I love you, back," I returned.

Joanna was driving, we informed Omar about changes around the way. But he basically knew who was locked up and who was dead already. Joanna took the first drive, and then I took over three hours later. Omar rode shotgun with me and Joanna was in the back taking a nap. My man was finally by my side, where he belonged.

4

Unless a man undertakes more
than he possibly can.
He will never do all he can...

Omar

An hour away from the city, I was too excited to even close my eyes and take a nap. I'd been up since five in the morning. The adrenaline flowing through me had me hyped. Being almost home in Queens had me feeling like a young boy on his way back home from camp.

I glanced at America, and she looked happy. She caught me checking her out, smiled back at me and blew me a kiss. The CD playing was a new young singer named Bobby Valentino. I gently bobbed my head to the track, *Tell Me*.

"What're you looking at?" she smiled.

"You," I said.

"Why…?"

"You look good, baby," I said.

"I always look good."

"Right now you're looking really good, indeed."

She smiled again.

"I can't wait to stretch my dick up in you," I said placing my hand on her thigh and gently squeezing.

"You best behave. I'm like a virgin again."

"Indeed, that's the fuck I'm talking about."

My fingers moved up her smooth brown skin, and wanted to continue. The bulge in my sweats became visible again. America noticed. I smiled.

"Tell him to behave, too."

America's foot pressed against the accelerator, slightly she opened her legs allowing my hand to slide up her skirt. Two fingers penetrated her tight, wet pussy. My index and middle fingers went deeper into her. She moaned and maneuvered the car through traffic. Her juices flowed over my hand, and felt my dick about to rip through my clothing as I continued to finger fuck her.

"Hmm, hmm, you better stop."

"I can't wait."

"You gonna have me crash if you keep this up," she said squirming around in her seat while trying to keep the Acura steady.

"True indeed." I said removing my hand and licked my fingers.

"You nasty boy," America smiled.

"Just trying to get a little taste before I get to the real thing," I chuckled.

"You waited over fourteen hundred and sixty days, another forty minutes won't hurt, hon."

"Tell that to my dick."

Hearing America chuckling made me even hornier. I wanted to grab her right here and end the drought but I glanced out the window and my attention was averted to NYC. We crossed the New York State Thruway Bridge and hit 87 south. Driving through the Bronx, the city seemed illuminated like a Christmas tree and looked alive. Lots of new cars were on the road. There were different models and makes of BMW's Mercedes, Lexus and SUV's. I used to push a black Lexus IS 300. I loved that car. I left it to my cousin, Greasy. I haven't heard from him in two years.

"I can't believe I'm finally home, baby," I said with a broad grin.

Joanna woke up as we crossed the Triboro Bridge; she yawned and peered out the window.

"Damn!" She said. "We home already…?"

"We're on the Grand Central, girl," America said.

"I know y'all muthafuckas were probably doing the nasty while my tired- ass was napping. I'm gonna roll down this freaking window. I ain't trying to smell fish all the way back home," she said.

"Joanna shut up. You always got sump'n stupid to say," America replied.

"Um okay, and you expect me to believe that. Omar ain't tryin' to talk, he tryin' to get busy," she countered. I smiled.

"See, he told on himself. Just don't be making me a Godmother anytime too soon."

Minutes later, we were in Jamaica, Queens, driving down the Van Wyck Expressway. I noticed the new Air Train in between the expressway. America told me that it's been up for two years and it took passengers from the Queens station, to JFK airport.

It was a quarter past nine when we dropped Joanna off at her crib on

Linden Blvd. It was a nice two level split home, with a backyard.

"Damn, Joanna, you living like this now," I said.

"Baby, this is all me, all day," she replied, getting out of the car.

I was impressed. It was still in Jamaica, but it looked respectable. I knew she was still getting some of her pops drug money. Even though her pops, Montana had been locked up for a minute. Joanna dated only get-money niggas, who were able to help maintain her lavish lifestyle. America made sure Joanna got inside safely and then drove off.

We drove to America's new place. She had a two-bedroom apartment on Merrick Blvd, and 109th Avenue. She had a new car, a new place, and a nice paying job working for Verizon Wireless and clocking fourteen fifty an hour. She was back in school, and making noise with her music. I even heard she put out a demo CD with six tracks. It was doing okay in the streets.

My baby definitely had stepped her game up. She knew some nigga with a studio in his basement and he looked out for her. But I knew sometimes a nigga ain't trying to look out for a bitch unless he trying to get some. I trust my shorty, and was convinced it was only business.

I had my seat reclined, and observed my past. We made our way down Linden Blvd, I tried to look for familiar faces and saw that they were putting up a lot of two family homes. It was still home to me and still my hood. We drove by some of my old spots and saw the bodega were still there.

"You heard from Omega lately?" I asked.

"Not in months."

I wanted to link up with him and find out what my crew been doing. Rahmel was concerned and wanted me to check on him. I had heard Omega was deep in the game. His name rang like bells and his rep was fierce around the way.

I followed America into her fourth floor apartment and was impressed by its décor and style. It was spacious, with ceiling fan and large window looking out on the city. A Dell 50-inch HD Plasma TV sat near a window, speakers were in every corner of the room, top with Nakimichi surround sound made me feel like you were at a movie theater. Parquet floors shimmered, and a large Isfahan area rug at the foot of a swanky leather sofa. Next to the kitchen chairs of contemporary oak and round table with a bouquet of red roses adorned her dining room set.

"Damn, baby, are you hustling?" I joked.

"This is yours too, baby," she said, walking up to me and wrapping her arms around me. "Welcome home." she firmly planted a kiss on my lips.

"I saved some of the money you left me before you got locked up," she whispered.

"What?"

"The fifty-thousand you stashed, I saved it and got us this place. I wanted you to come back home to something better. I didn't want you going back to South Road; you need a change of scenery, boo. And this is a new start for us and a family."

"I don't know what to say."

"Just promise never to leave me again. Be with me. I got you, baby. I got you. We can do this together. I want you by my side forever," she said.

We gazed into each other's eyes. Her eyes pleaded for me to leave the streets. She didn't say it directly, but I knew where this was going.

"I love you so much, Omar. I can't lose you again. I just couldn't bear it."

Her eyes became glossy, filled with emotions. We embraced. Her angelic features and soft touch made me commit.

"I promise I will never leave you again. I'm over the game, America. I've been doing a lot of thinking and I got too much talent to be wasting my life away on the streets. I fucked up once, and I ain't fucking up again. If it wasn't for you, I don't know where I would be right now. So you know what… Let's be a family and get married."

"Baby, are you…?

"I want you in my life forever."

She hugged me tight and confessed her love for me again. Her arms were wrapped tightly around me and she had tears trickling down her cheeks.

"I got a surprise for you."

"Pussy," I joked.

"No silly. Come here," she laughed grabbing my hand.

America led me into the second bedroom. I walked inside and got choked up. What she was doing for me is the epitome of what love should be. On the bed, she had dozens of gear sprawled out, Armani suits and dress shirts. At the end of the bed were Gucci and Kenneth Cole shoes.

"You is too much, baby. I don't know what to say," I said.

"My man, you represent me, and I represent you. We're a reflection of each other, and if I'm looking right, my man... No my husband is going to be right too."

We were wrapped in each other's arm, nestled together like an unborn in their mother's wound. I kissed her fervently. She was everything to me, and I wasn't trying to let her go.

After several minutes of endless affection, I pulled myself away from her and said, "Baby, I need a shower. I smell like that fucking prison. I want it off me. I ain't trying to be up on you an smelling like this."

"I understand, baby. Everything you need is in the bathroom. Go do you and I'll freshen up out here."

Her eyes stared into mines, reflecting love. She disappeared into the next bedroom and I walked into the bathroom. I quickly stripped away the unpleasant clothes that I had on, and was butt naked in her rose-pink bathroom. I stared at myself in the bathroom mirror over the sink. I had to admire myself. My physique was breathtaking. After four years of lifting weights with Rahmel and his peoples, I had a eight-pack, bulging biceps, defined triceps, and my back was muscular broad. I had one tattoo and that was of my girl's name, it was embedded into my right arm in bold italic scribble.

I reflected on my troubled life as I peered at my image. I was a thug, making at least a grand a day selling crack. I used to push guns. I shot people, even killed a man, unbeknownst to America. I drank, partied like the end of the world was coming, and cheated on my boo with countless of women. And yet through my wild ways, America still stood by me, treating me like her man. While the rest of the world saw me as a threat to society, she stuck with me. When I got dragged out my mama's crib by half dozen cops, America cursed them out like she was the one who birth me.

She was by my side when I caught a knife to my side because of beefing over a corner. She was in the hospital everyday, praying, asking God to heal me, and nurturing me back to health. She sat through my trial with me, everyday encouraging me to be strong and pray. When I got sentenced, she promised no matter how far they sent me she'd always write and visit.

I hated myself for putting that woman through so much. She didn't deserve it. I didn't want to be the same man I was four years ago. I wanted to be different and become better for her.

Rahmel coached me. He knew how I was feeling. When I first got jailed, all I could think about was America, wondering if she'd be faithful while I was on the inside. I was the only man she'd ever been with, and when you're alone in your cell, you think about all kinds of craziness.

I did her wrong, because I cheated on her with women that lusted after me since I was fourteen. And some I even had unprotected sex with, risking my life and hers. I didn't care. It was always about me, and with Omega, I felt invincible.

I continued looking at my image, and I didn't like what I saw. A handsome dude was my reflection, but on the inside, I felt ugly and deformed. I felt twisted with conflict. I wanted to change. I needed to change. The fear that I might be weak and fall back into my old ways gripped me. When I was in jail, there was no temptation for me. I read a lot of books and worked out, and took guidance from Rahmel. It was easy on the inside. I was home now and it was a different story.

I turned on the shower and got in. The warm water felt good. I was alone. I felt comfortable. It was quiet and tranquil. It had been a while since I had a long shower like this. I spent about twenty minutes in the shower, enjoying every minute of it.

I heard a knock and then America saying, "Baby, hurry up. Why you got me waiting?"

"I'm coming, baby."

Turning off the water, I jumped out and reached for my towel, drying myself. I looked at my reflection, wrapping the towel around my waist and promising to do right by my woman this time around.

I stepped out the bathroom and into the soothing and sexual melody of some R. Kelly's, *Honey Love* playing softly. The bass was bumping from the speakers at a comfortable volume. I looked down and noticed another dozen of silk rose petals at my feet leading a trail to the main bedroom. I smiled.

I followed the trail and walked into the bedroom, where it was dimly lit with four French vanilla candles burning, creating a soft, yellow vanilla fragrance in the bedroom.

"It's about time," America said with lust in her eyes.

She was on the bed, upright on her knees and naked with her honey brown skin shimmering gracefully in the candle lit room. Her nipples were hard, her long sinuous hair falling stylishly down to her shoulders and her pussy trimmed. She wore the diamond, seed pearl, sapphire, platinum and pink gold necklace that I bought for her before my incarceration. It stopped at the tip of her breasts. I took in all of her and felt my dick hardening under the towel.

"Come get what's yours," she smiled.

"Damn, you is looking extra right now," I proclaimed.

She smiled. It was contagious. Because when she smiled, I smiled.

I heard the CD changing to its next track, and Marques Houston, *Naked,* played. She gestured with her index finger for me to come to her, dividing her thighs apart a little bit, and had her other hand in between her thighs as she tenderly massaged her clit.

I walked up to the foot of the bed, and she came to me, still on her knees, and pulled at my towel.

"You heard what the man said, I want you naked baby. I miss big daddy. I want you to park that thing into me tonight," she whispered in my ear.

Her warm breath tickled my skin. She touched me while untying the towel from around my waist, it drop to the floor. I was blissfully hard. She pressed her luscious cherry flavored lips against mines. I felt her hand travel south, reaching for my thick dick. Her thin fingers coiled around my nine inches of thickness. She began moving her hand pleasingly up and down my long shaft as we kissed fervently, our naked bodies pressed against each other.

"Oh my God your body is so hard and muscular. Please fuck me, baby" she whispered in my ear.

I clutched her petite nude body and held her close to me. I moved my hands down her backside and rested them firmly against her ass. Cupping both cheeks, I lifted her up into my arms. She straddled me, and continued to saturate my neck, ear, and face with pleasant kisses.

I wanted to stick my dick in her as soon as we were vertical. I had other treats in mind. I pushed her down on the bed, her back meshed flat against the bed, with her knees up and legs spread. She just kept smiling.

"Do me, baby, take this pussy, please," she pleaded, her chest heaving up and down as sexual anxiety surged through her body.

I had her propped against two pillows, facing me. Opening her thighs wider, I penetrated her with my tongue. I began sucking and licking on her clit, while fingering her pussy. She squirmed and screamed as her legs quivered against my hard body.

"Ooh ah, ooh yes, baby, Omar...Oh, Omar, oh shit, ooh... Ooh yes...baby, baby!"

I went to work, eating her out feverishly. She gripped my head and held it in place, indicating to me that I was hitting her spot. She then clamped her thighs around my ears and dug her nails into my shoulders, screaming.

"Ohmygod! Ohmygod! Omar... Oh, I missed you so fucking much, baby!"

Her juices made my passion rise. Try as I may, I couldn't suck America dry. My dick got so hard it felt like my muscles were on fire. America gripped my throbbing rock hard penis and put it in her warm mouth. I was burning up.

I reached up and flipped her on her back, spreading her legs and getting in between. We locked eyes for a moment that said we truly loved each other.

Jagged Edge, *Promise* hummed in the background. I kept my weight off her and my arms outstretched in the push-up position.

"Baby please, I want you in me now," she pleaded.

Tears of joy mixed with our sweat. She ran her hands up and down my sturdy forearms. I almost cried but my dick took over and penetrated her. Slowly her walls opened up. It was tight like a virgin again. She moaned as I opened her gradually, spreading her lips wide apart with nine long inches of thickness.

Her juices flood me and I moaned, feeling the power of good pussy, tight, wet and ready. I pushed more of my dick in her and she grasped my arms tighter. My eyes rolled to the back of my head. Her love muscles contracted around my erection. I thrust myself into her.

"Sweet Jesus... Ooh, ooh, ooh... Yeah Omar. Fuck me good!"

Grinding my hips between her smooth warm thighs, our arms outstretched, I gripped her hands in mine. She pushed her pelvis against me, as I continued fucking her. Sweat poured. My hand under her butt, I raised her body close to me, making sure she felt every inch of my thickness. Her legs shook against my thighs. She dug her manicured nails into my back, leaving scratches that wouldn't heal for days. We panted and huffed, wrinkling the green satin sheets.

"Damn, baby, you got some good pussy... Whoa, whoa yes baby! You got some good pussy."

I grabbed her ass tighter as she bucked wildly. The position allowed me to have better momentum for a deeper, harder thrust. America let out a loud shriek. I wanted to take it nice and slow, but the feeling of pussy again after all this time, had me in a sexual frenzy.

I rolled onto my back, and America straddled me, pushing my dick into her love hole. She arched her back, grabbed my knees and went crazy on the dick, curving my shit inside of her. Now she was in control, and stretching my shit deep within her.

"Fuck me, Omar, fuck me! Fuck me! Ah, ah, ah, yeah!"

Her naked hips rocking backward and forward and gyrating against me, with her leaned forward and digging her nails into my chest.

"I'm... I'm coming, baby!"

I gripped her ass, pushing deeper and deeper into her, shortly after, I felt her juices pouring all over me. She shuddered, and hugged me tightly. I continued to thrust, pushing against her ass, and felt myself about to explode.

"Aw shit, I'm...!"

And soon afterwards, I burst into her. I fell against her my body trembling, making me feel like brand new.

5

Your love is all I need to proceed.
What's happening is so real in me...

America

Omar had me spent, as I lay nestled against my man with our bodies naked and sweaty against green satin sheets. After four years of being apart, we didn't miss a beat. When I felt his big dick open me up again, I started to cry. It was worth the wait. I knew he tried to be gentle with me, but I wanted him to be rough, and take my pussy like he was trying to win a fuckin' war. And he did, leaving no prisoners behind.

God knows I needed that. When I came, it felt so good, like a breath of fresh air and having the sunbeam in your face after being locked underground for a decade. I loved and treasured every minute of my orgasms.

I looked at the time and the red numbers on my nightstand. It was 11:50 pm. Omar was asleep and looked peaceful and handsome. I couldn't resist myself; I moved in closer to him and gently pressed my lips against his. I began kissing him lovingly. His lips were so full and soft. My fingers began dancing across his exposed muscular chest. I gently began disturbing him from his peaceful sleep.

I continued kissing him, moving my hand down his chest, under the sheets and began fondling his flaccid penis. I heard him moan as I smoothly began stroking up an erection again. I kissed on him again and teased his balls with my fingertips. He moaned, and squirmed a little, but his eyes still remained closed. While I caressed him below, I felt between my thighs tingling again and my pussy moist and ready.

Pressing my lips against his chest, I continued stroking him gracefully while working my tongue down his abs. I positioned myself under the sheets ready to give him a blowjob. His dick was hard in my grip and I wrapped my cherry flavored lips around the top of his dick. I coiled my tongue around the head.

I heard my man moan, as I started out sucking him off gently. I gave him a little lick there, a little kiss there, and a little suck underneath his nuts. Omar generously spread his muscular thighs nice and wide professing this dick is all yours.

Increasing my sucking gently, licking became longer I went from the tip to the base. I was in control of the dick. I sucked on it and stroked it simultaneously, spitting on his dick. I had half his dick in my mouth, with my tongue twisting around it and then I locked my arms around his waist and locked my lips making sure my man couldn't move.

"Oh shit!" he exclaimed, squirming in my grip. "Baby, you gonna make me cum like that."

My actions were rapid, as I slid my lips up and down his shaft, while I fondled his balls. He cried out, clutching the sheets. I swallowed him bit by bit and when I knew he was about to shoot, I went straight for his nuts; I put my mouth around his balls and started humming. Omar went crazy; his fingers ran through my hair. He went bananas and his legs quiver. I jerked him off as I chewed on his nuts.

"Oh shit!"

He raised his pelvis off the bed. Omar couldn't keep still. I wrapped my lips around the dick again, and deep throated him down to the base. I came back up and went down on him again, coiling my tongue around it. I quickly bobbed my head up and down, sucking his dick better than Super head.

"I'm ah... Ah! Ugh!" He roared.

He had a grip around my hair and clutched the bed sheets. I didn't stop sucking his dick until he exploded into my mouth and I happily swallowed. Coming up from under the cover, I wiped what was left of him from my mouth.

"You good, baby?" I asked with a content smile on my face.

"Hells yeah." He panted. "Damn, I love you."

I smiled and kissed him on his lips. "You hungry?"

He nodded.

After that episode, I was ready to cook my man a meal. I got out of bed and donned my navy blue hooded Velour robe with matching slippers. I went into the kitchen and began whipping together his favorite snack, a tuna fish sandwich, some eggs, and a glass of red Kool-Aid.

I served it to him in bed and he was like a big kid, devouring his food. I cuddled next to him, and let him eat while massaging his shoulders. I wrapped my arms around him.

"I love you so much, Omar."

"I love you too, baby. You the best," he replied, with a mouth full of food.

I chuckled and smiled. He was cute. It was hard to believe that the man I was holding in my arms was the same man who was charged with two counts of criminal possession in the second degree, and assault. My baby may have been a thug, but with me, he was the sweetest thing.

I know he did wrong in his past, tonight I pray to God that the man I was holding in my arms was a changed man. I wanted better for us. I believed that he was rehabilitated. I love him, and don't want my heart to be broken either by his thuggish ways or infidelity. I was well aware of back in the day. Love is a funny thing, you dance like nobody's watching, and love someone like you've never been hurt before. Well I plan to love my man that way, like it will never hurt me.

6

Living everyday like life's suicide,
corruption and murder he feels within.
Touched by his father's sins.
His heart beats wickedly inside him...

Omega

Sometimes, the only thing a nigga understands is violence. In the streets, it's the universal language. You put a pistol to a nigga's head and squeeze, or take a baseball bat and beat someone's brains out, and muthafuckas know you mean business. You gotta pull your weight around to let niggas know. I'm serious with this and I mean business. You show weakness and niggas will chew you the fuck up and spit you out like spit.

A rep meant everything to your game. If you didn't have authority and heart, you were dead. The game made no exception. You fuck up, and the game would come at you like a Mack truck, putting you flat on your ass. There ain't no room for mistakes, or half ass shit— you got beef, you come at it full force, or don't come at all. If you don't then the next nigga will. You respect the streets and the game, and she'll be good to you, until you fuck up.

My beef was one block away. I had buildings and heard hustlers from Baisley were trying to setup shop around my way. I already warned them to take that shit somewhere else, but niggas were fucking hardheaded and took my threats lightly. But it's all good, cuz what my moms always told me, if you don't listen, then you'll soon feel. And they were gonna feel my wrath real soon.

"Mega, what's good, why we just sitting here? Fo' real, fo' real… All 'em niggas is up da block," Biscuit said, ready to pop off.

"Nigga, I said wait, ya heard?" I replied irritated by his mouth.

"Ahight, nigga, you da boss," he said impatiently leaning back in the passenger seat.

Biscuit was my young protégé, sixteen, black, violent and just didn't give a fuck. He was thirteen when he first came on my team, putting in work for me. He knew how to handle guns like a Middle Eastern soldier.

I had a beef a few months back with Tiny. He had shop on Foch and Guy R. Brewer. He became greedy and wanted to stretch his business over into my territory, crossing that imaginary line of respect. His ego was out there, and he figured since he was a few years older than me, then it was cool to dip into my pockets.

Tiny's crew was on the corner of 155th street and 107th Avenue, chillin' out. I finally got the phone call that I was waiting for. Tiny's right hand man, Smoke just showed up and he was the nigga that I wanted to see. Without saying a word to Biscuit, I just started the car.

"We on it?" he asked.

I nodded.

"Bout fucking time. Fo' real," he said.

I slowly crept my whip around 156th street and parked it in the shadows of the block. I stepped out, so did Biscuit and we were greeted by three of my enforcers, Whistle, Tank, and Monk. They ran down the info on me and were ready to put Tiny's crew on the ten o clock news.

I had Biscuit by my side as we slowly approached the corner house near the bodega. Two rotweilers stood guard in the darkened back yard. I gripped a baseball bat, and closed in with Biscuit, .45 concealed in his waist. We went through the bodega, and hopped the neighboring fence to the yard with the dogs.

The dogs started barking as soon as they spotted us. They came charging and I whacked the dog across its head so hard. Biscuit took care of the other dog. I knew hearing the dogs bark would bring somebody outside to investigate. We pulled out our guns. And soon after, the screen door opened and two men appeared.

"What the fuck!" one men exclaimed, seeing his pulverized pups.

"Don't fucking move! Ya heard!" I ordered, pushing my Glock to his temple.

"Shit!" he mumbled.

"How many inside?" I asked.

"I don't know," he replied with boldness.

"You think I'm fucking playing with your ass? How many inside?" I asked going upside his head with the gat.

He was bleeding, his face was tight, and he reluctantly mumbled, "Four."

"Including Smoke?" I asked.

He nodded.

Whistle, Tank, and Monk appeared from out the store, guns in their hands. I told Tank and Monk to take care of the two we had. Whistle, Biscuit and I went inside to handle business.

We had an arrangement with the owner of the bodega next door. The two guards we had at gunpoint were forced down into the belly of the bodega, where they would be executed. Tank and Monk had their orders.

Inside was dark, and we were cautious. We heard movement and talking throughout the house, and I kept a keen eye on everything around me. My soldiers were right behind me. I continued to hear voices in the front room where there was a light on.

"Dominique, that's you? What's up with them dogs outside?" someone said.

Before they got suspicious, I leaped into view with my gun aimed at them. Whistle and Biscuit quickly followed.

"Fo' real y'all know what it is?" Biscuit shouted.

"What the fuck, yo!" someone shouted.

There were four of them alright, but I didn't know if the guard was lying to me or not. I nodded to Whistle. He checked all the rooms.

"Everybody, down on your stomach. Ya heard me? Now!" I ordered.

"C'mon now, Omega. You know Tiny gonna fuck your ass up for this," Smoke said.

"Get the fuck down, nigga!" I said, taking aim.

Smoke glared at me. He was tall, black, and ugly. They were all sprawled on their stomachs. Except Smoke, who felt he was too good to take instructions from a young hustler like me.

"Fuck you, nigga!" he spat.

"We fo' real. You think we playin?" Biscuit shouted, walking up to him and pressing the gat to his face.

"Go ahead lil' nigga, pull the trigger… Faggot, pussy muthafucka! You think I'm scared because this pre-school nigga gotta gun on me, nigga? I'll put this lil nigga over my lap and spank him with my dick….."

Pop. Pop. Pop. Pop.

Before Smoke could finish his insults, Biscuit blew his brains out and continued to shoot him.

"Fuck you, nigga!" Biscuit yelled. "Fo' real, nigga. You lookin' all fucked up now… Huh nigga?"

"Yo, yo… It ain't even gotta go down like this," one of the men said, still down on his stomach.

"What you say, nigga?" Biscuit asked, stepping to him.

"I said…"

Biscuit shot him twice in the head.

"Yo, fuck y'all niggas man!" the next man shouted. "Yo, I'll give Tiny the message not to come around here anymore."

"Omega, we gonna let him know not to fuck wit' you anymore," the second man said, backing his partner's plea.

"You know what, I appreciate that, but I'll give him the message myself now," I said, shooting both of them.

Whistle came back into the room. Nobody else was in the house. I told Tiny not to fuck with me and to prove my point, I murdered his right hand man, Smoke, to show him.

We left the bodies and headed back outside into the yard. Jumping the fence, we walked down into the bodega's basement. Monk and Tank had two butt-naked niggas tied up. They were bleeding and badly beaten.

"Fo' real, why y'all ain't kill these niggas yet?" Biscuit asked.

"Thought you might wanted to have some fun with them," Monk stated.

"Send one of them back to Tiny the traditional way, ya heard me?" I smiled and said.

Monk winked at me. Biscuit walked up to one of the fools, put his gun to the man's forehead and squeezed, blowing his brains out through the back of his head.

"That's word up, Mega, niggas ain't fucking with the team now, fo' real, fo' real," Biscuit said. "With me at your side, you know I always got your back."

Biscuit was my number one guy. He killed at will, and had more heart than most niggas I knew. He was my kinda dude. We cleaned up the store and walked back to the car. My cell phone started ringing. It was Greasy, Soul's cousin.

"Greasy, what's good my nigga?" I shouted out.

"Mega, you ain't heard?" he shouted.

"Heard what?"

"Soul's home. He got out the other day."

"Soul's home?"

"Yeah, he's out on parole. His girl drove upstate and scooped him."

"Word? Why he ain't let niggas know he was getting out?"

"Don't know. My nigga, Soul, is finally home!"

"I hear that, Greasy. But I gotta take care of some other things. Tell that nigga I'm gonna definitely get up with him."

"Ahight bet," Greasy replied.

"One."

I hung up kinda upset about Soul not telling anyone he was out, especially me. We've been tight since knee high and I could a thrown the phat welcome home bash. Been four years since I seen him. Soul back home made the crew even stronger. It was the perfect time to get at Tiny, and move his ass into retirement, permanently.

"Who was that, Greasy?" Biscuit asked.

"Yeah."

"What he had to say that got you smiling, my nigga?"

"Soul just got out."

"Fo' real?"

"Don't know, but I definitely gotta link up wit' my nigga, catch up on old times and shit. Ya heard?"

"I thought he was doing at least five?" Biscuit asked.

"Not anymore," I said.

"Fo' real, that's all good," Biscuit said.

I drove off, feeling really good. Goddamn, it was a new day. Tiny was almost out of the way. And with Soul back, it was gonna be like old times.

7

Two things to preserve in life;
your health followed by freedom.
You lose one you lose both...

Omar

The past few days back home felt like heaven to me. Being with America again was great. Everyday we made love and it seemed like the first time. We did it in the bathroom, in the shower, the toilet, on the floor, the sofa, against the wall, in the kitchen, the kitchen table, countertops—shit if we could fuck on the ceiling, then we would have done it there also.

I was home four days, and spent every last one of them with my girl. The only time we left the apartment was to eat. I only wanted to spend my time with America during the first few days back home. I didn't want any interruptions.

I knew my time alone with America would be short-lived. I ran into Connie in the chicken spot on Liberty Ave late one night. She recognized me on the spot and shouted me out, giving me a hug and was really happy to see me. It was cool seeing Connie again, but I knew she couldn't keep a secret for shit, even when I told her to keep quiet about me being back.

The very next day, my cousin Greasy called the apartment. America picked up and when she heard Greasy on the other end, her facial expression did not look too pleasing. She handed me the phone with a sigh.

"It's Greasy. How did he get this number anyway?"

"Hello…"

"What's up, cuz. Why you ain't tell anyone that you were getting out?"

"Greasy man… What's good?"

"You, my nigga… Yo, where you at right now? Greasy wanna come by and scoop you up," he said.

America was close by, listening to my conversation. He was so loud you'd think he was on speakerphone.

"Right now is not a good, Greasy."

"How 'bout tonight? There's a jump-off on Hillside. The crew's gonna be up in there. Soul, you need to come through. We missed you, man."

"I missed y'all. I'm gonna have to take a rain check on that. I'm chillin' with America."

"Damn, Soul, can't she let you off the leash for one night? We family, cuz."

"You ain't change one bit."

"Soul, you know how Greasy get down, pussy and makin' that gwap. I spoke to Mega the other day too… You know he's doing his thing and he took over shop while Rahmel's been locked down. He's doing it big."

"Yeah, I heard that."

I glanced at America and she had a look of impatience waiting for me to get off the phone. She walked up to me, pulled me slightly in her grip, and whispered in my other ear, "I'll be in the bathroom, getting things ready for us. Hurry up, baby."

"Ahight," I answered watching her walk away. "Damn…" I muttered.

Greasy always ran his mouth. I was happy to hear from my cousin again, but I was horny once more and America was waiting for me. I promised Greasy to link up with him over the weekend. I was still making up for lost time after being absent from her for so long. When I hung up, I smiled. It was good to hear Greasy's voice again, but then I cursed myself for forgetting to ask him what he did to my car.

I walked into the bathroom, and America had everything set up romantically. She was patiently waiting for me while lounging in the bathtub that was filled with bubbles and soothing warm water. Candles lit the room faintly and America stared at me with a seductive smile.

"You know the drill," she said, raising her leg out the water, and running her hand up and down her thigh.

"Damn baby, you ain't playing," I said, quickly getting out of my clothes. I got butt naked and slowly climbed into the tub and nestled against my boo.

Half-hour later, we both were still in the bathtub becoming wrinkled. America had her arms around me with her back against the tub, massaging my chest with her fingertips, with my back slightly pressed against her tits. It was such a serene moment, that I didn't want to get up from between her legs. The candles still burned dimly.

"You know, I was thinking," America uttered, breaking the silence in the bathroom.

"What's that baby?"

"Why don't you come with me to the studio tomorrow night?"

Her fingers still gently rubbed against my chest and I had my eyes closed enjoying her touch.

"That's you."

"And… You got talent, Omar. I know Kendal won't mind."

"This Kendal, how did y'all meet?"

"Through a mutual friend from work."

"Is that so?"

"I already know what you're thinking, Omar."

"I didn't say a word."

"We're just friends and do good business together. He looks out."

"I don't trust the nigga."

"You never met him before. What are you saying?"

"I'm saying, if a nigga is giving you free sessions in the studio, and you ain't even coming out of your pocket for that loot, he's after one thing," I hinted.

"Every man is not trying to fuck me, Omar. He's a friend," she assured me.

"Ahight, whatever… Have you seen yourself in the mirror, baby you look good, and if a nigga ain't tryin' to get at you, then he must be gay."

She chuckled. "You crazy, but that's what you want?"

"Nah, I'm just saying, nothing comes free in this world. You gonna end up having to pay one way or the other, either through cash or what you got between your legs."

"I've been going to see him for a little over a year now, and he gave no indication that he wants me like that," so she said.

"Indeed and maybe he's just subtle with his, baby. He ain't trying to scare you off. He knows you got talent. You're a gold mine to him, and he knows you gotta man you're serious with, but I guarantee, if I ever fuck up, and we become shaky, that's when he's gonna step off the sideline."

"All you gotta do then is don't fuck up, and we ain't gonna have no problems, right baby?"

I smiled. "You think I'm trying to lose all this and have the next man claim my glory."

"You better not. I love you too much."

"I love you too, America."

I felt my dick getting hard again under the water. Her touch always did drive my ass crazy. I wanted her again. I was about to turn myself over and position myself between her legs once more. But she stopped me.

"What are you gonna do with your life, Omar? You're twenty-five years old, and I love you too much to see you waste your life and talents."

"I know, I've been thinking about getting a job. But I ain't got no experience in shit but hustling."

"Why don't you go back to school and get your GED. I can help pay for you to go to a community college, or maybe you can learn a trade."

"A trade?" I laughed. "You mean something like becoming a mechanic or cook?"

"Whatever you feel comfortable doing, baby."

My future didn't look too good right now. Rahmel warned me that this would be the hard part, change. I was at a crossroad in my life, and knew that I needed to set a foundation for myself. If I didn't, it would be easier for me to link up with my old crew and do what I thought I did best. I wanted to see them again, but I was hesitant, because I knew they still lived that way of life, and that way of life could violate my parole and I would have to finish my five-year bid. I sighed.

"Whatever you plan to do, I'm with you all the way, baby."

She kissed me on the side of my neck and continued to massage my chest. There was a long pause. So many things were running through my mind. Then America hit me with, "Omar, promise that you will never go back to that life again? Are you done with the streets? Because if you're not, then don't waste my time. I need to know, will it be different now? Will it, Omar?"

I didn't answer right away. I thought for a moment then said, "America, all I'm gonna say is that I'm different now, and I'm gonna try so hard to do right by you. I can't predict the future, because I don't know the future. But I do know what I feel for you right now, is real. And I'm ready to accept the challenge by doing something positive with my life."

"I believe in you baby. I do."

I couldn't fuck up and break her heart. She didn't deserve it. If I got locked up again, there was no guarantee that she would continue to be by my side. A woman could only take so much from a man.

America began to run her hands smoothly across my skin, nibbling at my ear. I felt her nipples hardening against my back. Then she began to recite a verse from one of her songs in my ear. I remained still between her long legs as America sang softly, "The urge I have to feel you here with me. It leaves me breathless, for that memory. I have to have you more than once in life this situation boy it's out of my hands. The way you touch me, the way you caress me, the way your not afraid to get down with me, the way you look at me…ooh, the way that you move, says I'm always on your mind, our signs never lie…"

Her words were soothing and in my mind at the time nothing mattered.

The next morning we went down to Queens' courthouse to get married. It was the last day of her vacation, and America had to be back at work the next day. I wanted her to go back to her job a married woman.

I paid two strangers fifty dollars each to be witnesses. America wore the brilliant cut diamond 14k white gold mount with the platinum band on her ring finger. Even though it was purchased with drug money, the gift came from my heart.

I smiled, and America smiled back. "You nervous?"

"Nah, nervousness is for men who aren't sure of themselves. I'm very sure of myself today. You know I love you and will continue to love you."

"You better save that stuff for when we're in front of the judge."

"I got plenty more coming for the ceremony, baby. Don't worry."

"Come here," she said and planted a sweet kiss on me. "You are my everything."

Love & Gangsta

It was after one in the afternoon. We were finally called in the room for the ceremony. An elderly white man stood in a wrinkled suit clutching a bible. He smiled at us and encouraged us to come forward.

While he spoke, my eyes never left America. I had my hands in hers and never stopped beaming.

"Young woman, do you wish to say your vows now?" he asked America.

She nodded and looked straight in my eyes and said, "Omar, you are a man that I love and trust so much. You're my everything. You are the epitome of what love between a man and a woman should be. You are always the first thing I think about when I rise in the morning and the last I think about when I lay to rest. The first time I looked into your eyes, I knew you would become someone so special to me, someone so dear to me. And I promise to love faithfully. I promise to be one with you, together you and me bringing love, peace, and tranquility. I promise to give you all I can as your woman, because you're all I want in a man. Let us stand strong together. I love you, baby."

America had a few tears trickling down her cheeks as she said her vows to me. She gripped my hands tightly and I knew her words truly came from the heart. The Judge nodded, then he turned to me and said, "Your turn young man."

I gazed at America. I wiped the few tears from her face and smiled. I took a deep breath and said, "You know I love you, America. So let our hearts become one, tightly locked. Let there be no keys to unlock our trust, unlock our love, unlock what those will try to oppose. The first time I looked into your eyes, I knew that you would become someone so special to me, someone so dear to me. You always been there for me, got me hooked on your style and admit that for me, your type is just right, the one I'll soon have become my wife. You're my heart and soul, my boo, my lady, and angel in my life, a woman that makes me wanna exceed to become my best... I feel blessed with you and fortunate to have someone like you for my queen to my king. Give yourself to me and I will give myself to you. Placing you on the highest pedestal, then bow down on my knees to cherish and love my Nubian black queen. I promise to give you all I can as your man, removing the feeling of vulnerability, increasing the possibility of true uncompromising love. Now the sensation of your love covers my heart. The look in your innocent eyes, the touch of your innocent face, and I see my world, my all, the one I will always love. So as a man I try to close my eyes, so I can hold back my cries. But the harder I try, the harder I cry. Because the warmth of your touch, and the blessing of your heart, now have my eyes in tears, leaking wonderful soft cries for the love you and I share. Now falling in love I no longer fear and playa for life I no longer care, because I now feel more secure of what you and I share. So I wanna thank you for warming up a playa's heart, because now it's burning for just your love. I love you, baby…and today, I want you as my wife."

When I was done, more tears trickled down America's cheeks.

"Very well said," the judge said, nodding and smiling at me.

I held America's hands, facing her in my dark blue blazer, black slacks and wing tip shoes, feeling like I was on top of the world. The judge looked at America.

"Do you, Ms. America Stallings take Omar Stanfield, to be your husband, to have and to hold from this day forward, for better or for worse, for richer, for poorer, in sickness and in health, to love and to cherish; from this day forward until death do you apart."

"I do," America proudly stated, staring into my eyes with a smile.

He repeated the same vows and I looked at my beautiful woman and said, "I do."

The judge announced that we were officially married. I pulled America into my arms and gave her a passionate kiss.

"I love you," I proclaimed.

"I love you," she repeated.

It was official. She was my wife. Now I had to step my game up and do me on a more positive note. I had opened a new chapter in my life, and so far it was looking good.

8

Respect what's mine.
Know not to cross that line.
I won't have to get out of line
and clap you with my nine...

Omega

I ran Jamaica Queens with an iron fist. I wanted to be more feared than any gangster that came up before me. I acquired my reign in Queens violently through blood. My name ran thick through these streets like traffic and I had cash money longer than train smoke.

I was a street soldier for Tyriq's vicious drug crew and learned what I could from him until I set his punk ass up. Tyriq and Tip were gun down by Demetrius' hit men in New Jersey. I watched their brains spill and their blood splattered across the front seat and couldn't help but smirk. It was the beginning of my rise to power. Tyriq had fucked up and it cost him his life. He fucked up by bringing Vincent in the mix and a bloody war ensued with the Columbians.

In order for me to stay on top, I had to stay smarter, wiser, hungrier and more vicious than the next gangster. I couldn't look weak, and couldn't show any kindness. That was how I survived the war and proved my control on the streets.

There was a constant anger in me, driving me to care about anything but that money and my business. I had trust for no one, except for my right hand, Soul…who was released after doing a four-year bid. He was missed and I knew that I needed him by my side again. The two of us together again, we could own New York.

I rode around Queens in my candy red Lincoln Navigator with the vertical Ferrari style doors with the windows tinted and having the door handles, the gas tank cover and the exhaust chromed out. My interior was pearl white with red stitching and four small flat screens hung from the moon-roofed ceiling over each seat. And my truck rested on 26" chromed rims that made my truck feel like it was reaching to the sky.

I was showing my wealth, but not too blatantly. I didn't want the feds to come creeping up on me. I had enough enemies hating on me and didn't need the heat from law enforcement anytime soon.

It was a cool clear night and I felt this inward calm, knowing Soul was home and I had to go see my dude and show him a good time. We came up together since we were knee high. From playing in dirt and sand, slap-boxing each other in the streets, stealing snacks out the bodegas, fighting, running trains on bitches, we both got in the game together on the strength of my older brother, Rahmel. Soul was the one nigga that knew me best and the one nigga I would die for. We stood tall and held on to the attitude that we either gonna ride or die for each other. There was a promise that if one fell, then the next man would stand tall and hold the block down. I did that.

Soul was coming home to an empire that I had built over the years, and unfortunate for him, he caught a gun and drug charge and did that bid alone. I owed the nigga my life. The D. A. wanted to offer him a plea for exchange that he would testify against his brothers. They wanted me for years. I was lethal like the virus and had more bodies than a southern cemetery. I lived reckless, but lived smart. Soul had refused the DA's offer and even spit in his face for the offer. Soul was willing to ride out his time. I had much love for my nigga.

Navigating my truck down Rockaway Blvd, I stopped at a local bodega for a beef and cheese patty. It was reaching midnight soon. Four young niggas that were hanging out in front smoking and rolling dice gave me the nod of respect, knowing who I was and how fierce my reputation rang in the streets.

I wasn't alone. My 357 was tucked safely and concealed in the small of my back. I wore jewels with five-thousand cash bulging in my pockets and knew no one had the balls to step to me. I murdered many niggas coming up in this game and with the Jamaicans backing me and becoming my number one supplier, we quickly put the competition out. I was king of Queens.

Outside the bodega, I strolled confidently to my truck and quickly devoured my patty. Fifty Cent played and I turned up the volume to *Many Men*. My system blared and the young niggas bobbed to the bass, admiring my truck.

I was on my way to link up with Greasy at a spot on Linden Blvd. It was a good day. I had sent a message to Tiny— several of his men were now permanently resting in the morgue. I had to watch my back. This was war and I was a veteran on these streets. Soul was finally home and knowing that made my crew not only stronger but deadlier.

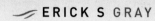

9

Let our hearts be one knot, Tightly locked,
Let no keys unlock our trust, Unlock our love,
Unlock whatever anyone opposes...

America

"I is married now… I is married now," I joked, imitating Shug Avery from the *Color Purple*.

Omar laughed at me as he carried me across the threshold into our suite at the Marriot. We were in downtown Brooklyn where we booked a room for the night. Going back to the apartment after our ceremony was a bit too ghetto for our taste. I wanted my first night as a married woman to be romantic. So I charged the two hundred and forty dollars a night suite to my visa.

Inside the room, we both looked around in awe. There was premium bedding, two flat screens, one in the bedroom and one in the open room, a mini bar, blackout drapes; the bathroom was bedecked with a hot tub and marble floors, granite countertops, and gold faucets.

"This is perfect indeed," Omar said, putting me back on my feet.

I wrapped my arms around him and kissed my husband, excited about our quick one night honeymoon. It wasn't the Bahamas or Hawaii, but it was cool. Soon the bellman came to drop-off our two overnight bags. Omar tipped him a twenty and he left with a smile on his face.

I picked up my small duffle bag and said, "Give me fifteen minutes, baby. I gotta look right for you on our first night as a married couple."

"All you need to do is come out that bathroom naked, and I'm good."

I slowly peeled off my dress and hung it on the back of the door. I washed up, then oiled myself down from head to toe, and sprayed some Eternity on me. I then slipped into a bright red stretch lace slip, with scalloped edging and a derriere-skimming length, with the matching thong on. And to top it off, I put on some hooker shoes, which were bright red five-inch stilettos.

I stepped out the bathroom and the lights were still on. Omar was shirtless, in his boxers, lounging on the bed watching TV. The remote fell out of his hand and his mouth dropped opened when he saw me.

"Damn!"

I turned off the lights and approached him seductively. Picking up the remote, I turned off the television.

"Tonight the only thing you'll be looking at is me."

He positioned himself comfortable on the bed, and I slowly removed his boxers.

"Damn, you look good, baby," he said, with his dick hardening in my grip. He moaned as I stroked him gently, massaging the muscles in his dick like a therapist.

"Hmm, hmm… Oh shit."

I continued to jerk him off until I heard him say, "Fuck this!"

Removing himself from my grip and positioned himself behind me. Curious, I watched him from my peripheral vision, with my pussy tingling for some dick action. Gripping my ass cheeks, Omar pushed me down on the bed, into a doggy-style. My legs on the floor, he ripped my thong off and tossed them to the floor. He pulled up my lace slip to my hips, bringing my animated pussy into his view.

Omar squatted behind me, holding the back of my thighs and putting his lips deep into me. His long tongue coiled inside me, penetrating every inch of me. I gripped the sheets tightly, and cried out, "Ah ugh, oh yeah, Omar. Oh God yeah!"

His tongue relentlessly attacked my ass making my legs quiver and juices rained heavily on his tongue, saturating his lips. I gasped crying out. I called out Omar's name numerous times, even screamed out, "Sweet Jesus!" as this sexual tyrant tore into me.

"Omar, you gonna make me… Oh baby, yeah! Yes!"

My manicured nails shredded the green silk sheets. It was so intense I was in a trance. For fifteen minutes, he didn't let up, not for air. He was a beast between my ass cheeks. He ate out my ass, sucked on my lips and chewed me up.

I panted, feeling my legs weakening. I was about to collapse. Tears began trickling down my cheeks. With my eyes shut, my husband took control of my body. I felt his big black hard dick sliding deep into me. I gasped again, with my grip never loosening around the bed sheets. His nuts slammed against my ass, as he pulled my hair, while he thrust his erection in and out of me. Piercing screams escaped the room walls, and I'm sure you could hear echoes of bliss in the hallway.

Omar pushed me down on my stomach, pressed his body against me, froggy-style and continued to fuck me. His body grinded against me heavily, his hands clasped into mine. My legs spread widely and he was like a tree trunk inside of me.

"Baby, I'm gonna..."

"Come in me, baby... Ooh yeah, take it. It's your pussy."

I wanted to feel him nut in me. Contracting my pussy muscles around his dick, the friction was almost unbearable. His grip tightened, and he rocked himself on top of me faster and faster, screaming, "Damn, your pussy is so, so good. Oh shit, baby... Oh shit! Ah... Ugh ah shit."

I felt him squirming around on top of me. He trembled, was breathless and sweaty all at once. Omar collapsed next to me on his back and looked at me with satisfying eyes. I couldn't move. The dick kept me paralyzed for a moment.

"What brought that on?"

"You're my wife now, it's gotta get better from now on." He smiled.

"Ooh baby, baby I'm not complaining baby. You did your thing."

He smiled and kissed me hard. I was spent and drooled all over him. I couldn't get up, or move. My first time having sex as a married woman and I loved every minute. Omar nestled against me, kissing me on the back of my shoulder, proclaiming his love for me once again.

I couldn't be happier. He had his arms wrapped around me, my back pressed against his chest, I felt safe and protected with him. He made me his wife, and I know not too many brothers in his position would be willing to make such a commitment.

Before I fell asleep, I whispered a prayer with my husband lying next to me. I wanted our marriage to last and we stay happy. We were going to have ups and downs, but I wanted our marriage to be strong. My aunt always told me, if you put God first, everything else falls into place. I was a believer.

10

If you aren't changing.
Then you aren't growing...

Omar

It was ten minutes after five when we arrived home the next afternoon. America took off another day from work. It didn't sit right with her going back to work the day after we had gotten married. She called her job and extended her time-off until Tuesday.

We were having a great time, breakfast in our hotel room, then touring the city via a nice long horse and carriage ride through Central Park. It was like our teenage years all over again.

As we walked toward the building, a 545 BMW rolling down Merrick Blvd on chrome rims, made a quick U-turn, coming back our way. The sudden change in direction of the car caught our attention.

"You know who it is?" I asked.

"No," America answered.

The silver Beemer stopped a few feet from us and three doors flew open. I was mentally getting ready for whatever. But it was Omega, my cousin Greasy and another young dude jumped out and started my way. I smiled.

"You been home almost a week now, and your ass couldn't come check your man…?" Omega smiled greeting me with open arms.

"Y'all rolling on a nigga like we got beef," I joked.

"What's good my nigga? It's good to have you home," Omega said as we rocked back and forth, hugging each other.

"Indeed, my nigga. It feels good to be back," I returned.

I looked over at my wild ass cousin, smiled and asked, "Yo, Greasy… where da fuck my car at?"

"You know Greasy crashed that back in 03. I had some bitch giving me head in the front seat on the Belt and she had some strong jaws," he laughed.

"Greasy, your weak ass owe me," I said.

My cousin smiled, gave me dap and hugged me. "Yo cuz, I missed you, man. I'm glad you home, my nigga," he said.

"Y'all niggas looking fly," I said checking out their gear.

"Soul, I'm telling you, money's getting great out here," Omega said.

Omega sported an official Mitchell and Ness; Reggie White's

Philadelphia Eagles throw back jersey, dark jeans, fresh tan Timbs and a thick, lengthy platinum chain. He had a giant multi stoned diamond eagle pendant. Diamond stud earrings were in both his ears and diamond pinky ring on his finger, blinging with no care.

Greasy wore Evisu denim suit, tan Timbs and leather Yankee cap. The amount of jewelry he had on made him look like a rap superstar. He was flossing a limited edition rainbow Tourbillion watch.

"Y'all niggas are making me look bad indeed," I laughed.

Even youngin sported Evisu jeans, red wife-beater and a long thick diamond chain around his neck. A platinum bracelet was frosty on his wrist.

"Biz is booming out here, Soul. Ain't shit change." Omega smiled.

"I feel you," I said giving him dap.

"What you got planned, my nigga?" Omega asked.

I looked at America, and then everyone suddenly noticed America and Greasy was the first to speak. "Hey America, you looking good as always."

America shot him the wicked stare and sighed.

"Damn, Soul, what's wrong with wifey? Why she grilling Greasy like-like she police or sump'n? America ain't got love for Greasy? We damn-near fam."

"Chill nigga," I countered.

"Ahight, you know Greasy was just joking wit' y'all," he smiled apologetically.

"Soul take a ride, ya heard?" Omega suggested.

"Yeah Soul, it'll be just like old times. You know…? Riding baggin' bitches getting our heads pop…" Greasy stopped realizing that America was still in our presence. "You know how we do?"

"Omar, may I have private minute please?" America asked, tugging on my arm.

"Give me a minute," I said to the old crew.

"Ahight," Omega said. He and the crew walked away.

"What's up, boo?" I asked.

"I know you're not thinking about leaving with them. We just got married. I took off from work. Today is still our day," she said, sounding angry.

"True indeed, boo."

"Well tell 'em to leave so we can finish with our honeymoon."

I sighed as America continued when she saw me looking reluctant.

"Omar, where were they when you were upstate? Not one of 'em went to see you. And I know you're not trying to get into the same shit that you were locked up for, right? I'm your wife now, so please take me serious. I love you. You start messing around with your cousin and Omega again, and you're gonna soon end up back where you just fucking came from. We're a family now. So start thinking like my husband."

"Indeed boo, I know. But listen, I'm a man, too. And you gotta trust my decision. You can't baby-sit me twenty-four, seven. I know where you're coming from, but there ain't gonna be no trouble."

"You right, you're a grown man and you're gonna do you regardless. I love you. But if you're serious about changing your ways like you say you are, then you need to change the company around you. And them over there," she paused looking directly at my old crew. "They are not gonna do anything, but bring you down."

I smiled, shaking my head and thinking.

"Baby," I said after a while. "I'll meet you upstairs."

She kissed me and walked away.

"It looked like you need permission from the warden, huh Soul?" Greasy laughed.

"Fuck you, Greasy."

"C'mon, let's be out," Omega said, motioning for me to get in the car.

"Nah, some other time for me," I said.

"You ain't comin' Soul?" Greasy asked.

"Not today, I got plans."

"That bitch seen you all fuckin' week since you been out... Fuck her!" Greasy snapped.

"Greasy, watch your mouth," I warned.

He sucked his teeth and looked at Omega.

"We came to scoop you, put you up on things. Let niggas know you's back. What's really good, my nigga?" Omega asked.

"Fo' real fuck that corny style nigga, and let's just be out fo' real," the youngin with them hollered.

"You know me lil' nigga?" I asked, glaring at him.

"Nigga, you don't fucking know me!" he retorted threateningly.

"Biscuit chill… You talking to my nigga here," Omega warned.

The look on Biscuit's face said he didn't approve of what Omega just said, but fell back and started minding his fuckin' business like he needed to do. There was something about him that I didn't like. He just rubbed me the wrong way.

"I hope prison ain't change you, ya heard me, Soul?"

"Mega, I'm still me. Believe that. I've been away from pussy, money, and my home four years now. Y'all niggas was eating while I was listening to 'em crackers upstate, like I was Kunta Kinte. America held me down. So don't step to me like I'm some off-brand nigga. I'm still Soul out this bitch. I can still put any nigga on his ass like it was still yesterday."

Omega looked at me for a minute, smiled then he said, "Ahight, my nigga. I thought you went soft on me fo' a minute. Had a nigga worried…ya heard?"

"Mega, Soul a fuckin' gangsta. That shit stays in our blood," Greasy laughed.

"Do you, my nigga. But we gotta link up and talk real soon. Don't leave me hangin, ya heard, Soul," Omega said, giving me dap.

"Indeed, we gonna link up, Mega. You got my word on that," I assured.

"Ahight, holla then," Omega said embracing me. "And welcome home, my nigga. When you ready to get this money again wit' your boy, you know where I'm at. Ya heard me?"

"I'm still mad that you're blowing us off right now, but Greasy understands. You still runnin' a marathon on that pussy, when you finish with America, come holla at you niggas," Greasy said giving me dap and a hug.

"Indeed…"

They all got back in the ride. Before Biscuit jumped in, our eyes locked for a moment. A chuckle escaped my lips. This little nigga probably popped off a few shots around the way and trying to step to me. I felt like bursting his fuckin' bubble.

The flashy Beemer disappeared down Merrick Blvd. Rahmel was right. When you first come home, everyone thinks it's the old you. Time stands still for no man. Only you have the ability to change what they think about you by your actions.

11

His seething thoughts causing distraught.
His mind burns as the world turns...

Omega

"Yo, Mega, we on the ten o clock news baby. Fo' real, fo' real," Biscuit shouted excitedly like a kid at the playground. He came running through the door, disturbing me. The nigga ain't had no manners and just turned on the fuckin' television even though I was chillin' with a shorty.

"What the fuck?" I shouted.

"We primetime, fo' real, yo," he said.

He turned to UPN 9 news, and there it was, 107th and 155th looking lit up like Christmas. There were police cars, camera crews and the coroners van doing work. I watched with Donna butt-ass naked next to me. She ain't give a fuck about Biscuit being in the room, the bitch was open like that.

"Mega listen…"

"Four bodies were found in Jamaica, Queens," the reporter stated. *"Police are now investigating what seems to be a drug hit of four black males found shot to death on the first floor of this home behind me. But what makes this case so much more shocking, is that in the backyard of this home, they have found two dogs beaten to death. It seems the suspects came into this place of residents through the back door to carry out their attack. Police have no suspects at this time, but believe the time of death of these victims occurred a little more than forty-eight hours ago. Homicide detectives had secured the crime scene, which is still fresh, and also paramedics were called to the scene to check to see if these persons were still alive and they were not found to be alive. Police are releasing no details on the cause of death at this moment and are still investigating. But once again, four bodies were found shot to death at this home not too long ago…"*

"You see that, Mega… We famous. We caught four bodies in one killin', fo' real. I bet you Tiny watchin' this shit right now, and shittin' in his fuckin' pants." Biscuit laughed.

"Yo, shut the fuck up! Ya heard?" I shouted.

"Fo' real, that's the first time I saw one of my murders on TV like that," he continued.

I jumped out of bed still naked and quickly grabbed the nigga by his T-shirt and pushed him against the wall with force that opened up his eyes in alarm. "Yo, what I say, shut the fuck up about it," I said scolding his juvenile ass.

"My bad, Mega."

This nigga, talking 'bout murders in front of a bitch, I warned him before to keep his mouth shut. I didn't care who Donna was bitches just talk too fucking much.

I dragged Biscuit into the hallway. "Wha' I told you about talkin' business in the open like that, 'specially round some bitch. You get too muthafuckin' hype and your mouth start running like a bitch on her fuckin' period. Ya heard me?"

"It's my bad. You know how I be?"

"Yeah, I know... Put that shit in check. Ya heard me, Biscuit?"

"I will, Mega. Fo' real, I will."

I let him lose and just looked at the nigga. "Go somewhere, nigga. I don't even wanna see you right now."

Biscuit was a good dude, but had a lot to learn. He was young and still inexperienced. I had to smile when he stepped to Soul the other day. The nigga got heart, but Soul would put him flat on his ass. I walked back to the bedroom and Donna was sprawled out with her tits exposed, channel surfing.

"Everything's okay?" she asked.

"Get dressed," I ordered.

"I thought we were chillin'? I got all comfortable and shit."

"Bitch, you ain't hear me? Do I gotta repeat myself?" I threatened.

She sighed, hopped out of bed, reached for her jeans and quickly put them on. I got dressed.

Half-hour later we were driving toward the Belt parkway. Just looking at her sexy ass, squirming around in the passenger seat got my dick hard.

"Yo, do me this special favor," I smiled, unbuttoning my jeans.

Unhooking her seatbelt, Donna leaned over in my lap. She pulled out my dick and wrapped her sweet thick lips around it, sucking me off. One hand gripped the steering wheel. The other was tangled in her hair forcing her head further down.

"Hmm… Hmm," I moaned, going fast on the Belt parkway.

I exited at Erskine and drove to Fountain Ave, parked under the bridge. Donna stopped sucking my dick, looked around and asked, "Why did you stop here?"

"I gotta meet up with some peoples… Just put your fuckin' head back in my lap and don't stop sucking 'till I say you can, ya heard me?"

I reclined and watched Donna's head bobbing up and down.

"I'm ah… Ugh ah…" I said grasping her hair tightly as my dick swelled in her mouth. A few more sucks and I exploded inside her mouth. She swallowed as semen still dripped from her lips. I firmly held her head positioned in my lap for a short moment. Soon after that, I glanced in the rearview mirror and saw a truck rolling up behind us.

"You done?" she asked, looking unsatisfied.

"Yeah, you did good," I smiled.

Monk and Tank got out the truck and were walking toward my ride. Donna uneasily, wiped her mouth and began straightening herself up. Tank quickly opened the passenger door and pulled Donna out the ride.

"Omega, what did I do? Please, don't do this to me, baby," she pleaded, screaming as Monk and Tank yanked her out.

She fell to the ground. Tank's swift, hard kick landed against her side. As she screamed, Tank pointed the .9mm with the silencer down at her and fired two shots into her dome. By the time I got out the truck, the bitch was dead.

"Yo wrap that up and put her in the back of your truck," I ordered.

"What the bitch did?" Monk asked.

"She heard too much," I said.

Tank and Monk began dragging the body to their truck where the back was lined with plastic covering. It had to be done and I couldn't risk it. Tank and Monk loaded the body in the back of the truck.

"Dump that bitch in Jersey somewhere," I said frustrated that the bitch with good head game had to go.

"You sure? You don't want me to make her disappear?"

"Nah, she deserves to be found. It wasn't her fault she heard what she heard."

Tank and Monk walked back to their truck, speedily backed up, and made a U-turn and drove off. I pulled out a cigarette and watched them leave. I sat in my truck for a moment, and then pulled off. I was on my way back on the Belt parkway when Greasy called me.

"Speak," I answered.

"Yo, I talked to my boy, he's down to link up Friday," he informed.

"Ahight, but you meet me tonight at the usual spot." I hung up.

I didn't like discussing business on the phone. I made my way back to Queens and met up with Greasy at the Wine-up, a small hole-in-the-wall bar, on South Road and 150th street. I felt comfortable there.

I pulled up to the place at midnight. It was a quiet night. A few locals were out lingering around on the corners, smoking, drinking, losing themselves in whatever drugs were available. I walked inside the joint and met Greasy in a backroom where we did business.

"Greasy, what you got for me?" I greeted.

"What's poppin', Mega?" he replied, giving me dap.

He took a sip of his drink and then reached into his jacket and pulled out a cellophane packet.

"What Greasy got for you— you gonna love. Check it out," he said handing me a pack.

"What the fuck is this?" I asked, taking it from him.

"That right there, Mega, is gonna make us twice as rich, ten times over. It's called ice." He winked.

"You mean crystal meth?"

He nodded.

"That shit right there, poppin' off big in the mid-west and south. White folks out there are goin' hard for that shit right there. We need to step up our game."

I continued to stare at the packet, clear crystal. Crack had made me rich. But meth was new to me, and I was skeptical about getting in bed with something new.

"That shit is more potent than crack. It's cheaper to produce. All we need's a connect. I got one out in Long Island. We can be the first out here to be pushin' this shit. Other niggas ain't fuckin' wit' ice," he continued.

"I see you did your research, Greasy," I said, tossing the packet back at him.

"You know Greasy's about that gwap, Mega."

"Ahight, let me think on it. I'll meet up wit' your connect Friday, and feel him out. If I like what I hear, we could be in business. And if this shit doesn't work out, it's on you… Ya heard that right? I hate changes, but since you're my boy, I'm gonna check it out."

"You know Greasy ain't never went wrong with that gwap, my nigga. You can count on that, Mega."

I studied Greasy's eyes. There wasn't a hint of doubt, I nodded then gave him dap. "Ahight, I'll see you tomorrow, ya heard me, Greasy?"

"Yessir."

I left the room and went back to my car. I didn't drive off right away. I always thought of crystal meth as white people's drug. And it probably would be a risk to introduce that shit to my regulars. They were fiends anyway and fiends would try anything if it could them high long enough. If this meth was potent like Greasy say it was, then the fiends of Queens were in for a rude awakening.

12

We came a long way baby and just to let you know. Our journey is not at its end...

America

My alarm went off at 6 am, and I sluggishly rolled over and cut that annoying sound off that echoed in my head. I was still tired from last night. I looked over at Omar, and he didn't even budge. He was asleep, dead to the world.

It was Wednesday morning, my first day back to work after a week's vacation. It was the best vacation that I ever took. My man, who was now my husband, was back in my life, and it felt so good. I couldn't ask for anything more, all we did was spend quality time together.

I stared at Omar for a moment and smiled. Kissing him gently on his chest, I reluctantly removed myself out the bed. I strutted to the bathroom to get ready for the day.

After a revitalizing twenty-minute shower, relaxing, for some strange reason, I started thinking about children. I definitely wanted some with Omar. I wanted a family. It was only right to give him children. I came out the bathroom wrapped in a towel, and saw Omar awoke.

"Gettin' ready for work?" he asked.

"Yeah," I sighed sitting next to him. "So, what you got plan for the day?"

"Don't know yet."

"Why don't you go see how your mother is doing," I suggested.

"Fuck that bitch!"

"She's your mother, Omar."

"And? That bitch ain't never did shit for me, I don't give a fuck about her."

"She gave you life."

"And that's all she was ever good for," he returned.

"Well, you need to do something. I don't want you sitting around this place all day while I'm gone. You can drop me off at the train station and take my car, and maybe look for a job or something. But just do something positive today."

"What time you gotta be at work?"

"Nine."

"You gonna make breakfast before you leave?" he smiled.

I looked at the time and it was seven fifteen. "Of course, I'll make some eggs, toast, and sausage."

"That's what's up. And can I get a quickie before you leave."

"Didn't you get enough of it last night?"

"Nah, your pussy is addictive," he said, pulling me close.

"Omar, stop. I gotta get ready for work. There's not enough time for me to fuck you, get dressed, and then make you breakfast."

"We can make time," he said, with his hand reaching under my towel.

"No."

"I need sump'n to hold me down while you're gone."

"Ahight, you want pussy or breakfast, you choose. You can't have both."

"Damn, you drive a hard bargain, baby," he said, his hand rubbing up and down my thigh while I sat on his lap.

I wanted some dick too, but I had a job to get ready for, and I wasn't trying to be superwoman.

"Man, fuck breakfast. I'll make my own," he said, pushing me on my back and unwrapping my towel. "And ooh, you smelling fresh too," he laughed.

"See, you gonna have me going to work smelling like sex."

"And, just tell them you got married and that your husband is a damn freak."

"You ain't got any sense."

He was already naked, because Omar never sleeps with clothes on. By the time he had slowly moved into position between my thighs, I was dripping wet with anticipation and Omar slid his morning erection into me. I panted, and gripped him as he thrust.

I looked at the time and it was a quarter to eight.

"Oh yeah, baby. Hurry, yes baby," I screamed with my legs tight around his waist, pulling him deeper.

"I'm coming."

We made love for ten minutes before he exploded in me. After we were done, I jumped up and went back into the bathroom to wash.

At eight thirty, Omar dropped me at the LIRR. I kissed him goodbye and strutted to the train station. I was on cloud nine. I took the nearest seat available, pulled out a good book to read and exhaled as I started to read.

It was nine ten when I arrived at the Verizon office ready to work. It was a cool job with good pay and benefits. And better, the hours weren't bad. I took a seat at my station and Monica was the first one to notice the huge smile on my face.

"You must have had a very good vacation," she commented.

"You have no idea," I replied.

"So tell me about him."

Monica was in her mid thirties, and been with the company for ten years. She was divorced, had three children, and loved to talk and gossip about anything.

I looked at Monica and said, "I got married."

"What, girl? Congratulations… When?"

"Thursday afternoon. We went down to the court house on Queens Blvd and made it official."

"Why didn't you tell me? I would have taken the day off to come and be your witness," she said.

"It was so spontaneous; we just did it, without even thinking about calling anyone. We wanted to be private."

"I'm so happy for you. Your man come home and made you his wife right away. He loves you very much. So when are the babies coming?" she joked.

"I don't know… The way we been doing it, I could be pregnant right now."

"Well if you are, you better let me throw you a baby shower. I already missed your wedding, I'm not trying to miss out on the baby shower," she said.

"Okay."

"Girl, he must be something else, because you're glowing right now. That man got you riding high."

"I'm in love, Monica. I'm his wife."

"America, you deserve the best."

"Thank you."

My day sped by and before I knew it, it was close to five o clock. I had promised Kendal that I'd stop by the studio after work. I was in the mood to throw some vocals down. I called the apartment, but Omar didn't pick up. He was probably out cruising in my car. I trust that he'd stayed away from his crew and his old stomping grounds.

On my way to the A train, I called the apartment again. No answer. I sighed thinking I need to buy my husband a cell phone. Monica walked with me to the train station. She lived in Brooklyn. We got a few snacks enjoying the evening. We stood on the platform waiting for the train to arrive, when a man walked by us in a gray suit and briefcase. He glanced at me, then looked back, and stopped. He walked back and said to me, "Excuse me, but you are truly beautiful."

I smiled. He was handsome.

"I just had to tell you," he continued.

Monica looked at me and chuckled.

"Um, I'm really lost for words right now... Are you involved with someone? Would you be interested in going to dinner sometime?" he politely asked.

I was still smiling, enjoying his graceful attention and then casually said to him, "I'm sorry, but I'm married."

The look on his face was priceless.

"Oh, congratulations. Your husband is a very luck man."

"He knows it," I said.

He nodded. "Well, here's my card. I'm a broker, if ever you think about investing, give me a call."

I took his card and he walked off. Monica laughed.

"Girl, you know what he meant when he said if you're thinking about investing. He wanna invest in something alright, and it sure ain't no stock or bonds."

"Stop it." I chuckled, feeling so good to tell him that I was a married woman, and I was off limits.

"America, you know what you are," she said.

"What?"

"You're a mobile red light."

"What?"

"That means wherever you go, you stop the fellows dead in their walk just so they can get a good look at you."

"Oh please, like you don't get your fair share of attention," I said.

"I get mine, but you got something in you that just brings too much attention. Omar is a confident man to trust you out alone, cause you know these playas are savages."

"We trust each other," I laughed as our train roared into the station.

I made my way down Fulton Street alone. I was in the heart of Bed-Stuy, dressed in a black long cutaway jacket and a sleeveless sheath dress with three-inch heels. It was hot, the fellas were out in swarms, and all their eyes were on me like I was from another planet. This was my first time taking the train to come see Kendal. I had always driven into Brooklyn. I hated the unwanted attention.

I crossed Fulton Street and a horn blew, some fool shouted, "You is lookin' good, ma. What's good? Let me holla at you for a minute."

Ignoring his feeble pick up line, I continued to my destination. Kendal's brownstone was on Macon Street. Kendal was so creative and experienced when it came to music that I always told him he was so underrated. His beats were on Dr. Dre, P. Diddy, or Swiss Beats level. And with my vocals, we were an ill duo. My name was definitely getting out there.

Walking down Macon Street, I saw Michael, Keith, Joe-Joe, and Tony out in front of Kendal's talking about they could rap better than Jay Z. They were always at Kendal's smoking, drinking, but they were garbage. Michael and Joe-Joe maybe, but the other two were garbage.

"America's in the house," I heard Tony yell, his little ass was always so annoying. He wanted to be a superstar, but he wasn't.

"All y'all don't have any jobs?" I questioned. "Every time I come around y'all always out here smoking, drinking... Doing nothing."

"That's what we do, workin' for the white man is wack," Tony said.

"Are you serious?"

"Yo, America, when I blow up, I'm takin' you with me," Tony added.

"Well, excuse me if I don't hold my breath." I had to laugh.

"Yo, what you doin' walkin', where's your ride?" Keith asked.

"My husband got it today," I happily informed.

"Husband?" all four of them exclaimed in unison.

I nodded. "Um mm, I just got married."

The look on all their faces made me wish I had my camera. I knew they really liked me, especially Michael, he did whatever I asked him to do—run to the store for me, watched my car at nights when it was late, or talked to me if I needed company.

"America, how you gonna do me like that?" Tony asked. "I told you I was gonna take care of you when I get my record deal. We were supposed to be Bonnie and Clyde on the tracks."

"You is married for real?" Keith asked.

"Yes." I showed them my ring and they were all taken aback.

"Man, I'm 'bout to cry, now I'm not gonna get my chance to discover America," Tony teased.

"You know y'all boys need to quit. I'm too old for y'all anyway," I said.

"I'm nineteen, ain't nothing boy about me, trust that," Michael said.

"Word," Joe-Joe said.

"Kendal is inside, right?" I laughed asking.

"Yeah, he in there mixing some shit up," Keith said.

"I'll talk to y'all later." I said heading up the stairs.

They all were cool, and respectable with me. I could have all their little hearts in knots if I wanted. Walking into the brownstone I headed to the basement. Kendal was in his studio. He practically lived down there.

I made my way down the steps, and heard the beat ringing out from downstairs. I liked it. Kendal was definitely doing his thang.

"I'm on that track, right?" I asked, nodding my head to it.

"You like it?" Kendal asked, bobbing his head up and down.

"It's tight, Kendal."

"I knew you would love it."

I got comfortable in his makeshift studio and was already thinking about a song to sing with the beat. Kendal smiled at me and started messing with the mixers.

Kendal was tall, cutie and stayed clad in throwbacks with a fitted. He's been producing for years, and once ran with Juvenile Delinquents, a rap group. They did their thang back in the early nineties. The group fell off due to bad management and money problems. Despite that, music was his heart, every track he produced, every rap lyrics he wrote, was pure platinum.

"You look nice, you just got off of work?" he asked.

"Yeah, but I can't stay too long."

"Why not?" he asked.

I took a deep breath, looked at him as he was busy on the keyboard and announced, "I got married last week."

"What?" Kendal shouted and the music suddenly stopped.

"I'm a married woman now," I repeated.

"To homey that just got out?" he asked and his expression wasn't one that was too pleased.

I nodded.

"Damn… Shit, I mean congratulations, I guess," he said hesitantly.

"You guess?"

"I'm just sayin', he just got out and y'all jumping the broom already. Are you sure about this? I mean, you about to blow up. I just don't want things getting in the way of your music career," he said.

"Kendal, me being married does not have anything to do with my music career. I love Omar, and we both felt it was the right time. Don't tell me you of all people are jealous?"

"It ain't even like that," he said, looking unsure.

I thought about what Omar had said about Kendal wanting something in return for hooking me up. My marriage would jeopardize us working together, making great tracks.

"You don't have a problem with me being a married woman? Because I respect our friendship, I don't want to start any problems between us. I've been coming here for over a year now, and we never allowed anything to get in the way of doing us. We both love what we do," I strongly stated.

"Yeah, I'm good, America. I was just caught off guard with it for a moment. You know we still cool peoples," he said halfheartedly.

Kendal turned the track back on and continued with his work. I stood there for a moment and observed him, and not once did he look up from the keyboard. I had this feeling inside me. He was jealous, and didn't want to show it. God, I hope my marriage to Omar didn't become a problem with Kendal, I thought. I love coming to work with him and chilling in the studio.

"You ready to get in the booth and lay something down?" Kendal asked. He glanced up at me and then continued messing with the mixing board.

"Yeah, I'm ready," I said.

I went into the padded booth, covered with foam stapled to the walls. I slipped on the headphones and pulled the studio microphone that hung from the ceiling closer to me and took a deep breath.

"Ahight, America, let's knock this track out," Kendal said and brought in the beat.

It was smooth with a piano sound to it, and more of a down tempo something channeling a Mary J. Blige song.

I snapped my fingers and thought about the perfect song for this track. My husband came to mind and I wanted to let the vocals lose with him in my heart and mind.

Why all you have to do is pick up the phone
    Dial my number (baby)
    And I'll come running like a child
    to his mother's cry. (I'm your lady)
    And when I leave your side
    my common sense start to counter
    my foolish pride.

I don't know why do I.

Why do I always come back to you?
No matter what I do
No matter what I say
Why do I always come back to you?
No matter what I do
No matter what I say

Every time I see you my eyes would smile
and then the tears start
because I know that you will
never be worth my while
but tell it to my heart
because it won't let you go that I
can't deny
I don't know why do I….

13

I'd rather be hated for who I am.
Than loved for who I'm not...

Omar

Life may not be the party we hope for but while we're here we might as well dance, my Uncle Ray used to tell me. He used to take me in when I would come running to him and cry about my mama. I was ten years old, and my mother's crack addiction was going strong at the time.

I remembered living in that house and sitting there watching my moms get high with her boyfriends. They didn't give a fuck that I saw everything. All she cared about was her high. No food or running water for weeks and sometimes days would go by without me seeing my moms.

Staying with Uncle Ray help me to survive most days. He would leave me in his crib alone while he ran the streets. I didn't mind, I loved staying at my uncle's crib. He had cable TV, food in his fridge, and even Nintendo. Sometimes I slept on the sofa but it didn't matter.

Ray was my uncle from my father's side. He was a down-to-earth, laid back hustler, who tried to avoid violence. He had a lot of talk to him, and was always around bitches.

I used to love it when my uncle brought these fine ass ladies home. Uncle Ray was so used to living alone; he never locked his bedroom door while he was having sex. Being ten years old, curiosity got the best of me. I used to hear the moaning. I'd tiptoe to his door and peek into his bedroom. Then I'd be rooted there watching the whole sex thing go down. My dick used to get so hard watching them butt naked ho's go down on my uncle and watching them being contorted in sexual positions. Studying him, I knew how to please a woman. And I learned how to be a playa.

My uncle used to talk to me about everything, from pussy to drugs; he taught me how to become a hustler and how to be a lady's man. My uncle was like my father. My biological father died before I was born. He was sick with cancer and passed away when my mother was seven months pregnant. My mother never used to talk about him, but Uncle Ray did. He always told me Melvin Stanfield, my father, was a good man. He worked hard everyday of his life as a welder working in the city. In his spare time, he played the saxophone and loved Jazz.

"Don't expect life to be fair, Omar. You start thinking that, and it'll bite you in the ass quick. Certain things happen, they just do. Your father was a good man. He loved your moms and couldn't wait till you were born. He would have been good a father to you, but that cancer ate at him like crazy. When he died, I felt guilty. I always thought that it should be me... I sold drugs, slept around with multiple women, even hurt people if it came to that, and your father was against my way of life. He should've been here for you, not me," my uncle once confessed.

I always thought about my father, and I always wondered how my life would've turned out if he were alive. I never cried when I thought about him—you can't cry for someone you never knew.

Uncle Ray helped to raise me. He was a career criminal, but the knowledge and wisdom he had was unbelievable. He could've been so much more if he didn't get caught up in drugs and women. Here I was, following in his footsteps. I even lost my virginity in his place when I was twelve.

I really missed Uncle Ray. The monster finally caught up with him and he died of AIDS five years ago. I cried and I rarely do that.

Driving north on Guy R. Brewer Blvd in America's Acura legend, I realized that I haven't been behind the wheel of a car in a long time. The radio was blaring, and the windows down. I had about hundred dollars in my pocket. It was one in the afternoon and quiet around the way.

Rolling through my old haunts, 164th street, at South Road and 107th Avenue, I saw a block that was notorious for drugs and violence. It was my home for twenty-one years. I was just curious to see if the block had changed.

Slowly, I rolled through the block then parked. I stared at the crib where I grew up. My moms stayed here, probably still getting high and turning tricks for drugs. I didn't care too much for her. I've been angry with my moms since I was young.

I sat thinking and staring at the dilapidated row of houses that lined the block. So much shit happened on this block, I hustled every day on the block, and got into so much trouble that cops knew me by my first name.

"Fuck that bitch," I hissed to myself.

I drove off with nowhere to go, checking out the young cuties on the street. By four that afternoon I was back at the building. Already the boredom was killing me. My wife was at work and I needed to do something, either get a job or hustle again. I thought about what Rahmel said to me. I needed to set some goals for myself.

I was making my way into the lobby and heard someone shout, "Yo, Soul let me holla at you for a second."

I turned around and saw Omega parked in front of my building.

"Damn, you stalking a nigga now?" I joked, making my way over to his ride.

He chuckled. "Just get in nigga."

I got in his plush Beemer and gave him dap.

"What you been up to, my nigga?" he asked.

"Gettin' used to things," I said.

"I see you pushing wifey's Acura around... Nice, America's doin' her thing."

"You know she holds it down. Where's my cousin?"

"Probably shacked up wit' some bitch, but I see you're lookin' fresh to death."

"She holding me down until I get back on my feet."

"That's what's up, but when you're tryin' to get back on your feet?" he asked.

"Soon as possible, why, what you got in mind, Mega?" I asked knowing Omega and wanted something.

"I wanna pull your coat."

"You seem to be doin' pretty good for yourself right now," I said.

He chuckled then asked, "You tryin' to get back in the game right now?"

The question finally came. I looked at him, thinking about what I'd promise to America. The temptation was burning inside of me. It was easy money and the streets were calling. But I couldn't break America's heart again. It wasn't right.

"Honestly, I don't know. Shit's fucked up. I wanna leave that life alone, I owe it to America."

"You're serious, Soul? I'm asking you this, because I'm thinkin' about investing into a new product and the money is right. I'll be the first out here to push it."

"What's the product?"

"You heard of crystal meth, right?"

"Yeah, vaguely."

"Your cousin hooked up a connect for me, some Mexicans out in Long Island. I did my homework — it's big out in the mid-west, cheaper to produce and it's more potent than crack. We move that shit into the cities and the fiends won't let go. I got a plan, Soul, and it's right. You and me, we could be the first muthafuckas up on this shit in Queens. I got the muscle, but I need niggas that I can trust to run this empire with me. The money we can bring in selling this shit is phenomenal. You wanna get back on your feet, we start pushing this meth, and you'll be flying. Soul, this is real money right here."

"How much we talkin'?"

"Forty, fifty thousand a day," he said.

"Damn!" I uttered.

"Yeah nigga, that kind of bread, we talking serious shit. Damn-near three hundred thousand a week in our pockets with this meth."

"You sure you ain't in over your head on this one, Mega, this ain't crack."

"Nigga, it's a new game. You gotta know how to play ball if you want in. Sooner or later this shit is goin' to pop off strong in the city. Let's be the first to get our hands on it."

"I need time to think. I just did four years in, and America…"

"Nigga, she wipe your ass too!" he barked.

"Fuck you! That's my wife you're talkin' bout," I snapped.

"Wife?"

"Yeah, we got married a few days ago."

"My bad. Congratulations. You could a told a nigga sooner."

"I felt it ain't really no one biz. What goes on between me and my wife is strictly between us."

"Yeah, I hear you. So now that you're a married man, you gonna have to start making that paper."

"Like I said, I need time to think on it."

"Soul, you ain't the type of nigga to watch the game from the sidelines, you're gonna want in sooner or later. And now is the time for us to really play ball."

"I'll holla at you man."

"Soul, I fuckin' owe you this, when you got bagged with all that work, you kept your fuckin' mouth shut, that's real right there. You ate those charges like a man. You could a snitched on me too, but didn't."

"What you gettin' at?"

"Soul, they don't make niggas like us anymore. I trust you with my fuckin' life. And I need a nigga like you to watch my back. Just in case shit gets ugly."

"Nigga, you know I'm on parole."

"We got that cover for you. I'm ready to pay off the right people, make some bribes, and do whatever it takes to keep muthafuckas off our backs. My money's long."

America was on my mind, but the offer was tempting. If I should become involved with Omega and it gets fucked up, I might end up back in prison. Then I may have to kill this nigga, we've been friends for too damn long. I love America, and I swear to God, I needed to start doing right by her. However, the inner demon was trying to bring the old me back out. I was a husband trying to keep on the straight and narrow. I made that vow to Raheem not to get involved in shit.

"I need time to think."

"Ahight my nigga, think on it," he said, pulling out a knot of bills from his pocket and peeling off four c-notes. "Here's a little sump'n to hold you down for a few days."

"I ain't no fuckin' charity case."

"I owe you, my nigga. As many times you done looked out for me and had my back. I'm just tryin' to help out a friend. You'd do the same for me. I know you need something to hold you down for the moment."

I hated to be indebted to anyone, because I hate returning the favor. He was right. I had the hundred America left for me before she went to work, but that wasn't going to last long.

"Soul, what you doin' later on tonight?"

"Why?"

"Come by the club over on Liberty and 150th street. It's called the Shack. People wanna see you and been asking about you."

"I'll think about it."

"You's a thinking ass, nigga. You feeling like Einstein and shit."

"When you locked up, you start thinking 'bout a whole lot of things."

I gave him dap and watched Omega peel off before a weird thought hit me. The whole time he never asked about his brother, Rahmel. Omega acted like his brother never existed. It showed a sign of disrespect. I shrugged it off and continued inside the building. I promised America I would pick her up at the train station later in the evening. I didn't want to miss her call.

I picked up America from the train station a little after eight that evening. She was coming from the studio. I had to admit it; I was jealous and made a small stink about it. America reassured me that it was only business and nothing more.

"Baby, I love you and only you."

I smiled and dropped it. When we got back to the apartment, I cooked up fried chicken and catfish, biscuits, and green beans, her favorite. I learned how to cook when I was twelve because mom wasn't doing it. I used to watch these cooking shows at my uncle's crib and write down the recipes. When I had the chance, I'd practice in the kitchen. There were a few near incidents, but nothing too serious to burn the house down.

We had a full belly and were sleepy by ten that night. America was in the bedroom getting ready for bed. I was in the living room contemplating Omega's offer. I had a ten o clock curfew with my P.O, but was willing to risk it. If he called or came by, and I was out, fuck it, I'd lie.

It was fifteen minutes after ten. I grabbed America's car keys and shouted, "Baby, I'm goin' out for a minute, be right back."

"Out?" America shot back.

She came rushing into the living room wearing a long sleeper white

T-shirt and glared at me. "And you're taking my car?"

"I gotta make a run real quick."

"Omar, it's after ten, pass your curfew with your P.O. What am I gonna tell him if he decides to call or worse come by to check on you?"

"He won't."

"How do you know that?"

"Because he won't," I snapped. "Don't worry, I'll be good."

She sucked her teeth and continued to glaring. "At least tell me where you're going."

I didn't want to tell her my location, nor did I want to lie to her. I was taking her car, and that made me feel less like a man. My silence made her even more irritated.

"You just gonna stand there and not say shit?"

"What you want me to say?"

"You know what...? Fuck it! You're a grown man, Omar. I'm not trying to keep you on a leash. Do what you fucking please!"

The pain in her voice was resounding. I didn't mean to diss America, but I needed some alone time. She went back into the bedroom and slammed the door.

"America..."

She ignored me. I stared at the door for a short moment.

"Fuck it!"

I pulled up to this hole-in-the-wall they called the Shack. A few people were milling outside. I parked the car and made my way across the street. It was a balmy Monday night, with graying skies and I sported a wife-beater, some denim jeans, and Timberlands. I walked up to a nigga mean grilling at the door and collecting money.

"I'm here to see Omega."

"Omega? Nigga, I don't know any Omega?" he replied with the screw-face and sarcasm dripping. "It's a dub to get up in this piece."

"What?"

I never paid to get into any club, and I wasn't going to start now. We had it like that back when I was coming up.

"You ain't got that dub; you ain't gettin' into this muthafucka. I let you know that now, nigga."

"Who the fuck you talkin' to like that?"

"Nigga, you best back the fuck down."

I didn't have a gat, but I had my pride and some hand skills to go with it. I was ready to knock this big mouth nigga flat on his ass.

"You know who I am, nigga?" I barked.

I was ready to bring it to this nigga. Suddenly, I felt an arm over me, I was about to react, but noticed that it was Omega.

"Soul, be easy, my nigga," Omega said calming me down.

"Mega, what's good?" I greeted him.

"Causing trouble already, Soul?" Omega joked.

"You know this nigga?" the bouncer asked.

"Nigga, you better back down, Dean. I just saved you from getting humiliated tonight," Omega said.

"Whatever," Dean said shooting me a smirk.

I laughed and followed Omega inside. It wasn't anything spectacular, but a comfortable spot for a nigga to chill and get his drink on. It wasn't crowded, but bitches were there.

The deejay was local and the bar was makeshift and stocked with beers, Hennessy, E&J, Alize, Grey Goose and bottles of Cristal. A few old bar tables were scattered around the joint.

I followed Omega to a small booth reserved in the back. Rap music blared throughout the speakers. A few girls were on the dance floor. We sat in the booth observing the place.

"What y'all fellows drinking?" a waiter asked.

"Bring us a bottle of Cristal," Omega ordered.

He nodded and walked off.

"I'm glad you came, Soul," Omega said.

"I had to come see." I said.

He smiled.

"This your place?" I asked.

"Nah, this shit is a dump compare to what I'm used to. I come here for business mostly; I like the people, and the owner, he good peoples."

A few of the ladies were clocking us hard. They were trying to be subtle. Moments later the bottle of Cristal and glasses arrived. We poured drinks and I downed mine quickly. Omega laughed.

Omega wanted to continue to talk business, but I didn't come for that. I came to chill, drink, and forget about any problems.

"Oh shit, Soul, what's good, my nigga?" I heard someone call out.

I turned to see Knocks. He came over and embraced me with a manly hug. Knocks was down to earth and stayed drunk the majority of the time. We reconnected for a quick moment and then he went to the bar to get himself another drink.

During the night I ran into several of the fellas, James, Loco, Mike, Tiffany, Norris, Pebbles, and my cousin Greasy came through with his wild ass. Kem and Kemp came through too, they were brothers that played ball and were almost drafted to the NBA, along with Monk, and Sky hollered at me.

It seemed almost everybody from around the way suddenly started to come through, showing me much love. Omega was confident I'd show up. He surprised the shit out of me by throwing a little welcome home party in my honor. I continued to get my drink on. It was good seeing everybody again.

"I hope you didn't forget about me, cutie," I heard a female say, as I was downing my fifth drink.

I turned around and standing in front of me was Alexis showing me some rhythm. She smiled at me and damn she was looking good. It's been years since we've been together. I thought she moved out of state and got on with her life.

"Alexis, what's good, beautiful? Been a long time," I greeted.

"I know, I missed you," she said, throwing her arms around me, trying to kiss me as if we were a couple.

I pulled back and told her to chill. I wasn't trying to go there and knew by her body action, she wanted to pick up from where we had left off.

"Why baby?" she asked with a confused look.

It was hard to resist, but I had to. She was dangerous for my marriage. I hated that I loved looking into those hypnotic light green eyes, and feeling on her long, brown hair, with her skin supple like honey wrapped around a curvaceous figure. She was one woman that made a nigga weak.

We had a thing that got real serious before I was knocked. Shit she was by my side early that morning trying to help me get rid of the drugs. She was in love with me, and so envious of America, that she got my name, Soul, tattooed over her left breast. But she knew America always came first in my life. So she played the hand she was dealt, my second bitch.

We used to fuck all the time. She even became pregnant twice for me. Both times, I made her have the abortion. I didn't love her like that and didn't want the trophies. Her feelings were hurt, but she soon got over it and gave me the pussy again.

Clad in short black glazed leather wrap mini-skirt, stilettos and halter-top, her tits were looking so nice. Temptation was a bitch.

"You still with her ain't you, Soul?" she asked, I could already see that jealousy seething within her.

"Let me buy you a drink, Alexis," I offered. Turning to the bartender, I said, "Grand mariner and Pineapple."

"You remembered my favorite drink," she said with a generous smile.

"Of course," I uttered. It was the most expensive drink in the place, thirteen dollars a glass.

Alexis stood by my side, sipping on her drink and chatting up old times. I decided not to reveal my marriage. She wasn't ready for the news. Alexis wanted to fuck me tonight. It was hard to turn down her offer for a quickie and a blowjob. The bitch had gotten me hard by barely brushing against me.

The night progressed and I met privately with Omega outside, near his ride. He was rolling a blunt.

"Mega, let me holla at you for a minute."

"Soul, you having a good time?"

"You know, it's always love wherever I go."

ERICK S GRAY

He chuckled and responded, "You conceited bastard."

"You still smoke?" He asked, taking a long pull from the weed.

"Yeah, I still get down with the haze."

I took the burning haze from his hand and took a long pull. It's been months since I sparked up and the effect was immediate.

"Soul, what you wanted to holla at me about?" he asked after a while.

Omega leaned against his ride and checked the time on his cellphone.

"You becoming larger than life," I said. "When was the last time you tried to holla at Rahmel?"

"Man, I've been hearing he changed and shit, tryin' to become righteous and shit. I ain't got time for that, Soul. Why you asking?"

"He misses you. You need to go check him or write him a letter, show that nigga some love."

"Man, I ain't tryin' to drive no seven hours upstate to some cracker town and walk up in no prison. You must be crazy. And then hear this nigga talk some bullshit to me, like he my daddy," Omega spat.

"Y'all brothers," I said.

"So? This nigga gets locked up and wanna start reading books and become righteous and shit, like he was never out here makin' money and murdering niggas. He the one that put me onto this shit, he made us, Soul and now I'm just takin' it to a whole new level."

"Yeah, but look where it got him."

"Man, I ain't my brother, Soul. What that nigga got in your head while you were up there? Huh? Fuckin' righteous muthafucka, if Rahmel came home right now, all that righteous shit would go out the muthafuckin' door. He'd be out here grindin and doin' what he do. Niggas get like that only cause they locked up, and them crackers be gettin' in their muthafuckin' heads. You see me, do or die nigga. I'm 'bout this money and I wanna know if you feel the same, Soul? You gonna preach to me like you my fuckin' brother and be on some broke shit? If so, then fuck you and fuck my brother!"

"You a cold nigga, Omega," I said, grilling him.

"It's a cold muthafuckin' world, my nigga, and sometimes the only

99

way to heat it up, is wit' this," he said, pulling up his shirt and revealing to me a black 9mm.

I had no words. He took another pull from the haze and looked around. And then he changed the subject by bringing up Alexis.

"Anyway, I saw you talkin' to Alexis, what's good wit that? You tryin' to fuck her tonight?" he asked.

"Nah, you know I'm married now... I done told you already."

"Nigga, pussy is pussy and Alexis is lookin' nice, nigga. You better stretch that pussy out. I know mad niggas that be tryin' to get at that, and she lovin' your ass nigga. Do you, nigga. America won't find out. I ain't gonna say shit."

"Yeah whatever. I ain't tryin' to let that be me anymore, sleeping around and shit."

"Nigga whatever, I give your ass a week, and y'all two gonna be fuckin' like crazy again."

A black Maxima suddenly caught Omega's attention as it slowly crept down the street.

"You know them niggas?" I asked concerned.

"Don't worry about it. I'm strapped. I caught some beef wit' this nigga named Tiny."

"Tiny? You mean Tiny Smalls, Demetrius cousin?" I asked.

"Yeah, him. Nigga thinkin' cause he got some weight around his way, he could just move on a nigga. I had to let the dogs loose on his boys. Make the nigga think twice about fuckin' wit' me."

"Watch your back. You know Demetrius and his peoples ain't no joke. Them Jamaicans ain't nothing nice to play wit."

"Soul, this is me, I don't run from nobody. I don't give fuck about Demetrius, that nigga could suck my dick, too," he exclaimed.

I had enough of Omega for one night, he was my boy, but that nigga had some issues. I went back into the bar to say goodnight to my peoples. It was getting late and I wanted to get home at a decent time.

It was around two when I staggered into the apartment. I went straight into the bedroom, plopping down in bed next to my sleeping wife. So tipsy, I didn't even bother to undress.

I was trying to get some sleep when I felt America getting out of bed and started untying my Timberlands. She gently pulled my boots off and sat them on the floor. Then she undressed me, and threw a blanket over me. Making sure I was comfortable, America whispered in my ear then she kissed me.

"I love you, boo."

Without even mentioning the time or the smell of liquor, she laid down. Guilt grew inside me like a muthafucka. I had left her at home alone without explaining shit to her about where I was going. And she still stood by her man. I became sleepless as my mind started racing.

14

Wanted to fade in the worst
way fallen by gunplay.
Outlaw since first grade.
Prison was his first date.
Blinded by a mother's hate...

Omega

The meeting with the Mexicans was in Hempstead, Long Island. We drove out there in a black Escalade with a small arsenal under our seats. Greasy was behind the wheel and Biscuit riding shotgun, I sat in the back, thinking, I didn't trust anyone. If it was bad, Biscuit was my insurance policy. I listened to the conversation going on in the front.

"Fo' real this stuff is the new crack, Greasy?" Biscuit asked.

"Son, it's a new day wit' this stuff, fiends be goin' crazy over that meth. Yo, I was in Texas one time, and you should a seen how hard they be goin' for a hit. Yo they would murder their own mama for this shit. Only thing, we gotta learn how to manufacture it right," Greasy informed.

"Fuck you man, Greasy?" Biscuit asked.

"This ain't mixing baking soda in water. You need muthafuckin' chemicals for this shit to come out right, and if you fuck it up, that shit will blow up in your fuckin' face."

"Fo' real nigga, you got us putting together some fuckin bomb," Biscuit exclaimed.

"That's how it is. But it's cheap to produce. And that gwap, yeah is definitely right," Greasy said.

"I'm riding wit' you on this, Greasy," I chimed. "But these Mexicans better not rub me the wrong way."

"They cool. You gotta believe Greasy on that," he assured. "They're about that gwap and handling their BI."

I didn't say anything else. I continued to ride quietly to the meeting spot. The morning meeting took place in a park next to Hempstead Turnpike. We parked in a sizable parking lot.

The Mexicans were waiting in a burgundy Lincoln Navigator nothing flashy about the truck. They were on time, and I liked that. Four men stepped out after we parked. They looked rugged, wearing wife-beaters, were heavily tattooed, and looking like they just stepped out of East L.A. I concealed the 9mm in my waistband.

"Let's do this," I said.

We walked casually over to where they were parked. Our eyes

stayed fixed on the four Mexicans. It was eight in the morning and the lot was practically empty. I looked around making sure nothing was out of the ordinary.

"What's good, Falco?" Greasy greeted, breaking a tense silence between our groups.

"Greasy, Greasy, it's always good to see you. Hope you came with some good news for us," he returned, shaking Greasy's hand.

"We came to hear you out," I chimed, addressing the man Greasy called Falco.

Falco looked at me and said, "You must be Omega."

I nodded.

"Come, let me and you, we go for a walk and talk, okay?" he said, already walking ahead.

I looked at Greasy and Biscuit and nodded. They stayed their grounds with Falco's men.

We started to cross a baseball field where the few people up early were jogging, exercising and walking their dogs. Falco remained quiet as he continued casually across the baseball field.

"I like baseball. It's a relaxing sport," he said

He had a slight Mexican accent, but his English was perfect. I understood every word he uttered.

"It's not rushed, like most other sports. Baseball is played with finesse and patience—America's favorite pastime," he said.

Falco was about my height, five-ten, slim with a bald head, a thick goatee, and looked to be in his early thirties. He was clad in a wife-beater, sweats, and white Nikes, and both his arms were swathed with tattoos from his wrists up to his shoulders and across his back. He sported no jewelry except for a diamond pinky ring on his right finger. He had a calm demeanor. Looking in his eyes I could tell he was ruthless.

"You know one of the reasons why I like baseball so much, Mr. Omega?" he questioned. He then answered his own question, "Because all the players get their turn at bat. You get to see all the players and watch everyone carefully. Each player holds his position with ease, either on base or the outfield; everybody got time to watch everybody. Every player watches and follows that white ball… Without it, there's no game."

"Yo man, we came out here to talk about baseball, or do business?" I spat agitated by his preaching.

"I like patience, Mr. Omega. The man who is in a constant rush, always fuck up. Sometimes you need to sit back, take time out to watch everyone and everything. When the ball comes, then you take action," he said. "You can learn a lot by just watching one game of baseball."

We walked and he continued talking.

"Mr. Omega, I've heard many things about you."

"I handle mines," I quickly replied.

"Are you familiar with methamphetamine? Or it's cousin, crystal meth?"

"Slightly."

"It's a growing drug, and popular in almost every state in the West and Midwest. I come to you, because I need my business to expand in New York. I need a man who can handle my work."

"I'm listening."

"I've done my research."

"You checking me?" I asked annoyed.

"Nothing personal, but I like to know a few things about a man and his family before I do business with them," he said to me, fixing his eyes on me. "You have a fierce and respectable reputation. I like that. And Greasy speaks highly of you."

"If you don't mind me asking, but how did you meet Greasy?"

"He was locked up with my amigo a few years back. This amigo of mine is a good judge of character. He's the reason I come to you with business. I understand that you're already a rich man, but I can make you a man of power and highly respected in unreachable places. You can be the first to really get this new product to customers. New York will have its first taste and have the fiends keep on licking your fingers for more."

"And what do I gotta give up?" I asked, knowing there was always some exchange.

"You do business with me only," he said with a commanding tone.

His cell phone suddenly started to ring. He picked up, checked the call I.D and said to me, "Excuse me, I have to take this call." He spoke in Spanish for a few seconds and hung up.

"Now back to business. You purchase a pound from me for fifteen thousand, wholesale price, and we start off with four pounds, nothing less. Or if you like, one hundred and fifty thousand for a ten pound batch, that can earn you retail price as much as fifteen million."

"Damn!"

"I've thrown the pitch. Are you ready to step up to the plate?"

His offer was tempting—hard for me to turn down. This was a new drug, and I wasn't going to jump in headfirst and be assed out.

"I'm gonna start off with the four, and if this shit works out, I'll definitely be back for the re-up," I finally said.

"Done deal, Mr. Omega."

"Another thing, how do you manufacture this shit, I'm used to crack. My peoples don't know nothing about this meth like that."

"I understand. I will link you up with mi hombre who will get you set."

Just like that, I found me a new connect. We shook on it, and I promised to have his sixty grand within the week. We then slowly made our way back to the parking lot.

"Everything good, Mega?" Greasy asked.

I nodded. Greasy smiled. "That's what I'm talkin' about."

Falco climbed back into the Lincoln Navigator followed by his men. After they drove off, Biscuit asked, "You trust these Mexicans muthafuckas?"

"Keep an eye out for me, Biscuit. You're my main guy for this shit on the street," I said.

"What about me? You gonna leave me out to dry?" Greasy asked.

"No, I want you in charge of the fuckin' labs that we're about to set up. Since you seem to know so much about the stuff. I want you and only you to deal with Rodriquez. That's who's gonna set it up for us. You hearing me, Greasy?"

"I got you."

"If this shit pops off, we're in for a really lovely year."

"What about Tiny? You know he's a greedy fuck, and if we're gettin' stupid rich, he's gonna make a move on us soon, especially after what we did to Smoke and his crew," Biscuit said.

"I know. I'm ready for that fuck," I stated.

"Let me handle the nigga," Biscuit suggested. "I can make it where that nigga won't ever see the light of day again."

"You a soldier Biscuit, but if we take out Tiny now, then we're gonna have a problem with Demetrius."

"He could get shot down too," Biscuit said.

It was complicated. Demetrius was a well-known drug supplier throughout the hood. He was South Jamaica, Queens' connect for coke. I didn't want to burn any bridges until I could walk on water or part the sea my damn self. I had a plan, and if this crystal meth popped off right, then I could say fuck Demetrius and Tiny.

The following night, Biscuit, Greasy, and I were having drinks while mingling with the bitches in the Shack. I had a small bundle on me and was treating these bitches to whatever drink they wanted. It was a good fucking thing while waiting for a call to get business started. I hated waiting on someone, especially some muthafucka I knew nothing about. I thought about what Falco said to me earlier, about rushing life and fucking up. I've been hustling since I was ten. I was a specialist at moving weight and making that paper.

I downed the Rum and Coke and eyed a piece of eye candy at the other end of the bar. She was talking to someone, but that wasn't going to slow me down. I wanted to go holla. I needed to get my mind off this phone call.

"Why you keep staring at me like that?" I asked her, ignoring the nigga.

"Excuse me…?" she answered.

She was looking good, hazel eyes, smooth brown skin, and dark black hair with blond highlights.

"You don't see me standing here?" the nigga she was with exclaimed.

"Step off, nigga."

"Nigga, fuck you!" he shouted.

"What?" I retorted.

"Fuck you, nigga!" he shouted, stepping to me like a threat.

Before I could react, Biscuit smashed a Heineken bottle over his head, and then Greasy ran up and began punching him in his face repeatedly. The guy dropped, and tried to protect himself from the blows bestowed on his dumb ass. He curled up in the fetal position when my Timberlands came across his face. I used the bar for support and crashed the heel of my boot down on his face.

"Talk shit now, nigga!" I yelled. "Huh? Talk that shit, nigga."

We fucked this nigga up for a moment, while everyone just stood around and watched. He was covered in his own blood, and whimpering like a bitch.

Biscuit pulled out his .380, ready to murder this nigga. I had to call him off.

"Nah nigga, chill. Not here. Too many people."

Biscuit's face was twisted with rage. He stuffed the gat back into his waistband. The nigga was unconscious and badly beaten.

"Yo, Omega, why you gotta disrespect my place like that?" The bartender asked.

"Shut da fuck up!" I yelled at his bitch-ass.

He didn't mumble another fuckin' word and went back to his business. I was heated, but it felt good to fuck a nigga up like that. I haven't done that in a long while.

I looked at honey and asked, "You wit' this nigga?"

"No not really, we just met," she said with uncertainty in her voice.

"Yo, let me holla at you for a minute in private," I said.

I led her to a back room, leaving Biscuit and Greasy to clean up the mess. I stared at her long legs and smiled. I took her into a backroom office, closing the door behind me. I couldn't even really call it an office. It was small with enough space for a few chairs, a table and some cases of beers and liquor stacked up in the corner.

"What's your name, beautiful?" I asked, staring into her pretty eyes.

"Jazmin," she answered coyly.

"I make you nervous Jazmin?" I asked, eyeing every inch of her figure.

"No."

"You sure, cause I ain't gonna hurt you. You just caught my attention," I said calmly.

"It's cool."

"I'm sorry you had to see that back there, but I hate when niggas get muthafuckin' disrespectful. You know who I am, beautiful?"

"I think," she replied.

"What you mean you think? They call me Mega. I run things in Queens, ya hear me? I saw you checking me out from the corner of your eyes. I know that clown ass nigga wasn't really sayin' shit to you. So I had to step to you. You like them bad boys, right? Don't lie?"

She smiled. I knew from the get-go, the bitch was gullible and I already had her in my pocket.

"How old are you?" I asked.

"Nineteen."

"Damn that's good," I laughed, staring at her figure once again. "And you got a man?"

"No."

"What you need, boo…? I got you. Ya heard? I'm feelin' you, ya feel me? I'm definitely liking what I see right now," I smiled, taking a seat on the cluttered table. "So what you like in a man?"

"You know, swagger, style, and his paper gotta be right," she laughed.

"So, you like what you see right now?" I asked.

"Huh, huh, most definitely," she smiled batting her long lashes.

"That's what's up," I said wanting only to fuck this bitch. "You ain't busy right now, right? I wanna chill wit' you for a minute."

"That's cool."

"Come over here, you ain't gotta be so far from a nigga. I need to get to know you a little better, you feel me?"

She walked up to me and I gently pulled at her shirt, and gripped her in my arms. She felt oh so soft. Her sweet scent brushed against my nostrils and my dick jumped.

"What you wanna talk about?" she asked in a gentle whisper, with my arms still wrapped around her.

"Some things, you know what I'm saying," I replied and moved my hands down to her ass and squeezed her phatty.

She continued to smile and asked, "How bout' you, do you got a girl?"

"Nah, I'm good right now," I replied.

"I don't know that, niggas be lying sometimes," she said with a sly smile.

"I don't need to lie," I returned, and then slowly began pulling up her denim skirt, and cupped her smooth butt-cheeks in my hands. "Damn, you're soft boo."

She chuckled, smiling at me, our faces barely inches apart. Her breath was fresh like scented gum and roses. I began moving my hand in between her soft thighs and brushed it against her pussy.

She was wet. I parted her panties to the side with my fingers and slowly pushed two of my fingers into her. She moaned, and said, "You gonna take care of me?"

"I got you, boo. Like I told you before, I'm definitely feelin' your style," I whispered in her ear.

My dick was hard like rocks and I was ready to fuck. She began unbuckling my pants and whipped out nine inches of black and hard.

"I see why they call you Mega," she smiled, and began stroking me gracefully.

I was in no mood for foreplay. I positioned myself behind her, bending her over the desk doggy-style. Hiking her skirt, I ripped off her panties from her moist thighs.

I quickly dropped my jeans and boxers. My dick was at attention, standing ready for the deed. I was tempted but wasn't stupid, I wasn't about to fuck this bitch raw. The manager always kept a pack of condoms in his drawer. He was always fuckin' his female employees. I pulled out a pack of Trojans. I rolled that tight condom back on my thick shit, then gripped Jazmin by her ass cheeks, spreading them and thrust inside her.

She groaned as I slid in and out of her roughly and then smacked her ass cheeks red just for the thrill. She gripped the table firmly throwing her ass back. I pulled her hair, and continued to slap her on her ass, feeling that tight ass pussy marinating all over my dick.

"Ooh, ooh oh shit… Oh shit. Ooh, ooh, fuck me!" she cried through clenched teeth.

Her legs were spread wide apart and her ass shaking fast. I was in a fucking trance, enjoying all of Jazmin's sweet pussy until I started to hear my cell phone ringing.

"Shit!" I roared and gripped Jazmin's ass check firmly.

My rhythm was going in that pussy and the phone was on the table in front of me. Quickly without missing a beat, I grabbed it.

"Who this?" I asked, with the phone pressed to my ear, while clutching that ass, still thrusting my dick in and out of Jazmin.

"You need to holla at me, right," I heard someone say, not knowing the voice.

"What?"

"Rodriquez," he said.

"Oh, yeah, yeah. What up?"

"You sound busy," he said.

"I'm into a lil' sump'n, but what's good?" I asked.

"Meet me tomorrow evening, top floor of the parking garage on Archer Avenue at six sharp. We'll talk then,"

"Ahight," I said but he had already hung up.

I tossed my phone back on the table and continued with my sexual onslaught. Tearing into that pussy from the back like a beast, fifteen minutes later, I was coming like a nut.

After the episode, we got decent again and strutted back out into the club. The blood was cleaned up and dude was nowhere around. It looked like the incident never happened. I saw Greasy by the bar and informed him of our meeting with Rodriquez tomorrow evening. He nodded. Jazmin remained by my side the entire night, and I was without a doubt feeling her company to some degree. Shit that same night, I took her to a motel and we fucked again. I blew that bitch back out again. I needed round two with her to release the stress that I was carrying.

The next evening, Greasy and I drove up to the top deck of the parking garage on Archer Avenue, between Guy R. Brewer and 165th street. The day was overcast and the top deck was sparse with a few parked cars.

Only Greasy and myself met with Rodriquez. We pulled up next to this pearl colored Benz sitting on 20" inch chromed rims with tinted windows.

"Nice," Greasy uttered, eyeing the ride.

A dark-skinned man with braids and clad in a dark suit stepped out. He didn't look Mexican. I exited my truck followed by Greasy.

"You sure this him?" I asked Greasy.

"I ain't never met dude before," Greasy replied.

"You Rodriquez?" I asked him.

He made eye contact with me before saying anything. He walked up to Greasy and me and said, "From now on, you only deal with me and only me."

"What happened to Falco?" I asked.

"He only wanted to meet the face of the man he's doing business with. After that, there's no more direct contact with him. I'm his right hand in N.Y, so anything you need you get at me," he informed.

"Not a problem," I said.

"Our first shipment for you will arrive next week Thursday. Four batches of crank for fifteen cents a piece," he said. "Now, I'm gonna teach your peoples how to properly produce and market the goods. Once you know the right chemicals to use, you'll be in business. This shit is addictive like a toddler on his mama's tit."

He passed me a card with only a phone number on it, and then handed me a cell-phone.

"It's pre-paid, and we're the only ones with the number to that phone. When it rings, and you see a 410 exchange, don't answer it, just meet us at this location and remember it," he explained to us, and then handed me a small piece of paper with a Brooklyn address.

"Remember the location and then burn that shit," he continued. "And another thing, we only deal with the two of you. From this day on, any new faces and we shut you down."

"I understand," I said.

"Any questions?" he asked.

I looked at Greasy and he looked at me, and then I looked at Rodriquez.

"Nah, we good for now."

"Y'all fellas have a nice day," he said, making his way to his ride and drove off.

"They tight wit' their shit, Mega," Greasy said.

"I know, a nigga could understand that," I said.

I stared at the Brooklyn address and started to remember that shit quickly.

"Yo Mega, let's get sump'n to eat, a nigga is hungry like a muthafucka," Greasy said.

"Ahight."

We got back into the truck and made our way out the garage. A new day was dawning for me. I was about to experiment with a new drug, but I also knew I'd be haunted by my past. A few niggas had to be made ghosts.

15

Only two places you should fine peace.
The grave and in your home...

America

Early Sunday morning, and the scintillating rays of the sun beamed colorfully through the luxuriant white clouds. I stared out my bedroom window still in my underwear and holding my belly gently. The morning looked so peaceful and calm. I wanted to get ready for church in Brooklyn where I've been attending on a regular basis. Getting involved in the church helped me deal with the stress during Omar's incarceration.

I peered out the window and my eyes became glossy. I had so many thoughts running through my head that I became overly emotional. Omar was still sleep.

He's been home a month now, and wasn't really doing anything for himself. He was looking for a job but I had my doubts. When I asked him what places he applied at, it was always Best Buy, Target, and Sears. I couldn't check behind him. It was his responsibility.

My period was a week late and I suspected that I was pregnant. We were fucking like rabbits everyday without protection and not once did he pull out of me. I felt that our situation just got crucial. I was happy but also a little worried.

Having a baby was a huge responsibility that required support emotionally and financially from us both. Omar needed to step up and bring in an income to this marriage. I've been supporting him for a month now, and there was only so much that I could do. I knew that it was hard on him, being a convicted criminal and having no education to fall back on.

He didn't even have a high school diploma or a GED. Omar wasn't doing much with his talents that he was blessed with. At nights he would write a few rhymes and poems and recite them to me. He hasn't lost his touch with his word skills. I felt happy for that.

I didn't want to pressure him, nagging him about getting a job. My biggest fear was that if I started doing that, it would pressure him to get back into the drug game again with Omega and Greasy. I pushed him but didn't try to make him feel less of a man. If a baby was on the way, I couldn't afford to have him locked up again. It would definitely destroy me.

I went into the bathroom, turned on the shower, immediately

undressed and got in. While in the shower, I prayed to God, asking him for help. I needed guidance and for my husband to understand that there were other ways to get paid beside hustling drugs. Omar needed a positive start somewhere.

I was in his corner, letting him know I had his back. But I needed help I couldn't handle this one alone. If something didn't come through for him soon, it would only be a matter of time before he started slipping back to his old ways. I was scared. I would love for Omar to come with me to church, but I knew I was pushing it. I got out of the tub and stared at my reflection.

"Life's going to be okay, America," I told myself.

The doctor's appointment was scheduled for tomorrow morning. I needed to find out how far along I was pregnant. I wrapped a towel around me and walked back into the bedroom. Omar was still sleep. I began getting ready for church without trying to disturb him. When I was almost dressed, my husband opened his eyes and stared at me.

"Where you going, baby?" he asked, stretching and yawning.

"Church," I said.

"Oh word…?" he asked, awakening from his sleep. "What time will you be back?"

"Around two or three."

"Have a good time then," he said. He then got out of bed, scratching his ass, and went inside the bathroom.

I sighed, walked to the bathroom door, knocked lightly and said, "Omar, come with me."

"Huh?" he shouted.

"I said come with me to church this Sunday. I want you to meet Pastor Moore and a few others. Maybe they can help with you with finding a job. Just come, it could do you some good."

He opened the bathroom door, looked at me and said, "Nah, baby, that's you. I ain't been to church since I was six. I ain't tryin' to hear about God and shit like that."

"Why not?"

"Don't start getting religious up in here today, baby. It's too damn early," he said closing the bathroom door.

I couldn't force my husband. So I let it be and went into the kitchen to fix myself a light breakfast. I made scrambled eggs and tea. I was drinking my tea, when I felt my husband's gentle embrace from behind as he slid his hand under my skirt.

"Omar, please stop… Not today," I firmly said.

"Why not, baby? Let's do a quickie," he persisted.

"I said no. I'm on my way to church and I'm not going smelling like sex," I said pulling myself away from him.

"Ahight whatever," he mumbled, walking back into the bedroom.

I watched him for a moment and then collected my things and walked out the door.

"Now faith is the substance of things hoped for, the evidence of things not seen… Hebrews 11.1," Pastor Moore preached to the crowded congregation.

"Faith is the substance of things, but hope is a necessity. Sometimes people say that you will not get anything just by hoping, and that's true to a certain extent, for there is no substance to hope…can I get an Amen church…"

"Amen," the congregation shouted.

"Hope is a imperative companion to faith. Hope is the goal-setter. Faith is the substance of things hoped for. What things? We hope for the things God has given. Without faith it is impossible to please Him. The Lord is not pleased when we don't enter into provisions that He has made for us… Do you hear me church?"

"We hear you Pastor Moore," a lady shouted.

"Some things we will never come into except through faith. We must know what God has given, or we can't have faith in the promise," he preached, arousing the entire congregation. "Train your spirit."

I was moved by his words. I really wished Omar was here to hear him preach. He needed to hear this instead of staying home.

After the service, I wanted to talk to Pastor Moore. He was talking to Mr. Jenkins, a well-known and respected man in the church and in my community of South Jamaica, Queens. Mr. Jenkins was my high school teacher in the tenth and eleventh grade at August Martin high school. The students loved him and he did so much for the kids and students.

"Sister Stallings, or should I say, Sister Stanfield," Pastor Moore greeted me by shaking my hand and kissing my cheek.

"Hello Pastor, and hello Mr. Jenkins," I greeted them both, smiling.

"How's marriage?" Pastor Moore asked.

"It's cool, I tried to get my husband to come to church," I said.

"Well, it's hard on a marriage when one spouse is saved and the other isn't. But you keep on your husband, and you let him know continuously that he has a good woman by his side. You pray for him, and be patient… Sometimes it takes time for someone to see the light. Remember, it took me a long time before I accepted the Lord into my life. You don't give up on him, because you know God will never give up on you."

"Thanks Pastor," I said.

"How're things going with him getting a job?" Mr. Jenkins asked.

"That's another problem," I admitted. "He says he's looking for work, but I don't know if I should believe him or not."

"Sister Stanfield, I have to run into my office, but talk to Mr. Jenkins and call me later and we'll talk," Pastor Moore said and then walked off.

"He needs to find something soon, Mr. Jenkins. I don't want him falling back into his old ways," I said.

"I may have something for him at the community center on Merrick Blvd," he said.

I smiled. "Are you serious?"

"It's part-time for now, but if he's a good worker and can handle a broom, a mop, and be around over three dozen kids, then he's the man for the job," Mr. Jenkins stated.

"I will definitely let him know, Mr. Jenkins," I said, and gave him a deep and loving hug.

"Tell your husband to come down Monday afternoon around four, and we'll talk then."

"He will, believe me, Mr. Jenkins, he will," I confirmed.

I was ecstatic. I couldn't wait to tell Omar the good news. When I walked into my apartment I was disgusted to see Greasy and my husband lounging in the living room with a few 40oz malt liquor bottles on the glass coffee table. The television was loud as they gawked at some big butt ho' shaking her ass on the screen. Greasy was smoking a blunt with his feet up on my furniture like he had no home training and stinking up my home with that foul weed smell.

"Oh hell no!" I shouted, glaring at the two of them. "I just came home from church and y'all got me cursing."

"Hey baby, Greasy just stopped by to say what's up," Omar said, getting out of his chair.

I gave Omar a sickening stare.

"How was church?" He had some nerve.

"Can I talk to you in the bedroom?" I said heatedly.

"Yeah, we can talk. Yo Greasy, I be right back."

"Ahight cuz," Greasy replied, with his eyes still glued to the TV. He then took a long pull.

I quickly snatched the smoldering cigar out of his hand and said, "Don't disrespect my home like this, Greasy, you can't smoke in here and pour that beer down the sink."

Greasy looked up at Omar and asked, "Yo cuz is she serious? What's good? How she gonna snatch Greasy shit like that?"

"This is my house. I pay the bills up in here," I said.

"Damn, and you just came from church and acting like you got the devil in ya. Y'all need to go talk that out fo' real. Go handle that, Soul." Greasy sounded like a damn idiot.

I glared at him and shouted, "Greasy, you shut up and leave my damn crib! I'm sick and tired of you! Get out!"

He sucked his teeth and replied, "Whatever, America. You actin' real unfamiliar, you got the Holy Ghost in you and now you wanna act like you ain't ever burned and drank before, you need to step off that fuckin' high horse you're on and…"

Before I could react, Omar stepped up and said to him, "Yo Greasy chill, this is my wife you're talking to."

"I know, Soul, but I'm sayin'."

"Chill, my nigga, it's my business and you respect her, ahight," Omar said.

"Ahight, Soul. I'm out anyway," Greasy said.

"Thank God," I said.

Greasy looked at me angrily and turned his attention to Omar and said, "Yo cuz, we definitely gonna link up later and talk."

He left the apartment without saying another word. I loved and respected Omar for that. Since we've been together, he's never let anyone disrespect me. But he still wasn't off the hook for treating my place like some ghetto fabulous pad.

"What you need to talk to him about, Omar?" I asked with serious attitude.

"Nothing too serious," he explained.

"What you mean nothing serious? You know what your cousin is into, Omar. He ain't any good, and he will never be shit. He's a drug dealer, a thug and probably a murderer too," I was sounding hysterical.

"Whateva, America. That nigga is family, and I ain't tryin' to turn my back on family," he angrily replied.

"I'm your family, Omar. We just might be a family," I hinted, giving him a clue that I might be pregnant.

"What? What you gettin' at, America?" he asked, calming down his tone to me now.

"What you think I'm saying," I replied back to him in a sarcastic way.

"You pregnant?" he asked incredulously.

"I might be. I have a doctor's appointment tomorrow morning to find out for sure."

"Oh shit, say word, boo? We gonna have a baby," he exclaimed, looking like a different person now. He smiled and embraced me.

I pulled back, my arm outstretched and said, "Maybe, but I want to know, what you and Greasy got going on?"

"He just came by to chill and talk about old times, America. I'm not into nothing, I swear, America. We were just chilling."

"I don't want him in this apartment anymore, Omar. Please don't have him in here anymore," I pleaded.

"Ahight, I promise you that, boo. What time is your doctor's appointment tomorrow morning?"

"Ten O'clock."

"I'm coming with you."

"You don't have to."

"Yes I do. I'm not trying to have you roll up there by yourself. We're going together so we can both find out for sure if you're pregnant."

He made me smile. I love him. This time I didn't pull back from him when he wanted to embrace me. He held me in his arms and said, "I'm gonna have a son."

"How you know it's going to be a boy?"

"Because I know. I'm probably gonna have a knucklehead boy to raise."

I laughed.

"I love you so much, America," he said holding me tightly.

"I love you too, boo. And if I'm pregnant, you know what this means?" I asked.

"I definitely gotta step up my game and do me."

"Do it right, Omar, for us and the baby. I don't want our child visiting you in some cell."

I felt so secure in his arms. I remembered the job that Mr. Jenkins wanted to offer him and I said, "Omar, I may have a job for you."

"Fo' real, where?"

"I know a good friend at the church, he's someone that I've known for a very long time and he informed me about a part-time position as a janitor at a community center on Merrick Blvd. It's not too far from us and he's really great, and I trust him. Are you interested?"

"Yeah, no doubt. I'll check it out."

"He told me to tell you to come down tomorrow afternoon at four and he'll talk to you. It may be part-time, but it's a start, Omar. And Mr. Jenkins have so many connections, that there's no telling where you might end up once you start working for him."

"I hear that, I'm gonna definitely check it out."

"Omar, you need something, especially if I'm pregnant."

"America, I'll be down there tomorrow afternoon and I'm gonna take care of us, you hear me?"

I hugged him tight and we both had a relaxing Sunday afternoon despite the small turbulence.

"Wear something nice. It means a lot to me," I said.

The following morning, I found out that I was three weeks pregnant. Omar held onto my hand and was beaming when we both heard the news.

"It's a boy, right doctor?" Omar clowned.

The doctor chuckled and said, "It's really too early for all that. Let's just pray that the baby is healthy."

"Thank you, Doctor Bryson," I said.

"It's a boy, I know it," Omar boasted again.

We walked out the private physician's office proud, expecting parents. Omar already had plans for a son.

I thought about my family and just wanted a healthy, loving family. We were already married, and Omar had a possible job lined up—even though it wasn't much, it was something, and something was always better than nothing.

16

Excellence is never an accident.
It's always the result of high intention.
Sincere effort, intelligent direction,
skillful execution and the vision to see
obstacles as opportunities...

Omar

It was a quarter to four when I walked up to this community center on Merrick Blvd—it kind of looked like a low budget YMCA. I was still happy from the news I've received this morning. I was going to be a father and the feeling that I had inside of me was so overwhelming, that I felt like an entire new man. Now I needed to do something with myself. I needed a job. I needed to get paid and help support my wife during her pregnancy.

I was having a boy, and immediately I wanted the best for him. I became a husband, and soon I was going to be a father. A month or so out of prison, and already two positive things happened in my life.

Greasy was trying to bring me back into the game. He was pushing a burgundy Mercedes CLS550 coupe and dripping with diamonds and platinum. Him and Omega were popping off with crystal meth. He told me of their Mexican connections. Looking at my cousin caused a bit of envy in me, but I shrugged it off. I owed it to my family to change my ways.

I stood outside, asking myself if I can really do this. I've never done a job interview before. Everything felt brand new to me during my first few weeks back home. I was seeing my Parole officer on a regular basis and trying to stay out of trouble.

Walking into the building, I was greeted by children running back and forth and a few counselors trying to maintain order.

"Can I help you, sir?" a young lady asked.

"I'm here to see a Mr. Jenkins," I said.

"Hold on for one minute," she said me, getting on the phone.

I observed the place and noticed some folks watching me—probably judging me already. I stood in my slacks, button down shirt and stylish loafers, my baldhead glistening like I just polished it with wax.

"He's busy in the gym. C'mon, I'll take you there," she announced, coming from around the desk and guiding me through the place.

"I'm Cindy and your name is?" she asked.

"Omar." I smiled.

She mirrored my smile and then asked, "Are you one of his students?"

"I'm here to see him about business," I said. I didn't want her in my business and thinking that I was some broke nigga coming into the center looking for a job, even though I was.

She walked ahead of me and I admired her backside. Her figure was banging. We came to the gym, and I heard some commotion going on inside.

"Nah, fuck that. He a ball hog, Mr. Jenkins," a young boy shouted.

"You ain't shit anyway, nigga. You can't handle the rock, with your scrub ass," another boy shot back.

"Now you two stop all this carrying on. And what did I tell you about cursing and using the N-word in this building," a man shouted.

He stood between the two feuding young men. "Young black men should respect each other. You two hear me? We work as a team in this center."

"Tell him to start passing the rock then, and it'll be all good," the first young boy shouted.

The second boy sucked his teeth and sneered.

"I want you two to shake hands and act like men in here, you hear me?" the man said. "What's the first rule in this building?"

"No fighting or cursing, Mr. Jenkins," both answered in unison.

"Okay, okay. I want the two of you to take a timeout from the gym and basketball, and do something more constructive with your time here. Go upstairs and see Ms. Tony, she'll give the two of you assignments that y'all can work together on. Until I can see the two of you work on something together without fighting or arguing. I'll allow y'all to come back into the gym," he said.

"C'mon Mr. Jenkins, I got a game next week," one said.

"I suggest y'all get it done quickly and prove to me that you both can work together."

With a show of attitude, they moved along without further beef.

"Mr. Jenkins, this is Omar, he came looking for you," Cindy introduced.

"Thanks Cindy," he replied.

"Not a problem," she said and walked out the gym, leaving me alone with Mr. Jenkins.

"Omar... America's husband right?" he asked incredulously.

"Yeah," I replied dryly.

"Nice to meet you young man. We'll talk in my office," he said.

I followed him down the corridor that was decorated with multicolored arts and crafts from all different ages, along with a towering glass trophy display case that was filled with awards, medals, plagues and certificates, the awards and medals for basketball and volleyball. There were pictures up of young men and women involved in different activities.

"America's been telling me so much about you," he said when we reached his office door.

I kept quiet. His office was cluttered with stuff. He had over a dozen framed pictures hanging on his wall. I noticed a picture of him with Al Sharpton, one with 50 Cent, Mayor Bloomberg, and LL Cool J. There were basketballs, bags of sports equipment, and other sports paraphernalia cluttered all over the place. His desk was chaotic with papers, books, folders, and more pictures. There was an old TV set with a VCR on top that sat catty corner near a closet. He had a bunch of folding chairs for furniture—some wood and other metal.

"Excuse the place, please have a seat Omar. I haven't had the time to clean up. I've been so busy with these kids, and I'm sorry that you had to witness that small incident in the gym. Kids will be kids," he chuckled.

He took a seat on one of the folding chairs near his desk.

I took a seat and said, "Nah, it's all good. I've seen worse."

He smiled. "So, America tells me that you're interested in finding work."

"I'm trying, but you know how it goes, black man just came home after a bid, ain't no company trying to give me a chance. They too scared of a brother."

"Are you ready to work?" he asked.

"Yeah, I'm ready to do something."

"When I mean if you're ready to work, I mean are you ready to work on the way you think, on becoming a positive brother for the community?"

"Where you going with this?"

Love & Gangsta

"I hear so many great things about you, Omar… that you're talented, gifted with words and music and I've also heard some other discrediting things about you. My kids in here they talk, and some are very familiar with your past," he said.

"I did me a few years back, but that was years back," I explained to him.

"So have you changed the way you think?" he asked.

His approach was kind of irritating. I came here for a job and this niggas was talking to me like he was my fuckin' P.O.

"No disrespect, but I thought that I was here for a job, not for some evaluation of my life."

"I apologize. I don't mean to pry into your business, but I do care. And I do respect that you became a husband to America. She loves you so much, and can't stop talking about you in church. Not too many brothers are willing to get married, especially right after coming out of prison. We need more men becoming husbands and fathers to their kids, and stop becoming a baby daddy to multiple women. So I commend you for that."

"No doubt," I returned.

"Now, as for the job, it pays seven dollars an hour, part-time, six hours a day, and you'll be working Monday through Friday from three to nine at night. You'll be working mostly with Jim our head custodian, probably mopping and sweeping, and doing minor repairs. You'll be around a lot of kids too, and sometimes, they can be a handful," he explained.

Mr. Jenkins seemed to be a cool dude. He kind of reminded me of Morgan Freeman with short grayish hair corresponding with his grayish goatee. He had a distinguished demeanor that went beyond his cluttered office. He was about mid-fifties.

"You interested in the job?" he asked me.

"Yeah, I definitely need it. It's something right, and I can get my P.O. off my back about finding a job," I said, staring at him.

"It is. The money may not be good from the start, but if you work hard and improve yourself, you can go a long way," he said.

There was a sudden knock at his door. "Come in," he shouted.

Cindy stepped into his office and informed him, "Mr. Jenkins, they need you on the second floor."

"What would this place do without me?" he said, smiling. Before he stepped out, he asked, "Can you start next Monday, three o clock sharp?"

"I'll be here by two-thirty," I told him.

"That's what I like to hear." He then walked out, and I followed behind him.

"New job, huh?" Cindy asked.

"Sump'n like that."

"Good luck, it's cool here. Everybody's nice. But the pay could be better."

"Thanks for the info," I said and kept it moving.

I knew Cindy was flirting. Smiling like she already had a crush on me. I had to move away and fast. I am a married man and needed to keep reminding myself. The best way to resist temptation was too stay away from it early.

17

Feeling like the sky blackened the day he was born. Been a pain in his mother's wound, Not too soon till he's poison to the world...

Omega

The past month been sweet for me, meth exploding on the scene so quickly, the fiends couldn't get enough of it. Tripling my investment by still pushing crack/cocaine and weed. With meth the money poured in like a waterfall. Within a month, I'd already sold twenty-five pounds of the stuff. I needed to re-up four days after receiving the first four- pound batch from Rodriquez.

He was on point with his, setting up shops through the hoods. Rodriquez put my peoples on how to set up and run a meth lab, without the explosion. Greasy was in charge of the labs. He took care of mixing, preparing, and overseeing the product.

When it came to receiving certain chemicals or ingredients like Pseudoephedrine, Iodine crystals, Red Phosphorus, cold decongestant, anti freeze bottles, and Coleman fuel we got it in bulks from the Mexicans. We supplied the gas cans, laboratory equipment, Bunsen burners, mason jars, glass tubes, and our time.

The product was easy to make, but time consuming and dangerous. It wasn't crack and not as safe to produce. One fuck up and you can find yourself in the burn unit suffering first-degree burns all over your body.

I had five meth labs set up throughout Queens within the month. Two in a basement near Guy R. Brewer, one in a garage over on Supthin Blvd, and two in a private house by Merrick Blvd. I stayed away from complexes and apartment buildings. The reason, too confining and it wasn't as easy to dispose of certain waste products in large quantities. Then there was the greedy or patriotic landlords to payoff, either way I'd have them killed for being in my BI.

Certain chemicals have a distinctive odor when mixed together. Sometimes there'd be a strong smell of chemical solvent lingering, tenants became suspicious. Private homes were discreet, with garages, driveways, and yards to get rid of trash. The disposal of waste like the type we had would be suspicious to the sanitation department, neighbors, or cops.

We hauled our own trash in vans and the Mexicans took care of the rest. The houses were a good distant from each other, and we tried to limit the amount of traffic throughout any one location.

Crystal meth was a drug that was potent and could keep you high for eight to twelve hours. It was beginning to become popular in the city. I went from a re-up of four keys, to fifty keys in one month. Just $500 worth of ingredients can yield a kilo, with a street value of $15,000.

The Mexicans were on point. Rodriquez was the number one guy in New York. You needed something you went to him, nobody else. Falco was the number one man coming from the Amezcua Cartel. He was from Tijuana and so was his organization.

The Amezcua Cartel had hubs set up all over the country—Atlanta, Dallas, Phoenix, Portland, Los Angles, San Diego, Guadalajara, Culiacan, Tijuana, and now they were moving into New York, with me as their backbone. Seventy-five percent of meth consumed in the country came from a Mexican Cartel. With this new drug on the block, it was looking like the crack epidemic all over again.

My crew was making money hands over fist. We had our share of enemies and rivals. One that was still a thorn in my side was Tiny. A week back, his peeps did a drive-by on one of my spots and killed a worker. Tiny needed to be dealt with.

I was in bed with the Mexicans now, and the prices they were hooking me up with were sweet. I cut my coke supply with Demetrius by a half and when I started buying less from him, threats soon followed. Demetrius was a very respected and powerful man in New York, and I knew I couldn't make my move on him yet.

I needed the Mexicans for support and back up. If my crew went to war, I couldn't go up against Tiny and Demetrius at the same time. I played it smart, becoming a loyal consumer for Rodriquez and the cartel. Soon I became an investment to them. I needed the Amezcua Cartel to see that I was a money tree for them, and New York was gonna make them richer than ever. Then they would see that my enemies were their enemies.

I had money to burn and I needed protection, not just from the streets, but the law also. My money was long, and I had to spread some. I retained the best defensive lawyers. I had a team of cops in my pocket, couple from the 113th precinct and the 103rd.

One of the cops, a woman, was on the force for three years. Judy was from the 113th and we met a few days after I hooked up with Jazmin.

I met Judy at a mutual friend's party. Judy was light skinned with frizzy reddish hair, an agreeably petite figure, and no tits. She was cute, sported wired framed glasses and had a small acne problem. But she was a benefit to my organization.

Judy was turned on by my continuous cash flow. I had no idea she was a cop. I paid for all her drinks and we hit it off lovely. Despite being a cop, Judy was into bad boys. I knew she had some idea of what I was about, but that didn't stop her from getting to know me better. I took her number and linked up a week later for drinks, mingled at a lounge in downtown Brooklyn. Later that night, I got a suite at the Sheraton and fucked the shit out of her.

That night she admitted she was a police officer. I saw it as an opportunity. Then I find out that her pops was a Lieutenant in Brooklyn, and she was daddy's little girl. I had to keep her around.

I was on my way to running the city. There were heads to exterminate in order for me to step up my game. I had to let other drug crews know, meth was my thing. If they tried pushing weight in my area without copping product from me, then there was a problem. My first problem was Tiny once again.

Late Saturday evening, Biscuit and myself spotted one of Tiny's soldiers over on Supthin and Foch. He walked into a barbershop with a friend.

"Yo Mega, that's the nigga that robbed your spot the other night," Biscuit said.

I watched Biscuit pulled the .357 from under the driver's seat and cocked it.

"Let me handle that nigga. Do him right there in the barbershop… Fuck him up bad," he said fervently.

I looked at him and nodded. He smiled, stuffed the gat down his waistband, and jumped out the car. We were parked across the street from the barbershop. Word got out that Flop, Biscuit's target, just got out a few months ago and had become one of Tiny's hired gun. Tiny set him lose on me, but Biscuit was about to put lead in him.

I sat in the passenger's seat, nonchalantly watching Biscuit crossing the busy Blvd. The barbershop didn't look crowded, only a few heads lingering around talking and bullshitting. The front of the place was strictly glass and transparent with a clear view from where I was parked.

Flop was sitting in the barber's chair about to get a haircut. Biscuit stood off to the side smoking a cigarette, waiting for the right moment. My cell phone rang and I answered.

"What's good?"

"Hey baby, are you seeing me tonight?" Judy asked.

"When you getting off?"

"In a few hours. It's Saturday, and I miss you."

"We can definitely work sump'n out."

"Are you busy?" she asked all polite.

"Not really, just chillin'. Just call me when you get off work and we'll link up."

"Definitely, baby."

I hung up as two men exited the barbershop. There were now two barbers inside with Flop. Biscuit took one more drag from his cancer stick, pulled out his gat, and casually walked into the shop. Flop was in the chair running his mouth.

Biscuit walked in and without hesitation shot Flop twice in the head. Flop tumbled to the floor. Biscuit quickly pointed his gun at the two men then began walking backwards to the door, his gun trained on the barbers. He stuffed the gun down his jeans and began walking back to the car. He jumped in the driver's side, and drove off.

"You a lethal nigga," I noted.

"I just do what I do… Execute niggas to prove a point," he replied with a sadistic smirk.

"Yo, his barber cuts nice. I might have to check him some day for a shape up," he joked.

"You a wild boy, nigga," I laughed.

My phone went off again. It was Jazmin.

"What up, shorty?" I answered.

"Why you ain't call me today, baby? I called you twice, and it went straight to voicemail both times," she complained.

"Bitch, don't call me wit' that bullshit, I've been busy," I chided.

"I'm sorry baby, but I miss you. I didn't get to see you all last week, and you know how I get when I need some," she whined.

"So you coming through later?" she asked, sounding a bit desperate.

"I'll think about it."

"Omega, why you playing me?" she barked.

"Bitch, don't get fuckin' loud over this phone. You fuckin' hear me?" I snapped.

"I'm sorry, baby. I'm sorry."

"I'll check you tomorrow, but tonight, I'm busy," I said and hung up.

"That was Jazmin whining ass?" Biscuit asked.

"Fuck that bitch!" I cursed.

Jazmin was hood, and down for whatever. She helped my crew stash drugs and guns, and was ready to kill for me. Her young naïve ass was willing to prove her undying love to me by any means necessary and stood tall with me through a few incidents during the short time we met. But she could be needy sometimes and had some issues that really pissed me off.

Jazmin and Judy didn't know about each other. And I kept it like that. If they knew about each other, then jealousy would kick-in, and jealousy will make a bitch emotional. When a bitch becomes emotional, she'll start doing stupid things, and that's where troubles begin. I was no doubt using Judy, but when it came to sex, she was a wildcat, and there were no limits with her.

Biscuit dropped me at Judy's crib after midnight. I reached her apartment and I was in the mood for some pussy. Her two-bedroom, well furnished, basement apartment in Freeport, Long Island became one of my chill spots outside Queens. I rang the doorbell, and she answered the door in panties and bra.

"It's about time, baby," she greeted me with a hug.

Gerald Levert was playing and incense was burning. She began tugging at my shirt, moving her hand across my chest and unbuckling my pants eagerly.

"You got that for me?" she asked.

A devilish grin escaped and I reached into my jacket pocket. I pulled out the meth for her to snort. Judy smiled.

"You're the best, boo," she said then pulled out my dick, stroking me gently.

I moaned, feeling my rock hard erection rise to her touch. Sprinkling some crushed meth on my dick.

"Suck my dick," I ordered.

She did without hesitation, sucking my joint with the meth, and snorting the drug in one motion.

"You want more?"

I dangled the drug over her head and she looked possessed. The bitch was about to go into overdrive. She swallowed me whole, sucking and chewing on my genitals.

Her sex-drive became excessive because of the meth. It turned the bitch into a crazy ass nymph. I was staring down at NYPD at its best, kneeling, kissing and pleasing a king.

"Um uh... Um hmm."

She slobbered me down, and deep throat every inch. I had my hand tangled in her frizzled reddish hair, forcing myself down her throat. The bitch coughed and gagged, but continued to suck me off.

I stared at her, loving it. Judy had a taste for bad boys and the drugs. That gave her extra boost. I definitely had my way with her, taking advantage of her high. I came out my pants and backpedaled toward the couch. I needed to sit down. Judy followed. She was now horny and really fuckin' high off the meth.

I was slumped on the couch with Judy spreading my legs wider. She kissed between my thighs, and tickled my balls with her tongue, then shoved my dick down her throat for the thrill. Saliva ran from the corner of her mouth as she hummed against my nut-sack.

I told the bitch to stop and go get her gun. She didn't ask questions. She came back a short moment later with a Glock17 in her hand and handed it over to me. I had to smile. I had Judy lie across the couch on her back and spread her legs. I then took her gun and gradually pushed it into her pussy, mixing hard deadly steel with runny warm soft flesh. I pushed more of the barrel length into her and she cried out, clutching the couch. Her legs began to quiver. I thrust the gun in and out of her like a fast discharge having her juices spill out all over the gun.

I loved doing her with her own gun. It was the biggest turn on for me. I used mine once, but it wasn't the same. And what was crazy, the shit was still loaded. Judy quickly came out her bra and removed her panties and was ready to lose herself in the nastiest way.

"Fuck me, Omega! Fuck me now," she cried out in a heated pitch, showing me how strong her sexual craving was.

I tossed the bitch the rest of the crystal meth, and she snorted that shit within a minute leaving her nose red. I protected myself with a magnum and gripped that bitch by her slim waist, shoving my dick into her ass and made her teeth sink into the couch from the heavy pounding.

"You a dirty pig bitch, right?" I exclaimed.

"Hells yeah, baby."

"Bitch, let me hear you scream like pig."

"Oink… Oink… Oink…Oink… Ooh… Oh," she chanted.

Judy was high on crank, and it made the sex much more exhilarating. She would have been able to go all night. But I wasn't on drugs and had my limitations. When I had no more use for the bitch, I called up Biscuit and had him come pick me up around three in the morning and drive me to the crib.

They call me the devil's pawn. Look at me and see
hell is born. The new walking fury

18

Immorality is in the air tonight
infecting the weak and sinful
soon before the day is light...

Omega

The following morning I was asleep. Jazmin was nestled butt-naked next to me. My cell phone rang. It was on the nightstand nearby. I glanced at the time. It was noon. After my episode with Judy, I came here. Despite our small beef, Jazmin was my ride or die chick.

"Yo, why da fuck you calling me so early?" I barked, without knowing who was calling.

"It's Greasy, we need to talk?"

"'Bout what?" I asked.

"Demetrius came to me last night; he wants a meeting with you."

I stood upright in the bed, with my back on the headboard and the phone still pressed against my ear. "What that Jamaican muthafucka saying?"

"He just wants to talk. What you wanna do?"

I had to think. I was still at war with his cousin Tiny, and I shitted on him by cutting my product from him in half. He had to know about my deal with the Mexicans. I never trusted Demetrius. It could be a set up. I had witnessed how he wiped out Tyriq's whole crew overnight and used me to set it up. Spoon was dead and Vincent locked up. The Columbians were in the federal pen. Demetrius had full control over the city with the brutal Shower Posse at his beck and call.

Demetrius was a greedy bastard. Everything was cool as long as he was making plenty of money off you. He hated problems and betrayal. My deal with the Amezcua Cartel would be a problem and a betrayal. I wasn't in the position to war with the Jamaicans just yet. Demetrius had rained destruction on my former bosses and without the Mexicans support a war would be an uphill battle.

"You want me to set sump'n up?" Greasy asked.

My mind was in a spin. I had to do sump'n. The Jamaicans were a threat, but I needed to be an even bigger threat.

"Go ahead, set it," I said.

"How you wanna play it?"

"I don't trust that nigga, Greasy. Set up the meeting somewhere

141

mutual and in the public, but not too much public. You feel me?"

"I feel you. I'll get back to you with that," Greasy said then he hung up.

I turned off my cell phone thinking. It was game time now. I definitely needed Soul, but he was acting funny, still straddling the damn fence. He was a married man now. Prison may have actually changed that nigga. He needed a push, some kind of reason to come back in the game, but I couldn't think of anything.

"You hungry baby?" Jazmin asked waking up and rubbing her eyes.

"Yeah," I responded, my mind elsewhere.

She smiled and straddled me, gazing at me with her soft brown eyes.

"What you want for breakfast?"

"I don't give a fuck… Cook anything."

"Whatever nigga!" she retorted.

She hastily got her naked ass from off my lap and marched into the bathroom, slamming the door.

Around six that evening, Greasy called back and told me the meeting was set for eight tomorrow evening at Baisley Pond Park. It was close to home, in the public, but not too many people were around where they would be in the biz. It was a perfect spot.

Monday evening we pulled into the small parking lot of Baisley Pond Park. Dusk was settling, and Greasy pulled the truck into one of the many open spots in the parking lot. Biscuit sat in the back holding onto an Uzi, for that just in case reasoning. I had a .357 in a stash box, and Greasy carried a .45 concealed.

"Fo' real, you should let me air out his greedy ass and see if that nigga bleeds green like his fucked up Jamaican flag," Biscuit said.

He wanted to shoot everyone, but it couldn't play out like that.

The game had to be played like chess; every move had to be strategic and careful. Believe me, I really wanted to just kill everyone and take over this muthafuckin' city.

We sat and waited patiently, watching cars pull in and out. The parking lot was thin with cars. Around fifteen after eight, a black Yukon on polished 22" black rims came cruising into the parking lot. I nudged Greasy, pointing out the truck.

It pulled up about four spaces from us. The windows were tinted and we heard the system bumping reggae. It was Demetrius. I became even more alert—remembering how Tyriq and Tip was caught off guard and gunned down a few years ago. I wasn't going to be caught napping.

The three of us stepped out of the truck and approached Demetrius. He slowly emerged from the backseat of the Yukon clad in a pair of beige cargo shorts, with a netted green, yellow and red tank top displaying a weed plant across his chest. He stood about six-five with a stout build and his long dreadlocks hung from his head, twisting like thick rope down to his back.

Demetrious and a crew of three, including his right hand man, Jagged approached us. I walked up to Demetrius feeling tension so thick; you could slice it with a butter knife.

"Brethren, why yuh bring da little youth to grown folks business. Him no need to be hurr. Mi will deal with him real soon," Demetrius said, pointing at Biscuit.

"Fuck you, Ja-fake-can ass. Fo' real, nigga! You see me smilin'?" Biscuit retorted, getting ready to wild out.

"Little one, you will come upon mi wrath real soon for killing me cousin Flop. Mi gwine teach ya a lesson," Demetrious continued in his thick Jamaican accent.

Demetrious and Biscuit exchanged hard stares and I knew Biscuit was itching to take a go at him, but I had to restrain my dog.

Biscuit reached for his gun. Jagged and his men started to pull out. But I intervened and got Biscuit to be calm. The Jamaicans knew Biscuit was responsible for killing Flop.

"Omega, keep dat bitch on a blood- claat leash where it belongs, cuz him gwine see me vex real soon," Demetrius warned.

"Let's talk," I said to Demetrius.

"Mi listening," Demetrius responded.

We took a short walk. Before leaving, I looked at Biscuit and gave him a warning to chill. I knew Greasy had him under control. Demetrius and myself began walking down the cemented path that ran parallel to the lake.

The park was tranquil. The meadow covered with ducks. A soft breeze shook the leaves. This pleasant surrounding should put a nigga at ease, but dealing with the Jamaicans had a nigga on edge.

"Why ya fuck wit' me, brethren? I'm da one that started yuh, and now yuh wan betray mi and leave da nest to get in bed wit' dem raas-claat Mexicans. Mi run dis city. Yuh hear and yuh disrespect mi? Mi get rid of dem Columbians and yuh see what we did to yuh other boss, Tyiq. Brethren, I think da man smarta than that."

"Your city?" I chuckled. "First of all, nobody owns me. Ya heard me? You owe me. I'm the one who helped build your shit, selling, and spilling blood. Now it's my turn. I ain't fuckin' wit' you anymore Demetrius!" I barked.

"Watch yuh bombo-claat mouth 'round mi. Mi will chop yuh down. Yuh think da Mexicans will back yuh when I rain down war on yuh whole blood-claat crew. Mi cut yuh a good deal and now yuh stand here before mi and spit in Shotta's face?"

"You finish? Business is business," I said.

"Mega, yuh in over yuh head. This a man's game."

"It's a new day. I'm stepping up, and I no longer need your services. Ya heard me, dreadlocks?"

"Brethren you realize there's no turning back."

"Do what you gotta do, muthafucka."

Demetrius shot me an evil smirk that would put fear in the average man, but I wasn't average.

"Mi will find yuh and gut yuh like da blood-claat pig."

"You and your cousin better watch your back. This my town, nigga. I'm running shit now! I ain't fuckin' Tyriq or Vincent, ya heard?"

"Yuh made yuh own blood-claat bed, now yuh gwine bleed in it. Tell Biscuit mi gwine finish what he started wit' mi cousin. Mi nah feget this,

Mega."

"Yeah, whatever nigga. Fuck doing business wit' you too!"

I started to step away from him, never taking my eyes off of him. His eyes stayed fixed on me with a cold chilling stare. A war was brewing. It was only a matter of time before Queens became Iraq. I motioned to Greasy and Biscuit. It was time for us to go.

"Batty-boyz unu better behave," Jagged said in his thick Jamaican accent. "I don't wanna have to take off my belt and spank yuh lickle asses…"

Before I jumped into the truck, I looked fiercely at Jagged and held his stare for a beat without responding. I got in and Greasy drove out the parking lot.

"Why we leave 'em breathing?" he questioned.

"Chill, Biscuit," I urged.

"Even Stevie Wonder could see that Demetrius wasn't too happy," Greasy laughed.

"Fuck that nigga. He want war, I'll give him fuckin' war," I said.

"What about the Mexicans, they gonna have our back on this?" Greasy asked. "We gonna need extra guns."

I had to come hard to show that I'm somebody you didn't want to fuck around with. I was in this game to win it all. I had to go hard or I was gonna die trying.

19

Absence is to love what wind is to fire
it extinguishes the small, it kindles the great...

America

I kept my pregnancy quiet. My music career had suddenly zoomed off. There was a buzz on the streets about my CD that Kendal dropped. I was also booming, doing hooks, verses, and ad-libs for rappers, mostly underground.

My sudden exposure came with an emotional price tag. Everyday after work, I was in the studio, and on weekends. I was seeing less and less of my husband because my career was growing. I spent more time writing and had so much to say and felt that there was so little time to say it.

I was now two months pregnant and knew I couldn't hide my pregnancy from Kendal and friends for too much longer. I was worried that my pregnancy would intimidate my rising fans and sudden admirers. I loved being pregnant, but felt that now it came at a bad time.

Kendal kept me running everywhere. I was doing shows with him and his crew, recording in different studios. Everywhere throughout the city, listeners were in awe and my beauty and charisma had them digging my style.

Independent record companies had their eyes and ears on me, looking to sign me. Kendal happily informed me that an A&R from Def Jam wanted to meet. It was happening so fast, my talent was causing a buzz. People started thinking that America was my stage name.

Omar appeared happy for my success, but being on the go constantly started to wear on him. He worried about my health and the baby's. Omar often warned me about going so hard. We'd argue and he'd be so angry that he'd shout then leave for hours. I was spending more time with Kendal and Omar was becoming jealous.

My dreams of breaking into the music business were coming through. I just couldn't walk away. Omar had a job at the community center. So it seemed he was finally getting his life right and leaving the streets alone. We were becoming a family, and I prayed every night for us to stay together.

Friday evening, I was hanging with Joanna. We planned on shopping in the city along Fifth Avenue followed by a late lunch. Joanna did most of the shopping. She spent over two grand in four different stores. Later, we dined at Magic's Chef.

"So bitch, when are you due?" Joanna asked.

"Excuse me," I replied incredulously, choking on my sandwich.

"America, how long have we been friends, and you think I don't notice. Why are you trying to hide it?"

I smiled.

"Are you smiling? So how far along are you?"

"Two months," I answered meekly.

"Two fucking months? We ain't friends anymore," Joanna barked. But I knew she was kidding.

"So bitch, you just got married and right away, a baby? I'm hearing you're starting to do big things with your music. So I assumed this meal is on you since you couldn't tell me the good news."

I chuckled. "I wanted to keep my pregnancy a secret for the moment."

"Why?" she questioned.

"Because my career is starting to pop off. Who's gonna want to sign a pregnant singer. You know how it is in this business? Sometimes as long as guys think they could hit it, they ready to open all kinds of doors. Once they see that I'm about to have a baby, they gonna try to find the next—"

"America, bitch please. That's nonsense. You got talent, girl. True fucking talent, and if niggas tryin' to put you on because they only want to fuck you, then leave them alone," she said cutting me off.

Diners at the neighboring table turned to look at us, shocked to hear Joanna, who appeared to look like a rich white girl used the N-word to me.

"What, y'all muthafuckas shocked because I said nigga; well I was born in the hood and got Spanish blood running all through me, so get the fuck over it and mind y'all fucking business. I swear America, muthafuckas are nosey up in this piece," she spat.

I laughed, seeing these people blush with embarrassment.

"But anyway, like I was saying bitch, keep doing you and remember when you walk up on that stage to collect your Grammy. Bitch you better have me standing right next to your ass and thanking me first," she laughed.

"Girl, you know it." I slapped her five.

We continued to dine and I paid the bill. Joanna only had plastic on her, so I paid cash and gave the waiter a ten-dollar tip.

A few hours later, I met up with Kendal at the studio in Brooklyn. I came in some sweats and a T-shirt, and was ready to get to work. I knew I wouldn't be able to hide my pregnancy from him for too long. I was really starting to show. And it was a shame that women could notice a girl was pregnant faster than any man. I couldn't hide it from Joanna or my co-worker Monica, but here I was working with Kendal everyday and he didn't have any idea until today.

I walked down into the studio and Kendal was working with one of his rappers. His name was Vision he was a lyricist who reminded me of Nas. Kendal looked up at me, and went back to working with Vision. I walked in on him while he was playing with the mixer.

"What's good, America?" Vision greeted me with a smile and a hug.

"Hey baby, I heard you're doing your thang on the mix tapes now," I said.

"You know it. But congratulations to you. I'm hearing all about you through the grapevine. You know we gotta collaborate on sump'n," he said.

"That's what's up, Vision," I replied smiling.

"Hi Kendal," I greeted cheerfully.

"What's good, ma?" he answered dryly.

An eerie silence wedged itself between us. Vision's ringing cell phone broke the tension.

"Oh shit, this my shorty right here. Yo, I'm gonna take this outside," he said. Before walking out, he hollered, "Yo, Kendal, I'm gonna continue our session tomorrow, ahight?"

Kendal nodded, Vision waved and bounded out the studio. Silence returned immediately after Vision's departure. It was clear that Kendal was agitated by something. I didn't know the reason.

"Are you just gonna ignore me for the rest of the evening?" I asked.

"When was you gonna let me know about the baby?" he asked sarcastically.

"So you know."

"Yeah, a lil' birdie told me. Why you be hiding shit from me, America? Damn, this is fucked up. You've got record labels lookin' at you and you about to blow up, and you get fucking pregnant!" he barked.

"Well that what usually happens when two people have sex," I retorted angrily.

"You keeping it?"

"Of course I'm keeping my baby. It's my husband," I shouted becoming really annoyed with his mannerism.

"No disrespect America, but you got a lot going on for you right now, and dude comes home and boom— everything changes."

"It doesn't have to. I can still move forward. I'm only pregnant, that doesn't affect my voice and the way I sing," I said.

"But you know how some of these dudes can be, they want beauty along with a voice and with you pregnant, they just might turn the other way and find someone else."

"Well it'll be their lost, not mine. I'm still beautiful. I'm pregnant not deformed, Kendal."

"We came a long way, America. And now I feel shit's going down the drain right now. Damn, I had so much invested into you, I trusted you and you fucked me!" he spat.

"I fucked you? Kendal, what's really going on with you?" I asked with a perplexed look. "This is more than music and me being pregnant," I said. "We've been friends for over a year now, and I came down here almost every day laying down tracks and bugging out with you, and there was never a problem with you. We're good together and we connect with music on so many levels, that I don't want this to end."

"I don't either."

"Oh, I see," I said. It finally dawned on me. "Are you jealous of my husband?"

Kendal didn't answer me right away. He turned away, avoiding eye contact.

"So what's the deal between us?" I sighed. "You don't want me down here anymore?" I asked.

"I never said that," he answered sounding annoyed.

"So what are you saying?" I asked staring him down.

His gaze held mine long enough for me to see his eyes becoming cloudy.

"America, I'm in love with you. I tried not to be, but I can't help it."

"Kendal, but you knew about my situation from the jump," I said.

"I know, and when Monica introduced us, it was just business... Believe me. You have a great voice, and I have the right tracks. Together I know we can do big things. I try to deny my feelings for you, but it came to a point where I was looking forward to seeing you in my studio, even if it was for a short moment. I love everything about you, America... Your laugh, your talents, you're so caring and you're so beautiful. I hated knowing that I might never have you. It was magic the way we connected, and when you talked about your man, I felt jealous. I hated hearing about him, especially in my place. But I listened to your problems. And the shit this nigga put you through, I always questioned myself, why are you still with him? I wanted to give you so much more than just good beats and tracks. I wish I was the man in your life, not him."

He stood close to me with his eyes never leaving mines. I didn't even know how he felt about me until recently, when the attitude and sarcasm came out. Kendal's a cutie and had a lot going on for him. I'd be lying if I said that I wasn't a little attracted to him. But not enough, I kept it business with him. I've been with one man, Omar, since I was fifteen, and I'd never cheat on my man. Kendal took my hands into his while gazing in my eyes.

"I'm trying to let it be business only between us, but my love for you is making it hard."

"I don't know what to say to you, Kendal. I'm married, and we're having a family. I never wanted to mislead you. I love and cherish our friendship and your honesty, and I don't want that to ever end. But us, it can't..."

Before I could finish the sentence, Kendal grabbed me into his arms and started kissing me passionately. I was shocked by his sudden boldness. I was more surprised with myself when I didn't resist. I should have slapped him blind and cursed him out. But didn't. My arms were draped around him, embracing him. His lips were soft as butter as his warm, fresh breath filled me up.

He picked me up, and without thinking, I straddled him. This couldn't happen, but I wasn't trying to resist. I was married, pregnant, and this was a sin—infidelity was wrong. But my attraction to him with the curiosity of being with another man sexually was winning.

Kendal walked me over to the brown sofa. My back was pressed against it, and my legs wrapped around him. I felt my tongue slipping into his mouth. A river was flowing between my legs and my nipples were erect from his touch.

Kendal pulled at my sweats, trying to remove them. I held on with a weak grip. Minor resistance to his persistence, my heart pounded rapidly, and my conscience ate away at me. Omar weighed heavily on my mind. Briefly.

With a quick tug, Kendal pulled my sweatpants off. My Victoria Secrets followed quickly. His hand expertly grazed my trimmed pubic and my pussy throbbed uncontrollably. Kendal pulled up my shirt and gently kissed me on my pregnant belly. I felt his hand reach down in between my thighs and grabbed a handful.

I moaned enjoying the guilty pleasures. My eyes were closed and I bit my lips, enjoying Kendal's lips sucking on my nipples while fingering me. He began unbuckling his pants as he stared at me in the raw. He hurriedly came out his jeans and boxers and I gasped. Kendal's dick was hard like a long steel pipe.

Fear struck me and breath seemed caught in my throat. I needed to put this escapade with Kendal in check, I thought, spreading my legs wider for him. I gazed up at him with pleading eyes. He slowly positioned himself between my thighs, and slowly pushed his erection into me.

"Ugh!"

The grunt escaped both our mouths simultaneously. I held onto his arms as he plunged his hard thick flesh deep. He gripped the couch trying to get his rhythm going. Kendal danced between my thighs. My eyes were closed and guilt suddenly overwhelmed me.

It felt good, but in my mind, I was thinking about my husband. Our love and his trust for me hit me like a sledgehammer. He cheated with countless women beforehand and I probably deserved this one quick good fuck from another man, just to see how it feels. But two wrongs don't make a right. Omar was finally getting his act right and trying to better himself for us to be a family. Now I was doing wrong by him.

Kendal gripped my hips and was fucking me with burning passion. He fondled my breasts, kissed me tenderly on my neck and whispered in my ear.

"I love you, America."

Oh God, this is wrong. Wrong, so wrong. I pledged my love to another man and tried to be a woman of God, despite all the wrong Omar's done in his life, he deserved another chance. He deserved all my love and trust and this pussy belonged to him.

Kendal's dick was swelling up in me, tightening my walls with each thrust. It had to stop. It shouldn't go any further, but lust, temptation, and curiosity plagued me and I wanted to let him finish. But each thrust betrayed something stronger, something that lust and temptation shouldn't be able to break.

I made a vow to my husband and God. I questioned myself, how can I be celibate for four years and then slip up after Omar's return home. I had his trust, and he needed mine. I wanted him to do right for himself and the baby. Tears were running and I hated myself. This couldn't continue. I gripped Kendal's shoulder while he was still plunging himself into me, enjoying every moment.

"Kendal, stop," I said, slowly trying to push his sweaty body off me.

He was tenacious and didn't hear me. I pushed him harder by his shoulders.

"Kendal, stop, please!" I begged.

He looked at me confusedly. "What?"

"I can't continue," I said.

"What you mean, America? I'm almost there. I need this, please don't do this to me," he pleaded.

"I - I can't. I'm a married woman. I'm carrying his baby, and I love him too much."

"What the fuck?"

He pulled his dick out of me and jumped off the couch. Backing off, Kendal had an incredulous look on his face. He was still hard.

"Why are you doing this to me, huh? We're good together."

I had fucked up and crossed the line. Knowing Kendal had strong feelings for me, I had gone there. Sitting upright on the couch. I picked up my panties and sweatpants off the floor and quickly began getting dressed.

"America, you know I love you, right? And I'll never hurt you. So why you gotta hurt me? You could have let me finished at least. Why are you doing this to me?"

"Kendal, I'm so sorry, I shouldn't have started this. You've been so nice to me and you helped me so much with my career that I just got caught in the moment. Omar's the only man I've been with and…"

My voice trailed, I didn't know what else to say to him. It was now awkward between us. Kendal reached for his clothing and began getting dressed. When he fastened his belt, he looked at me and said, "You know what, it was mistake… You, me, the music and me hoping for sump'n I know will never happen between us. To hell with all this shit. You know what? Just go on and get the fuck up out my studio!"

"Excuse me…?"

"You heard me, get the fuck up out. I ain't trying to deal with you on any level anymore. Go be with your nigga, and when he breaks your heart again, I ain't here for you anymore, go cry on someone else's shoulder," he barked.

I was shocked and in awe. I stood up and said, "So, it's like that between us, Kendal? It was a mistake what we just did. I'm sorry that I allowed it to go that far. But please, let's not end it this way."

He didn't even acknowledge me. We came so far and I didn't want to leave his studio with him mad at me. I wanted to salvage some type of friendship or business arrangement between us. But Kendal was truly upset.

"Fine," I uttered, collecting my things.

Kendal was in the booth, tweaking with the mixer without looking up at me. I was prepared to leave. I looked at him for a moment and then walked out the door. Everything was going so good and now it was going so bad. I had myself to blame. It was the first time I cheated on Omar and it felt sickening. I lost so much, my friendship with Kendal, and now I had a guilty conscience. I sat in my car crying.

When I got home, Omar was in the kitchen making dinner. I tried to hide the look of guilt from my face. It wouldn't leave my mind. I dried my tears and walked into the kitchen to see Omar cheerfully toiling over the stove.

"Hey baby?" he greeted, turning to look at me.

Shockingly, I smacked him across his face. He was shocked and replied, "What the fuck is wrong wit' you?"

I was deeply hurting inside. When I looked at Omar, I knew he committed the same actions against me multiple of times with different women.

How? I thought. I felt so fucked up just letting Kendal get a taste of it and here was Omar who I knew allowed plenty of women to get a taste of him. And I thought to myself, did he ever feel as guilty as I did now?

"America, what the fuck did I do now?" he asked.

"Nothing," I replied.

"So why'd you slap me?"

I was still burning inside. I grabbed him by his shirt and pulled him closer to me. "Fuck me now, baby!"

"What?"

"I wanna feel you in me right now," I pleaded, unbuttoning his shirt and pulling at his belt.

He was confused for a short moment, but then got with the program no longer questioning my actions. We both dropped to the kitchen floor and stripped away our clothes. I felt the coldness of the tiles against my back as Omar climbed in between my legs with us being in the missionary position. He was so hard and inside me, opening me up with his width. My fingernails tore at his backside, leaving long scratches down his back.

About an hour later, we were still sprawled out naked on the kitchen floor. I gazed into Omar's eyes and then gave him a kiss on his lips. "I love you," I said.

"I love you too, baby, even though you be buggin' out sometimes," he said.

I laughed.

"We gonna be a family, America."

Kissing my belly he rubbed it. I smiled so hard that it hurt. That's all I needed to hear from my man. I stared at him as he played with my belly. Then he pressed his ear to my stomach listening. I smiled and laughed.

"Baby, it's too early to hear or feel anything yet."

"I know, but I just enjoy touching you. You and my son are so precious to me. I definitely want this family to happen. I did something last night that I never did before, America. I got on my knees and prayed for us to be a healthy family. You believe that, I prayed. I feel this baby changing me already," Omar said.

What I felt at that moment warmed me like the sun itself. I was speechless, but so moved. Tears trickled down my face.

"You've been good to me since the first time we met. It's time for me to return the favor," he said wiping away my tears.

It felt oh so good making love again and again in the same spot on the kitchen floor. I was never happier.

20

Our life is simply a reflection of our actions.
If you want more love in the world,
Create more love in your heart.
If you want more competence in your team,
improve your competence.

Omar

Peace to you and yours black man. I hope all is well with you. I received the letter that you sent me and I'm happy to hear that you finally became a man and committed to your lady. Marriage is a big step my brother, so take it one day at a time and live every day with her as if it was a new day. The two of you are a team, she's your partner Soul, and let it be 100/100 with each other in all your endeavors—through the good and bad. You share and become one. A woman's love is something no man should take for granted, you hear me my brother.

I miss you though, my brother. But I rather miss you knowing that you're free physically and mentally, than being in here with me. I'm also free Soul, I'm free mentally and no matter where they put me, my mind and soul will always journey free to strive for better and attain knowledge and understanding. They will never take that away from me.

I think about you and Omega constantly…and I regret bringing my younger brother into this life of crime. I thought I was being a good older brother to him by teaching him the way of the streets, how to push drugs, shoot a gun and make money. And now I hear he's spiraling out of control. I can't do much for him in here, and I'm glad you had a talk with him. But don't let him change you, Soul. Don't let my younger brother bring you down. I know he's like family to you, but sometimes we gotta let family be and let them learn the hard way. You can't change a man until he wants to change himself. Omega needs to be stripped away from everything and hurt like I've been hurting over the years. I pray for my younger brother everyday and you should to, Soul. Please pray for my brother. He is lost.

Enough of me rambling, I feel blessed to receive a letter from you and glad that things are working out for you. Keep focus, Soul. Life can be hard, and a struggle, but with good positive people by your side you can soften the journey and make it a bit easier. But before I go, you know I gotta leave you with some jewels. This relationship applies to everything, in all aspects of life. Life will give you back everything you have given to it. Your life is not a coincidence; it is a reflection of you.

Reading Rahmel's letter nearly sent me into tears. Upstate, he held me down and I was glad to hear that my dude was doing okay. I had written him a letter three weeks after my release and informed him what was going on with me. I couldn't keep him in the dark. He helped me so much and I definitely needed to keep in contact with him.

The job at the center was going good. It kept me busy. Mr. Jenkins helped keeping me focused. When he had the chance he'd counsel me on everything and always inquired about America.

The kids at the center took a liking to me. Some had heard of my past reputation and respected me. They even questioned me about being in jail. We discussed aspects of the streets. There were those who wanted to know about how to get paid. There I'd shrugged and continue with my work with Jim, the senior janitor.

Jim was a comedian. He was in his mid fifties and survived Vietnam, the civil rights movement, the crack epidemic and and his ex-wife.

"You wanna know why a divorce is expensive, Omar?" he'd asked.

"Nah, why?"

"Because they're worth it," he joked.

I laughed.

"Shit, the bitch would've probably had one of my nuts too, if they weren't attached."

I continued to laugh at his antics about his ex wife.

"Omar, what you call a redneck farmer with two sheep under his arm?" he asked.

"What?"

"A playboy," he replied.

He was a riot. We were checking the lights in the hallway when Cindy walked by in skintight jeans and a T-shirt.

"Hi Omar," she greeted cheerfully.

"What's up," I replied nonchalantly.

She smiled at me and continued down the hall. Jim and I paused for a moment and stared at her backside.

"Damn," Jim whistled. "Problem with me and 'em young girls is soon as I'm in, I'm out. Beating up pussy's overrated for an old dude like me.

I'm gonna need Viagra and a jump-start to get at that pussy," he laughed.

"Jim, you too much," I chuckled.

"I see she wanna throw some o' that at you, Omar. I can tell," he said.

"Too young for my blood, Jim, what she's like seventeen, eighteen?"

"Eighteen and a sweetheart," he smiled.

"Besides, I'm a married man now."

"I said that to myself four years ago, and then the bitch divorce me a year later."

"How long you been working here?" I asked.

"Ten years now. Mr. Jenkins he's a good dude, Omar. I have nothing but love and respect for that man. He looked out for me, helped me out through rehabilitation and then got me this job after I was two years clean."

"You were on drugs?" I questioned.

"Man, after Vietnam I got married to my wife and moved in with the needle. I spent my honeymoon sick in the bathroom in a cheap ass motel. I got my wife hooked on heroin soon after our wedding and we both went through hell. Turned around and got on the pipe in the eighties. I was more faithful to crack than I was to my wife. Reason being it treated me better, Omar," he said.

"Yeah, hmm."

"My wife got cleaned in ninety one, after our kids were taken away from us and put in a group home. She went into rehab and threatened to divorce me if I didn't do the same. Like I said, I couldn't leave the crack alone, man. Just thinking about getting high used to get my dick hard."

"You got kids, Jim?" I asked incredulously.

"Three, my oldest is about your age, twenty-four. Last time I saw him, he was on trial for murder. He shot a man to death for a dime bag. Twenty-five years to life they gave him. Twenty-five to life."

"Damn!" I muttered shaking my head.

"I wasn't around to raise him. I was either in jail, or too high to even care. My second boy is twenty, and I haven't seen him in six years. Last I heard about him, he was doing stickups. I gotta sixteen-year-old daughter.

She's a bitch like her mother. Can't even keep her fuckin' mouth and legs close long enough to walk and talk straight. She already got a one-year old son. And she's pregnant again by some old muthafuckin' hustler type," he said.

I was quiet, as he talked. There was anger in his voice.

"Yeah, Omar, we far from them Cosby's." He shrugged. "I can't blame the kids for being so fucked up. I have to shoulder the blame. If I was any type of father, their lives would've been better. But I wasn't around to guide and talk to them when they were young. I didn't care; I was stupid. I took better care of my drugs than I did with them."

"What happened to your ex-wife?"

"That bitch been clean now for over fifteen years. She got her life together, remarried, and moved down to Charlotte, North Carolina and started another family with another husband."

"She just forgot you and her kids just like that?" I asked.

"I guess the bitch wanted new memories and so on. We haven't talked in years. She was a fine piece of ass when we got married in ninety-three. Met her after I left detox. We clicked and the bitch got pregnant a year after we met. But the baby died due to complications during my wife's pregnancy. After that, I stopped trying to have any more kids. Besides, the three that I had were fucked up anyways. Mr. Jenkins supported me through some hard times and once I got this job, I never looked back," he said.

"I'm sorry, Jim…"

"What you sorry for, Omar? It's all my fault. You don't apologize to a man unless you have to. My choice cost me my family. That's what drugs do; they make you forget about all-purpose and reality causes a man to be selfish in life. You're young, so learn from your mistakes, and learn from mines too, Omar."

After saying that, Mr. Jenkins came casually walking down the hall. He looked at me and smiled, then asked Jim, "How's he coming along, Jim?"

"He's workable, Mr. Jenkins. Trying to educate the young man. You know?"

"Sometimes it's best to observe things with your own eyes than to listen," Mr. Jenkins laughed walking down the hall.

Jim and I continued with the task at hand. We always talked and shared stories. He knew about my past as a hustler. Shit, I may even have sold him drugs during his drugged-out years.

It was after nine and I was getting off the job. The night was quiet. Most of the kids and staff had already left the center. I walked outside and Greasy was posted up, talking to one of the young girls from the center. Business seemed good. He was pushing a new silver Lexus and he sparkled diamonds and platinum. Greasy saw me and shouted, "There goes my nigga right there. What's up cuz?"

I walked over and gave him dap. I'd seen the young girl he was with at the center a few times. She was a cutie, and was into thugs.

"That's your cousin?" she questioned, staring at me with an inquisitive smile.

"Yeah, this nigga is a muthafuckin' OG," Greasy said proudly. "But now this nigga got a job and shit, thinkin' he Mr. Rogers. You fucking around with these young bitches up in here, Soul? Tell me that's why da fuck you up in here."

"What you doing 'round here, cuz?" I asked.

"Nigga, Greasy came to check you. I wanted to see what's really good wit' my nigga," he said, with shorty clamped tightly under his arm.

"How'd you find out I work here?"

"Nigga, you know we got fuckin' eyes everywhere. We got young soldiers up in this piece too, my nigga," he informed. "And you know how I do? Greasy stay lookin' for some bitches to grease."

He looked high, talking all loud and erratic. The young girl he was with was only seventeen, and been passed around the young homies from the block a few times.

"Soul, we 'bout to party tonight, I came to get you. It's been a minute since we hung out together; you know what I'm sayin'…?"

"I'm a pass on that, Greasy," I said.

"Nigga, what…? Get the fuck outta here! That Leave-It-To-Beaver-shit ain't working here. I'm your family, nigga and I got you."

Greasy pulled out a wad of hundreds, flashing them in front of shorty and me kind of recklessly. "I got the gwap… Everything is on me tonight. You down, luv?"

"Yeah, you know I'm down, baby," she answered, teasingly pushing up against Greasy.

"What's up, Soul? We haven't really chilled together since you came home, nigga. Don't disappoint me on this tonight. We waiting for her friend to get off. Nigga it's a nice night, Greasy's paid, and I got me a fine shorty right here, and her friend is just as fine. We do it like ol' times, my nigga. "

"Here comes my friend right there," shorty smiled and nodded. "Cindy. Cindy, over here."

I turned around. And oh shit, it damn sure was. It was Cindy from the center, looking sumptuous. A tense sigh, sounding like a whistle, escaped my lips.

"There you go cuz, shorty's nice." Greasy smiled, looking at me.

Cindy waved at us, smiling when she saw me standing with her friend and Greasy.

"What's up y'all…? Hey Omar, what you doing standing out here with my home-girl, huh?"

"We 'bout to roll, girl. You coming, right?" Greasy said.

Cindy smiled and nodded enthusiastically.

"See, there you go, Soul. Greasy got his and you got yours," Greasy said, tossing me the keys to the whip. "I'm feelin kinda twisted, cuz. You gon have to drive. Me and Gina be in the backseat. Besides, Greasy owe you, since I crashed that nice ride you had back-in-the-days. Shit used to ride smooth like a bitch on top."

This situation seemed unavoidable. I got forced into this shit because Greasy looked to be in no condition to drive. I walked around to the driver's side. Cindy jumped in the front seat. Greasy and Gina occupied the back.

I drove off, and Greasy wanted to stop at his crib for a moment. He wanted to be a showoff and impress the two young ladies that he had wit us with his spacious three-bedroom crib in Elmont

"I've been hearing much about you, Omar. So you are the famous Soul, huh?" Cindy asked, trying to start a conversation.

I nodded. I could hear Greasy and Gina getting it on in the backseat. I was thinking, this is trouble waiting to happen. I didn't mind hanging out with Greasy, but when it concerned bitches, he acted stupid. Greasy always stunted hardest in front of the bitches, flashing money, jewelry and talking shit. He wanted to be the man.

"I heard that you were locked up," Cindy interrupted my thoughts.

"Yeah… A small bid."

"How long were you in?"

"I did four…"

"I got a cousin who did ten years. Maybe you know him. He goes by the name, Breezy," she said.

"Nah, that name don't ring bells with me," I said, trying to keep my conversation short and simple.

She was trouble for me. Cute, young, and I knew she was ready to drop the panties for me.

"So, you gotta girl?" she asked smiling.

"Yeah, I'm married."

"Oh, wow."

The news shocked her. Greasy seized the moment and immediately intervened.

"Yo, shorty, Soul's a real nigga. He don't give a fuck…"

I wanted to smack the shit out of his mouth. But shot Greasy my coldest stare through the rearview mirror as I continued driving.

"So, you love her?" Cindy asked.

"No doubt."

"That's nice. You look like you would make a good husband to someone. I just broke up with my man a few weeks… These young niggas be actin' stupid all the time. I want a man that's able to hold me down. I'm not the one for the BS. I'm tired of these niggas out here that ain't about shit," she said.

"Cindy, you're young. You in school?"

"I'm a freshman at York College."

"That's what's up, keep doin' you."

Things were really heating up in the backseat with my cousin and the girl. I watched Greasy smiling, pulling something out of his jacket.

"Yo, cuz, you down for a hit?" he asked.

I saw the pack and wanted to wild out on Greasy.

"Nigga, what the fuck is the matter wit' you? I'm out on papers and you got me driving a dirty car!"

"Nigga, stop being so paranoid. It ain't that much drugs. And we ain't gettin' pulled the fuck over. Why the fuck you trippin'?"

"Cuz, I'm on fuckin' parole, nigga! And if I'm violated, I'm back upstate."

The girls were startled by my sudden outbreak. I didn't care. My cousin was being an asshole, risking my freedom. I didn't want to catch some small-time possession charge.

"What else you got in this ride?" I asked.

"You know how we do, cuz. There's a nine-milli under the seat," he informed.

"Fuck you, Greasy!" I shouted. "For real nigga, fuck you, nigga!"

I wanted to pull over and get the fuck out. Then I caught a glimpse of Cindy and there was a worried look on her face. So I continued driving.

"Yo, Soul, just fuckin' drive. Shit is ahight, my nigga. Greasy got you. We ain't too far from my place anyway. Make this right at the next light," he instructed.

While I drove, him and Gina were getting high off of crystal-meth in the back. Cindy was quiet next to me. She stopped asking me all her damn questions.

"Cindy, you want some of this?" Gina asked.

"No, I'm good."

"Bitch you sure? I'm ready to fuck." Gina whispered loudly to Greasy.

Suddenly I felt really uneasy. I just had a positive talk with Jim about drugs, and now here I was chauffeuring my cousin, the drug-dealer to his home. I pulled up to Greasy's two-story Victoria-square home in Elmont. The immensely silent neighborhood was lined with trees and manicured lawns.

"Cuz, welcome to mi casa," Greasy said as he made his way up the steps with Gina clinging to him.

I was overwhelmed when I walked inside. Who knew my cousin had good taste in decorating? The foyer alone was lined with marble floors, as was the rest of his crib. He had a three-bedroom, two and half bathrooms, with outdoor deck, a fireplace, and pool table in the great room. There were two crown-ceiling fans, one in the kitchen and one over the great room. His leather furniture was buttery soft, there was a granite kitchen counter.

"Shit's nice, right Soul?" he asked of me.

My mouth opened but nothing came out. I was definitely impressed. And I thought America had our place decorated nice.

"Mega and I are making big things happen. You see all this shit, Soul?" he asked, pointing to the plasma TV with a play-station type remote in his hand. "Paid up to five grand for this, in cash," he boasted. "My nigga, you should be living like this too. We got the fuckin' world in our hands, my nigga. Ain't no muthafucka fuckin' wit' us, Soul. We makin' sure our shit is on lock. I'm the man, right baby?"

"You sure are," Gina smiled, walking into his embrace.

His swagger was high. Cindy and I just stood there looking lost in the sauce. This mix could prove lethal.

"Chill, make y'all selves comfortable. Y'all family, mi castle, su castle." Greasy laughed.

Rap videos played on a luxurious home entertainment center with a 62" HD plasma screen. Greasy walked into the kitchen. The speakers that encircled the room were deafening. Cindy took a seat on one of the many plush couches that lined the room. I stood gawking for a minute.

"Ooh, this my shit right here," Gina cried out and started dancing to a G-unit track blaring through the room.

"I get in… I get in…" she sang off-key.

The bitch was high off meth, all excited and horny. She started seductively grinding in front of me. Slowly pulling up her denim skirt, gradually exposing her black thong.

"Girl, you're so crazy," Cindy laughed.

"You wanna dance with me, Soul," she licked her finger and teased.

She got up on me, real close and personal. Her skirt hoisted, and began fondling herself. This bitch was a freak but I wasn't with it. I just shook my head.

"Um, 50 could get it," she said loudly, continuing to dance. Then she did the unexpected, pulling off her thong and tossing it at me.

"I'm wet, baby," she said to me.

Cindy looked at her girl Gina disturbed attitude and said, "Gina, I think you need to chill out right now."

"Nah, I'm tryin' to have a good time. It is so hot in here. Ooh, I need to cool off, girl. My pussy is itching. Soul, come scratch it for me," she laughed, pulling her shirt over her head. She was now only clad in bra and skirt.

It was getting real hot up in there and I was becoming more uncomfortable. America entered my thoughts and I knew I had to leave. Gina continued wilding out. Soon she was out of her skirt and when Lil John, *Get Low* started playing on the screen and blaring out the speakers, the bitch went loca. Completely naked she started booty shaking.

Gina was high as a muthafucka, wiggling and slapping her booty. She bounced it around then dropped it like it was hot. I had to admit that her young body was tight, with her thin curvy waistline, a phat ass, and tits like ripe grapefruits. A few years ago, if I was in this same situation, I would have had that bitch bent over the couch, and dug her back out. Things were different now. My life was important to not only me but others.

"Damn bitch, you couldn't wait for a nigga," Greasy hollered, coming out of the kitchen clutching a Moet bottle and more meth.

He went over and started dancing and grinding behind Gina. They snorted more meth and continued wilding. Cindy and I stared at them shaking our heads. Gina curved her naked body over, grabbing hold of the couch and backing it up on Greasy. Greasy grabbed her hips with one hand and downed the bottle of Moet.

"I'm 'bout ready to fuck this bitch," Greasy said, unzipping his pants.

"Damn nigga, chill the fuck out. You're high," I said.

"Nigga, I'm horny. You want dibs on this, Soul?" he asked.

"You wilding, now."

Greasy dropped his pants and thrust his dick into Gina raw. She panted, gripping the couch tightly and sweating profusely.

"Y'all crazy," Cindy shouted, looking on wide eye at the crazy sexual performance.

"Umm, ugh… Ugh, Umm hmm, shit! Fuck me! Oh yes fuck me!" Gina cried out from the doggy position.

Her back was curved over the plush leather sofa and throwing it on Greasy. His ringing cell phone on the glass coffee table interrupting. He picked it up, and answered the call without missing a beat.

"Yo…? Ahight… I got you Mega. What time? Bet… One." I heard him say, as he still continued ramming Gina.

He hung up and looked at me as he continued fucking Gina. "Yo, Soul, do me a favor…? I need to drop something off to Mega. Can you do that for me?"

"Like what?"

"Some cash. It's in the trunk of my ride."

"How much cash we're talkin' about, Greasy?"

"Nigga, it's only a small gwap, twenty-thousand in hundreds. He's at this club on Liberty. Just take my shit, do that for me and have fun. I'm gonna be a minute wit' this bitch. And plus, I owe you a Lexus."

I was skeptical. But I didn't want to hang around and watch Greasy continue to fuck this young bitch. Greasy tossed me his car keys while still pounding Gina.

"You know Greasy got you, my nigga," he added.

"Whateva! I'm out," I told him.

"Good lookin' on that, cuz," he said.

Greasy and I then looked over at Cindy, who was still seated on the couch. Then Greasy came out of his mouth and said to her, "You want me to break you off too, bitch? You know your friend is lovin' this dick right now." He pulled at Gina's hair and smacked her on the ass.

"That's okay, I'll go with Omar," she said, and got up to leave with me.

My cousin was a wild boy and too much pussy was never enough for him. Since we were kids, he's been a playboy and been fucking bitches since ten years old. He wasn't changing his promiscuous ways anytime soon. I wanted no part in what he was in.

Jumping into the Lexus, I drove off knowing that there was twenty grand cash hidden in the trunk. Cindy was quiet towards me for the first ten minutes. The radio was low, and the only thing on my mind at the time was, why the fuck did I say yes. I did five miles over the regulated speed limit down Merrick Blvd.

"So, how long have you been married?" Cindy asked, breaking the silence between us.

"A few weeks now," I replied.

"And how long have y'all been together?"

"Ten years."

"Damn, that's what's up. I hope I can find a man that's like you. So if you don't mind me asking, what's your type of woman anyway?"

I chuckled. "My wife."

She laughed. "I mean, what she look like. I know she pretty, cuz you are fine. If you weren't married, would I be your type?" she asked me, getting bolder with the questions.

I glanced at her and smiled.

"You're cute, and yeah, I like your style. But you're young and I'm a married man," I said.

"Age ain't nothing but a number, and I don't kiss and tell," she stated.

I smirked catching her drift. This bitch was smart, and in school trying to get a degree from York College. But there was another side to her, she loved thugs, and her friend Gina was a wreck waiting to happen.

"We could do us, Omar, and nobody ain't gotta know," Cindy boldly said.

I looked at her briefly thinking, a few years back, it would have been on. Now I couldn't do it.

"Can I ask you sump'n?" I asked.

"What…?"

"Why would you short yourself like that?"

"Excuse me?"

"You're a beautiful girl, and you got a lot going for yourself. I'm always seeing you fucking around with these clown ass wanna-bees. I ain't gonna lie, I been hearing about you and your girl's reps."

"What kind of rep?" She sighed.

"You know what I'm talkin' about."

"Niggas be lying," she said with attitude.

"But you fucking around with them to get quite a name for yourself."

"It's my business," she snapped. "Who are you now, Mr. Jenkins. I thought you was supposed to be this gangsta. Shit, since I met your ass, you've been acting scared!"

"Damn, you be acting all nice, but when I start telling you the truth, you spaz the fuck out. Just chill with all that."

She just looked out the window and kept quiet without saying anything else to me.

"You want me to take you home first?"

"No, I wanna roll. I wanna have some fun tonight, with or without you," she said scornfully.

That's when I should have taken her ass home. It was out the way, and I didn't want to stray too far with twenty thousand in a trunk. I pulled up to the Shack and it was poppin'. There were many cars and people hanging about, and I felt inside me that there was trouble in the air tonight. I parked the ride somewhere safe then Cindy and I headed for the entrance.

It was close to midnight and I knew I needed to call home and let America know that I was okay and would be home soon. I had gotten so wrapped up with Greasy and his foolishness that the time was flying by. I navigated my way through the thick crowd that was lingering outside and got through the bouncers with no problem this time.

I walked into the club, and it was definitely live. The dance floor was cramped with sweaty revelers, and the DJ was spinning Biggie mixes. Cindy's face said that she was open. I noticed her catching the attention of males in the place. She was eating it up, flirting and smiling back. I had to shove a few knuckleheads out the way as I walked to the back. Cindy stayed close behind me.

One of Omega's men was standing outside the roped off VIP room. It was a room the club rented for private parties. The guard knew my face and let me through without hassle. Word around town was that I was home, and soon the face came with the name. He nodded as I walked by him.

The room was filled with beautiful women, and a handful of Omega's notorious crew. The music was loud, and so was some of the jewelry and platinum niggas were sporting. I knew a few in the room and they gave me respect, and the ones that I didn't know, minded their business.

I spotted Omega at a table with a woman seated on his lap. Bottles of Moet, Cristal, and Grey Goose cluttered the table. Omega saw me.

"Soul, what's poppin' my nigga?" He greeted me with dap and a hug.

"I see you're doing it big," I said returning his greeting.

"Always, my nigga. I almost thought you forgot about your peoples," he said.

"Nah, just doin' things differently," I replied.

"Yeah, whatever... You slowing your roll for a minute, I understand. You know Kemistry, right?"

"What up," I said, giving Kemistry a head nod.

He nodded, lounging and clutching a bottle of Moet. I've seen him around when he was younger, and remember Kemistry being some young wannabe gangsta, now turned rapper.

"Yo, my boy is about to perform tonight, I'm sponsoring my nigga. And I'm glad you came through. Yo, Kemistry, you think you can fuck wit' my nigga Soul in a freestyle battle?" Omega asked, putting me in the spotlight.

I didn't come there for that, but Omega was always instigating something in the hood, either it being a fight, or a freestyle battle that he was always pushing me into.

"I ain't come here for that," I said.

"I want you to school this nigga real quick, Soul. You nice nigga, and Kemistry gotta go against the best to be the best," Omega said.

Kemistry was sizing me up, with this cock-sure smug look on his face.

"Yo Omega, what your man here like a retro Run DMC," he joked.

"Ooh-wee," a few people shouted.

"Soul, he callin' you out my nigga. School this nigga, son. He my boy, but show him what you working with on your lyrics." Omega exclaimed, he was hyped.

"C'mon, Omega, I'll bury this dude. Don't have him get embarrassed up in here tonight," Kemistry boasted.

A small crowd gathered trying to see what the buzz was about. I was now getting hyped, because this nigga Kemistry was coming out of his mouth like he was Jay Z or some shit. And I knew he wasn't at all. He was a small time studio gangsta.

"Nigga, you talkin'. C'mon, the only thing hard you will ever see in your lifetime is your teeth hittin' the concrete, after I put your bitch ass down," I spat.

I was into this now. And hated to turn down a battle, especially from niggas that thought they were the next icon in Hip Hop.

"Yo, them sound like fighting words to me. Fuck that, we takin' this shit up on stage. Y'all niggas better bring it," Omega stated.

He made his way into the party and on the stage, grabbing the mike then announcing to the crowd that it was about to be on.

"I didn't know you could rhyme." Cindy was so excited, she gushed. But she didn't know the half.

If I hadn't been so involved into the streets, I knew I would have been the next Jay Z or Fifty. Shit, I knew I was up there with them or better. I even had a few labels willing to sign me back in the days. But the choices I made in life, fucked everything up.

The crowd in the club was hyped when Omega announced that Kemistry was about to battle. Some folks in the crowd knew me and what I was about and some were clueless to who the fuck I was.

Kemistry made his way toward the stage first, followed by his little entourage of young wannabes. He took the mike from Omega and announced, "Y'all wanna see a nigga get his ass chewed out tonight. Y'all know who I be, right."

The crowd went bananas, shouting and screaming and waiting for the battle to happen. I made my way toward the stage and jumped on there and grabbed the mike from Kemistry and said, "He ain't ready for this. I'm 'bout to school this Fabolous wannabe."

The crowd roared, and the DJ started playing the instrumental to Mobb Deep's *Survival Of The Fittest,* I was hyped.

"Who's first?" Omega asked.

I stared at Kemistry and said, "Lady's first."

"Ooh," the crowd chanted.

"Fuck this! I'm a finish it before it even begins," Kemistry returned, grabbing the mike from Omega.

He nodded to the beat and began.

"Yo, yo, yo… Take a look at this dude, his gangsta is retro, like tokens on the muthafuckin' metro, how you gonna come up against a king, when I heard you was someone's bitch up north, stayed goin' south up north, your rep is soft son, like the tits on my bitch, this nigga is so pussy, I'm ready to fuck this bitch, nah let me get a rubber and protect this bitch, look at this nigga, thinkin' he flossin', what are those, boss jeans he's in, c'mon now, I'll bury you like dirt, shit on you like earth, then spit you out like birth, cuz mixin' wit' Kemistry is toxic and you don't wanna get it poppin…

Now peep this scene and know who I be, that nigga that ends it before it starts, so don't envy me, player hate me, even come against me, cuz you need to be on your knees and applaud this king, because your bitch be loving it, to her your just another itch, and with me, I be having her scratching when she sees the dick, have her cry out…aye papi! Makin' the little winch flinch when she sees the twelve-inch, having her jump on my dick, run up all in her shit, making sure she feels the dick. Then when she's finish, she can kiss on my dick, then go home and kiss you on the lips and have you come back over here and tell me how sweet my shit is…"

The crowd went berserk. He had skills. Omega took the mike from him.

"Oh shit, Soul, I think it's on. You got competition son. He brought it kinda hard, yo. You ready?"

"Yo, give me the fuckin' mike," I said, staring at Kemistry.

The same beat played, and I had everyone waiting. Gripping the microphone, I was going in.

"Okay, you finish screaming my son…? Shouting over the mike like you really bussin' guns, like your rhyme is on point… Now stand still, don't run, take this ass whooping like a man and let me oust this punk. Omega why you put me against this fool, him and his weak crew lookin' like Blues Clues, bunch of dykes, who's fuckin' who? Now I'm gonna stand here, and break down the Kemistry in you. You're soft like baby shit, you watered down like liquid mist, all that huffing and puffing, nigga you still full of shit, so nigga don't stand here vex, you tryin' to be creative I give you that at best. Let me breathe a rhyme in your face and now you overzealous… You dare stand before a king and now I'm a have my words shake up your rap career, make you mock more than laugh in here… You and your bitch kids running around town wit' water guns, and you still ain't wetting shit, you come up in here talkin' hard, and rhyming about drama, when none of your beefs don't even exists. Now what you gonna do when I bring the streets to you, look at him, I got him cringing n' flinching son, acting like a fool, he wanna stand tall, but this dude ain't cool… even got your boys asking… *what's up with you*… nigga so pussy, I ready to get money n' pimp this bitch…look at him sweating, tryin' to come up here and run a mile on my dick n' play wit' the big boys toys… he tryin' to hold it down in his mother's costume jewels… You a straight character, holding props like an amateur, disgrace fool, now it's lights out for you and your pussy ass crew. Nigga let me recollect you to back to my words in VIP… The only hit you'll ever see in existence is your face hittin' the floor, after I lay your bitch ass down faster than the towers came down, then I'm gonna go over and hug and fuck your bitch and have her know what a true man is."

The crowd was loud, going berserk after I destroyed Kemistry on the mike. I shut him down where he stood.

"Yo-o-o, that's my nigga, Soul. Oh shit, Kemistry, I don't know… Nigga brought it," Omega shouted through the mike. "I don't think you ready."

"Yo, fuck that nigga, I'm the one with the record deal," Kemistry retorted, and walked off the stage.

"Oh, shit, do I detect some hate in my boy," Omega said, always instigating.

I stood there proud with anther notch on my belt for destroying the competition. Omega gave me dap and hugged me.

"You definitely got skills my nigga. I watched Kemistry shut down many rappers, and in one night, you came up in here and shut him down like it was nothing," he said.

"That's because it was nothing," I returned.

"That's my dude, though. I got money invested into that nigga. I got his album dropping in a few months. You down to do a few tracks wit' him and get your name out there," Omega offered.

"I'll think about it."

"Do that."

Omega and I walked to the bar and he treated me with drinks. I told him about Greasy and the money I had for him in the trunk of my cousin's car. He wanted to get that later. Right now he just wanted to have a good time.

I got a lot of love that night for my verbal battle with Kemistry. It bothered me that Cindy was playing it really close to Omega. I wanted to take her home, but she insisted on staying and continued having a good time.

It was after one in the morning when Omega told me he wanted to talk to me privately. Cindy was sitting on his lap, tipsy as fuck. It was getting late and I knew America would be worried about me. Omega and I walked into the club's back office, and when the door shut, Omega handed me a black Glock 17.

"Hold this, Soul. It's yours," he said.

"I ain't got no use for that, Mega." I was annoyed.

"I got beef wit' these Jamaicans and I feel that everyone close to me needs to be strap," he informed.

"Nigga, I ain't in the game anymore... You know this, Mega. I'm a married man, workin' a legit job," I told him harshly with my eyes fixed on his.

"Yeah, and you think Demetrius gives a fuck about that, him and Tiny knows how close you and I be. I ain't sayin' that he's gonna come at you, but you never know. And I want you to be armed just in case."

"Mega, I'm on parole, I get caught wit' a gat on me, I'm back upstate, plus more years added to my time."

"Nigga, I rather you be judge by twelve than be carried by six. Take the joint and stash it, Soul. You say you out the game, but you still got enemies out there that don't like you. And they might use you to get at me."

I thought about it. There were the pros and cons. I was running around naked without protection. Knowing my past, who is to say that someone I did wrong to won't hesitate to come up on me and put a bullet in my head?

Omega told me he was watching my back, but maybe he had other motives. He wanted me back in the game with him. My life now was cool. I had a legit job. It was slow money coming in, but I finally had peace of mind. It was something I haven't had since I was five or six.

Reluctantly, I took the gun from Omega. This nigga done put so many thoughts and worries into my head that it felt like I shot a nigga yesterday. I concealed the Glock in my waistband and we continued to talk for a moment. He was telling me about business being good. He was making crazy Arab type money, and flaunted his riches.

After our talk, we went back out into the club and I ran into a stunning looking Alexis. She was in a sexy red halter style neckline dress and a pair of four-inch sandals. Her long hair fell gracefully down her shoulders, as she sipped a drink.

"I see you still got talent, Soul," she seductively smiled. "So when are you gonna use some of that talent on me, baby?"

"I ain't in the game anymore, Alexis. I'm straight, and you was always the type to be wit' a nigga wit' a lot of money."

"There's always that one exception. The way you used to do me, I'm ready to bend the rules just for you Soul."

Her hand was pressed against my chest and she was close enough for me to smell her perfume.

"You know I need to chill. I'm not wit' that anymore."

She smiled at me and said, "So, you really have changed or think you fuckin' changed. I must admit that I'm still jealous of her, Soul. You and I should have been an item not that bitch. I heard that you married her, is it true?"

"Yeah, a nigga like me done finally jumped the broom," I said.

I saw the look of pain and hurt on her face. I felt bad somewhat, but she had to understand that I was becoming a changed man, and our sexual relationship was fun while it lasted.

"Well, I feel like a fuckin' floozy, standing here throwing myself at you. I was ready to suck your dick again and have you fuck the shit outta me. I had two abortions by you, Soul. I wanted to have a baby by you so bad, and you made me give it up. And now you're married, you think it will last?" she asked with a lot of hope in her voice.

"Alexis, you need to chill."

"Fuck you, Soul!" she barked. "I love you, nigga. And you went and married that bitch. I wanted to have your kids and be your fuckin' woman, and you did nothing but dissed me."

She was starting to cause a scene.

"Alexis, chill the fuck out," I said.

"I did everything for you… Stashed your drugs and guns, lied to police for you, gave you pussy when you wanted some, I even made runs out of town for you in my own fuckin' car, and all I gotten in return from you was nothing. Now I'm standing here asking for some dick, and you got the nerve to tell me no!"

I was losing my patience with her. I stepped to her, grabbed her arm and said, "Ain't no need for you to get loud up here! Keep your fuckin' mouth shut, Alexis."

I saw eyes staring at us, all in the business, watching this raving tall beauty cursing me the fuck out.

"No, I won't keep my mouth shut, Soul. I'm tired of you treating me like some second rate cum collector for your ass. You toss me to the side to run home to that bitch!"

"Alexis, you really need to chill and watch your fucking mouth," I warned.

"No. Fuck you, Soul! Does your wife know about how we used to fuck like crazy? Or should I go and tell the bitch about the two abortions I had and how you used to eat my pussy out real good Soul… Real good."

I punched her in the jaw, spewing blood. I was pissed at her.

"You muthafucka!" Alexis screamed, throwing her drink in my face and charging at me.

Before anyone else could get a hit in, two men came between us. Omega was pulling me back from her with a smile on his face. He escorted me outside and said, "Damn nigga, you must have been laying pipe in that bitch like a plumber for her to react like that."

"Mega, I ain't in the mood right now," I said.

He just laughed like it was a joke. I felt bad about hitting the bitch. But threatening my marriage about some bullshit that happened in the past? I didn't need her shaking things up between America and me.

"Since we're out here, let me get that from you," Omega said, referring to the cash in Greasy's trunk.

"Yeah, I'm parked over here." I pointed.

The night was calm. A few folks lingered outside the club. Omega and I walked across the street to Greasy's parked Lexus. As we walked, I happened to stare at my reflection in one of the parked cars and noticed a shadowy figure slowly creeping up behind us.

He was dark like the night, and my suspicion told me that we were in danger. I saw him raise his hand and saw a gun gripped in the image coming from the car window. I pushed Omega out of danger, screaming, "Get down, it's a hit!"

A loud shot went off soon after. The bullet whisked by missing me by mere inches, and shattering the driver's side window.

Omega and I scrambled for cover, the sound of gunfire going off around us.

Pop! Pop! Pop! Pop! Pop!

Shots were missing us by inches. The killer was dressed completely in black and he was tall with a mask covering his face, shooting at us erratically.

"Muthafucka!" Omega shouted.

He had his Glock gripped in his hand, and returned fire quickly. People scattered hastily, and I heard screaming and panic, and the night suddenly turned chaotic. I pulled out the Glock 17 Omega gave me. I felt the coldness of the street coursing through me again. This nigga almost killed me. I was seething.

I returned fire with Omega by my side and noticed the shooter was now running away. He fucked up and missed, and was running like the bitch he was. But I took aim carefully and fired off two shots in his direction. I saw the shooter stumbled suddenly and collapsed.

The incident was quick. I had saved Omega's life, and he was grateful. But I knew that I probably just killed a man. What the fuck...? The shooter was lying lifeless in the street and I became extremely nervous. Omega's crew started to pour out the club, guns in hand, looking around.

"Mega, you ahight?" one of his peoples shouted.

"I'm good," Omega returned.

"What happened, nigga?" one asked.

I just stood there, gun still clutched in my hand and gazing downheartedly at the body sprawled out in the middle of the dark avenue. Suddenly sirens were heard. It was time for me to be ghost.

"Soul, get the fuck outta here," Omega said to me. "We got this, my nigga."

I rushed back to the Lexus with the gun still on me, and drove the fuck off before seeing one cop car racing by with its lights sounding and blaring. I was nervous, but tried to play it cool. I hid the gun under the driver's seat and made my way down Liberty toward Merrick Blvd.

I drove carefully and made it to my building moments later. I parked the car and got out. It was two in the morning and the lobby felt still. I got in the elevator, and noticed this warm runny feeling near my right ear. I was bleeding. I wasn't hit, but the first shot scattered car glass and nicked me, enough to have my fingertips smeared with blood. I rushed upstairs to the apartment.

America was up when I walked in. She came out the bedroom and glared at me as I walked in. She spotted blood coming from my small wound.

"Ohmygod, Omar, what happened to you," she shrieked.

I was sweating and looking like a mess. This whole night was just bad news for me, starting with running into Greasy. America quickly came to my aid. We were in the bathroom and the wound wasn't anything serious, but just a small nick from the bullet or exploding glass that neared my face.

"Omar, what happened to you? How did this happen?" she demanded.

I didn't want to tell her the truth. I tried avoiding eye contact with her by staring at myself in the bathroom mirror. She stood behind me with a worried look on her face. I pulled out bandages from the medicine cabinet and wiped the blood from my face.

"What happened, Omar?" America asked again, in a more hysterical tone.

"There was a shootout at this club," I said faintly.

"What? Was you involved?" she asked. I heard the panic in her voice and knew she was scared to hear the answer.

I stared at her in the mirror and said, "Nah, I was just leaving, and niggas started wilding."

Even though I lied to America countless of times before, this time it was different for me. I was involved and denied telling her because things were going so good between us and I didn't want her to panic. Besides, I think I just killed a man, and that was news America wouldn't be able to deal with. I wasn't ready to accept the truth. And even though I'd bodied niggahs before, this time it was different.

"Omar, are you telling me the truth? You weren't involved, and what club was you at till two in the morning? Are you back in the streets?" she nagged.

"I'm not, and I wasn't involved in no shooting, America!" I barked. "I was just in the wrong place at the wrong damn time. I told you, I ain't wit' that roughneck shit no more."

"Don't put me through this hell again, Omar. I don't deserve this, I don't have the strength anymore," she said before walking out the bathroom.

I continued to stare at my reflection, nursing my small wound. I'm out of the game, so how did I get caught up in this bullshit tonight? That was the million dollar question.

21

Can you kill a man who's not afraid to die?
All he sees is mayhem and destruction...

Omega

This is the part of the game when it gets really ugly. Someone tried to murder me the other night. And if it wasn't for my nigga, Soul, I would have been dead. This was the second time that he saved my life. He had my back, for real. He was always cautious, keeping an eye out and aware of his surroundings. That nigga is definitely my right-hand man.

The hit had to come from Tiny, because them Jamaicans don't miss. They'd sprayed the entire block with Uzi's and automatic weapons wiping out everything in sight. The shooter missed. Now it was my turn to hit back, and I planned on hitting back hard.

"I should a been there. Yo, I'm ready to murder these nigga, yo, fo' real," Biscuit exclaimed furiously.

"You know who it was?" Greasy asked.

"I have a clue, I'm gonna handle it," I said to them.

The game was about to get ugly with murder and mayhem. The streets belong to me, and I was ready to take it to the next level. I set up a meeting with Smitty, a gun dealer from North Carolina. He always came through with the heavy armor, firepower, and equipment for times like this.

Greasy, Biscuit, and myself met with Smitty at a discrete location in Brooklyn. It was two in the morning when Smitty drove up in his black Cadillac, sitting on 18" chrome.

Smitty was a white boy from the south I'd been dealing with since my brother ran the streets of Queens. He served in the marines, did his time overseas, and had access to almost any gun. He was straight from the trailer parks of North Carolina and grew up poor.

We stood outside our truck as Smitty came to a stop in front of us. He stepped out his ride, fresh in a dark blue three-piece suit, wearing dark shades.

"Omega, it's been along time since we did business together. I thought you was doin' a bid," Smitty said smiling.

"Had to lay low. What's good?" I said greeting him with a handshake.

"Business is business. I got some nice toys for you and your crew to play with, for the right price," he said.

"You know what I'm about, Smitty. I want the best. I got a beef wit' some muthafuckas who needs to be laid."

"What I got for you is no joke. Whatever you shoot at— you hit. And they'll stay down for the morgue to pick up," he joked. I smiled.

"Let's do this," Biscuit intervened, looking like an eager eight-year old boy on Christmas Eve.

"I got some firepower in the trunk of my car that I know you and your friends will definitely enjoy," he stated.

We followed him to his Cadillac. He opened his trunk and pulled out the biggest gun that he had.

"Aw shit… That's the fuck I'm talkin' 'bout," Biscuit exclaimed, his eyes glued to the weapon.

Smitty gripped the weapon in both hands and said, "This right here will lay an elephant down. I just picked it up. It's the SMG PK. It's one of the most reliable and compact sub machine guns in production. It shoots both in single shots and automatic. The rate of fire, 900 RPM and has a muzzle velocity of 375m/sec."

"Damn," Greasy uttered.

"Yo, let me hold this cannon," Biscuit said.

Smitty slowly passed him the gun, and Biscuit held the weapon in his hand trying to look like a professional.

"I got his brother too," Smitty said. He then pulled out the SMG PK1, which looked similar and Greasy picked up the SMG PK2. You feelin' it, Omega?" Smitty asked, smiling.

"Most def," I said.

He then went on to show us the Heckler and Koch MP-5, and a few Uzi's. I wanted it all. Biscuit didn't want to let go of the SMG PK.

"What's the damage for everything?" I asked.

"I knew you wouldn't let me down, for you, bro… Give me fifty even," Smitty smiled.

"Ahight, bet."

I nodded to Greasy, and Greasy tossed him a small bag filled with fresh hundred dollar bills that totaled to fifty grand.

"That's your money right there," Greasy said to him.

"Yessir."

We started loading everything into the back of our truck. Biscuit was happy.

"You know what, I wanna get rid of this too," Smitty said.

"What's that?" I asked.

He pulled out a Rocket launcher from the backseat of his ride.

"Is you fuckin' serious?" I asked.

"Take it for an extra five-hundred," he suggested.

"Yo, we can definitely fuck shit up wit' that right there, son," Biscuit said. "Take that shit, Mega."

"Ahight, I'll take it."

Smitty put the rocket launcher back in the case and passed it to Biscuit. I gave him the five-hundred.

After everything was loaded into the back of our vehicle, we drove off. I was ready for anything that came my way.

A week after the attempt was made on me, everything seemed cool. I was laying low for a minute, getting my head right and my strategy correct. I wanted those niggas to suffer. I was thinking, riding down Rockaway Blvd. in the passenger seat of a black polished Denali sitting on 22" chromed rims. It was evening and the hood was quiet. Greasy was driving and we were on our way to get our eat on. Jay Z was pumping and I was chillin'.

"Yo, Mega, is that po-po behind us?"

I turned to look and saw the marked blue and white following us.

"Fuck they want?"

We had two Glocks concealed in a crafty stash box over the glove compartment. But besides that, we had nothing else that could incriminate us.

"Just play it cool, yah heard son? Let's see how the fuck they play it."

Greasy kept the ride going at a moderate speed. He then turned right onto a residential block, using his signals. They followed right behind us. I knew what was coming next. *Whoop-whoop*

I heard the cop car echo out with its overhead lights blaring behind us.

"Fuck!" Greasy muttered.

He pulled over to the right in the middle of the block and put the truck in park. I remained stretched out in my seat, wanting to get the harassment over with.

"You good, right?" I asked Greasy.

"Yeah, I'm good."

I didn't even bother to turn around to see who was coming toward us. I already had the passenger window down and stared out the windshield.

"Hey baby."

I was stunned and turned to see Judy standing by the passenger side. Her partner, Ivory was by the driver's side.

"Shit Judy, why you gotta nigga stress right now? I'm thinkin' you real police and shit," I said.

"I am the real deal," she smiled.

"You know what the fuck I'm sayin. What's good though?"

"I know you've been busy, baby, but I wanna know, you got that for me sometime soon?" she asked.

Her partner Ivory was a meth addict too, so it wasn't a problem for her to been in our conversation.

"You know I don't ride dirty, baby. You gotta get at one of my boys for that. I'll make a call for you."

"Cool. So you down to see me tonight? It's been a minute?" she asked.

"Tomorrow night, I'll come through," I smiled, asking. "Everything's cool out here?"

"Yeah, it's been quiet. We only had that call about a man shot dead at some club on Liberty a few days back," she revealed.

"Yeah, what you heard about that? Any news?"

"Nothing, no witnesses came forward and the dead man had a sheet a mile long," she joked. "You don't know anything about that right?"

"Nah," I lied.

"Mega, remember we got that thing to take care of in a half," Greasy reminded.

"Ahight baby, I know you're busy and all, so I'm gonna let you be. If I hear anything about that other thing, I'll let you know. Be careful, okay," Judy said. She then leaned into the window and gave me a kiss.

"Peace," Greasy said.

We watched them walk back to the radio car, and I was thinking, even in uniform, that bitch got a body.

"Why you ain't say shit to her, Greasy. Damn, you fuckin' the bitch almost every night," I said.

"Yo, as long as Greasy see that bitch in that uniform, I ain't got shit to say to her. But when she's outta that pig skin, it's fuckin on," he sucked his teeth and said.

I laughed. Greasy put the truck in drive and drove off.

As always, to ease my mind from the drama in the streets, I went to pussy. That was my drug. It gave me a high. It made me feel good. I linked up with Cindy, this bitch that Soul brought to the club the other night. She was a young cutie who was moved by niggas like me—thugs and hustlers. Just looking at her made me want to fuck her. It was so easy that it was almost a turn off.

Three days after we met, I had her see me at the club. I wasted no time taking that bitch into one of the backrooms and had her on her knees sucking my dick. She was ahight, but I had better.

She was sucking on my dick, and I was thinking about the drama that was playing out. Tiny had gone into hiding. None of my peoples had seen that bitch-ass-nigga on the streets lately. I was going to put the squeeze on him and his crew. I was still seething from the previous shootout and I had to retaliate quickly so I wouldn't begin looking weak.

I put my boys, Whistle and Monk on the job. With the two of them hunting and preying, it wouldn't be long before they came back with a kill.

"Hmm, hmm… Oh, ugh, ugh."

Cindy was going to town. I grabbed her hair and enjoyed the bliss. While she was still sucking on my dick, there was a knock at the door.

"Who?" I shouted.

"It's Biscuit."

"Come in."

Biscuit walked into the room and he smiled. "Damn nigga, can I get next?" he asked.

"Nigga what you want?" I asked.

"We got sump'n," he said.

"Like…?"

"Whistle and Monk got two of Tiny's men. I thought you might want to hear that immediately."

"They alive right?"

"Yeah."

"Tell 'em we'll be there in half."

"Ahight."

Biscuit stared at Cindy still blessing me and said, "Shorty a freak and shit. Mega, can that bitch suck me off, too?"

Cindy stopped and looked up at Biscuit with contempt and said, "No, I don't think so."

"Bitch, I'll take that weak pussy from you!" Biscuit snapped at her.

"Biscuit, be out nigga, and make that call," I ordered.

"Ahight, fuck that weak ass bitch," he said to her before leaving.

On the streets, Biscuit was skilled, ruthless and feared, but when it came to the ladies, sometimes this nigga used his wrong head. I've seen this nigga raped bitches before, because it was one way of him getting some ass. They never reported him due to his reputation and fear. Despite his street savvy, Biscuit was still young and dumb.

After he left, I pulled Cindy up off her knees. I had her out of her tight jeans and panties. Cindy's ass was in the air. I was curved over the desk, fuckin' her doggy style with the magnum on. I was rough with her, pulling at her hair, and smacking that bitch on her ass, while sliding in and out of her.

Later that night, Biscuit and I met up with Monk, Whistle and a few other soldiers at one of my undisclosed locations. I used to get truly needed information from niggas who liked to keep a tight lip. We walked into the faintly lit, underground seedy area, exposed pipes overheard, asbestos baring ceilings and walls. There were two of Tiny's men bonded with duct-tape around their wrists, ankles and over their mouths. The pair was butt-naked on the hard concrete.

They saw Biscuit and me walk into the room, and started to squirm, mumbling incoherently. Their eyes wide with fear, bodies were already beaten bruised and bloodied.

"Y'all fucked up!" Biscuit said glaring down at them.

We stared at them knowing their fates. I needed information. It was a no-win situation for both. They could either die slow and screaming, or quickly. It didn't matter.

"Remove the tape," I ordered.

Monk crouched near them, and ripped the duct-tape from their mouths.

"Ah, ah, ah, ah, shit," one of the men screamed out, wiggling.

"What's good, fellas?" I asked.

"Fuck you, nigga!" one boldly shouted.

The second man remained quiet. He was scared shitless. His boy, on the other hand wanted to be hard. His end will be very painful and agonizing. I smiled.

"This nigga talkin' shit," Biscuit exclaimed.

"I ain't telling you all a got-damn thing! Fuck you, Omega!" he shouted.

"Nigga shudafuckup!" Biscuit yelled.

The man then spit out some teeth along with blood, compliments of Biscuit's Timberlands cracking his jaw. He screamed in pain, but it was only the beginning for him.

"Why you gotta make it difficult for us?" I shook my head and asked. He didn't say a word. He just continued spitting out blood.

"Don't get that shit on my boots, muthafucka!" I warned turning my attention to the second man, "You good?" His facial expression was frozen in panic. I looked down at him and asked, "What's your name, yo?"

"Mike," he replied.

"So Mike, we can make this easy on you. You wanna go home right?" I asked, sounding so sympathetic.

"I ain't do shit, man. I was just chillin' wit' my nigga and I got caught up in this shit," he explained.

"This your boy?"

"We cool, but yo… I don't know nothing," he pleaded.

"Somehow Mike, I don't believe you."

"Yo, man, c'mon man, I'm begging you…I ain't do shit to you. I got kids, yo. My girl just had a baby. She's two months. I don't wanna die, man… Please. What you wanna know?" he asked, begging for his life.

"I don't give a fuck about your kids, Mike. I care about my biz. I almost lost my life the other night, Mike. You care about me, Mike?"

"We supposed to be brothers, yo," he exclaimed.

Everyone started laughing.

"Brothers?" Biscuit replied. "Nigga, we ain't your fuckin' brother… This bitch ass nigga…"

Mike had tears streaming down his face as he stared up at me, awaiting his fate.

"Don't cry, nigga," I said to him. "Just tell me what I need to know, and it's all good wit' us."

"Man, I don't fuck wit' Tiny like that," he exclaimed.

"I don't believe you," I said.

"Yo, this ain't me."

"Ahight whatever, the truth shall be set free tonight," I said. I then turned to look at Mr. Tough Guy and said, "You finish spitting up blood?"

"You gonna get yours, Omega. You don't know who you're fuckin' wit!" he barked, still having some fight in him.

"Ahight, whatever… Y'all niggas break out the toys. We gonna get sump'n from these niggas one-way or the other. I tried being nice to muthafuckas."

"Hey, they wanna make it last, then I'm down," Biscuit said.

"C'mon man, I don't know nada yo," Mike shouted.

"Well, we're definitely gonna find out for sure," I returned.

I had Whistle plug in a hot steaming iron. We picked up Mike from off the floor and suspended him up from the ceiling, having his arms outstretched, and every part of him exposed and vulnerable. His body was limp and bloody from the beaten bestowed.

"C'mon man, please don't do this to me… Please, I beg you. I just wanna go home to my girl and kids. I never did shit to you man," he pleaded, sobbing like an infant. "If I knew shit, I'd a told you already."

I gripped the burning hot iron and held it to my side. Mike knew what was coming next. Sometimes the simplest household appliance can be the most perfected methods of torture on a muthafucka.

"Mr. Tough guy, you got sump'n to say, to save your boy from this shit? I can make it quick for him and you," I said.

"Fuck you, and that bitch-ass crybaby," he spat.

"Yo, you just don't fuckin' learn," I scolded, getting upset. "Ahight nigga, you wanna be hard, fuck this!" I said pressing the hot iron to the side of Mike's face and holding it there.

"Ah… Ah… Ah Fuck this! Fuck this. Muthafuckas… Ah-ah-ah-ah!" he screamed.

I pulled the iron from the left side of his face and left a disfiguring burn mark there with his skin melting like hot caramel.

"Anything?" I asked again, being upset.

Nothing from neither, Mike was whimpering, and his boy remained glued to the ground feeling no remorse.

"Fuck it, again," I said.

I pressed the iron to the other side of his face, and Mike let out a piercing loud scream that echoed beyond these walls. But he couldn't be heard, because there weren't any neighbors around. My location was far off and isolated. Mike cried out, he was ready to fall and crash to the ground, but he was still shackled to the ceiling from his wrists, with his body sagging from the pain.

"Please stop…please," he faintly cried out.

"Anything?" I asked again.

Once again, no one knew a damn thing. I pressed the iron to his face again. Then began working down to his chest, eventually I had to press that scorching metal iron against his genitals. The scream he let out after that hot metal iron came meshed with his skin and nuts, made my ears pop. Mike started to smell. And still he didn't budge.

"Yo, Mike might be telling the truth," I said.

I mean after something like that, he would have been told a nigga something. The pain was too unbearable. I looked at Mike, and he was a mess. His skin was burned badly, and he could no long support himself up.

"Mike, you okay? Hang in there wit' me Mike, we're almost done here," I said to him, sounding like an assuring friend. He was whimpering, his speech incoherent. His skin was red and blistered, and bruised.

"Yo, that nigga is done, Mega," Biscuit said.

"Let him loose," I instructed.

Whistle and Monk unshackled him, and he collapsed to the cold ground. He looked dead, but I knew he wasn't. I looked over at the next nigga. "It's your turn, muthafucka!"

I wanted his ass, this brazen fucking loud mouth nigga. He knew something. Monk and Whistle picked him off the ground and shackled him to the ceiling, suspending him.

"Ahight nigga, I'm gonna take my time with you. You got sump'n to say?"

"Fuck you!" he spat in my muthafuckin' face.

I was furious wiping his saliva and blood from the corner of my mouth. I punched him and spit back in his face.

"You dare spit on me muthafucka?" I shouted hitting him again, and again, until his jaw was twisted.

I was winded, glaring at this asshole, coughing up blood and his face looking like something from a butcher's shop.

"Yo, pass me those muthafuckin' vice-grips," I ordered.

Monk put them in my hand with pleasure. Now this shit was personal. He disrespected and spit on me. I wanted him to feel pain like he never felt before.

"Open your fuckin' mouth, nigga!" I demanded.

He was resistant. Biscuit came over to help me. He punched him the jaw, and then with his help, we began prying open his fuckin' bloody filled mouth. I had on latex gloves and so did Biscuit, and one by one, we began pulling out with the vice grips the few teeth that he had left in his mouth.

"Ugh… Ah… Ah. Yow… Ah… Ah… Ah…" he cried in agony as we pulled out three of his teeth with the tool.

"You spit on me, nigga," I shouted in his ear.

I put the vice grips near his exposed genitals and clamped the tool around his nuts as tightly as possible. He sounded like a wounded animal.

"You want me to stop, muthafucka? Huh?" I taunted. "Go ahead, say 'fuck me' one more time and watch what happens up in here tonight. I guarantee it's gonna last for hours."

He was whimpering. I clutched the tool and felt his nuts bursting gradually. I was about to pop them like a pimple.

"No, no. Oh God," he cried out in a high pitch tone.

"Say sump'n nigga, you better hurry the fuck up!" I barked. "You ain't talkin' that shit now, right? You think you big, huh? I'll break you down like the bitch you are."

"Oh God…" He cried out. "Ahight, ahight," he managed.

His body was collapsing from the pain. His face contorted and he was barely conscious. I removed the vice grips from his nuts and gave him a moment to catch his breath.

"Tiny, where is he?" I asked.

Mr. Tough Guy's mouth was coated with blood making his words mostly incoherent. But he was getting friendlier.

"I can make the pain go away, just tell me what I need to know, and I can make it stop. You have my word. I'm not such a bad guy, just give me the information I need and maybe we can be mans and all."

He began coughing and spitting up blood. I stepped back because I didn't want any getting on my Evisu jeans. I gave him a few more seconds, and then I was back to being impatient again.

"Biscuit pass me that fuckin' iron," I ordered.

He handed me the burning hot iron and I held it to my victim's face, urging him to speak up.

"C'mon nigga, just fuckin' tell me and all this will be over with."

Biscuit pulled out the 9mm and pressed it against Mr. Tough Guy's head.

"Yo, this muthafucka is being real stubborn. Let me end it for this punk-ass, Mega," Biscuit shouted.

"Nah, he's gonna talk. Right yo," I said, pressing the iron against his chest.

"Ah... Ah... Ah... Ah...Ugh fu-u-uck," he screamed.

"C'mon, nigga, you said you was gonna talk. I can make this hurt all night, nigga. You didn't feel a damn thing yet," I warned.

I placed the iron next to his exposed genitals. Finally he bitched up.

"Okay! Ahight, he's with a bitch in Yonkers. He got a crib up there," he exhaustedly informed me.

"Now, was that so fuckin' hard, why you wanna be a tough guy for a bitch nigga like, Tiny," I said to him.

He was out of it, slowly losing consciousness.

"Just do it, kill me nigga," he said in a soft gasp.

"Biscuit do this nigga a favor," I ordered.

There was no hesitation. In one quick motion, Biscuit raised the gat to tough guy's head and blew his fucking brains out. With a loud explosion, his body sagged. His carcass hanging from the ceiling, his arms outstretched.

"Ahight, let's do this," I said.

"What about our boy here?" Biscuit asked, pointing out Mike. He was still sprawled out on the cold ground, looking a hot mess—bloody and tortured.

"End him too. We got what we came for," I instructed.

"No doubt," Biscuit said pointing his 9mm down at Mike's head and squeezed off two shots.

I ordered Monk and Whistle to dispose of the bodies. They knew what to do. Biscuit and I left. I had to make a few phone calls and take a trip to Yonkers.

22

Shit's real who cares?
Death's near who's sincere?
Shed the last tears, No one really cares.
Feeling screwed. Looking inside you.
Eyes desperately in need.
I see the pussy in you.
You're weak. Copping pleas...

Omega

I had a small crew with me in a black Range Rover on our way to Yonkers. We got word on Tiny's exact location and I wanted him gone. Armed with the infantry supplies Smitty hit us off with, we were ready for anything. We drove north on Interstate 87 observing the speed limit. The last thing I needed was to get pulled over by state troopers.

By eight that evening we were in Yonkers. Tiny was staying in the suburbs. Word was that he owned a two-level three-bedroom home and stayed with this bitch named, Tianna in Park Hill.

It was mid-summer and folks were still out making use of what was left of the daylight. I wanted to creep through during dusk, so I had my crew lay low for a minute. We stopped at a nearby Burger King and had some whoppers and fries. Waiting around for hours, being inconspicuous as possible really tested our patience.

It was just before midnight we slowly pulled up to his block. Tiny had the last crib at the end of a dead-end block. There were no lights on in the lower level of the house, but I noticed that his bedroom lights were on.

"How we gonna get at this nigga?" Biscuit asked, cocking his 9mm.

I had to think. The place probably had a security alarm. Tiny was known to be a very cautious dude. Even though he was miles away from Queens and thought no one knew about this place, he'd have this shit airtight.

"Groggy, go check around the back and be subtle about it," I instructed.

A year older than Biscuit, Groggy was another one of the up-and-coming soldiers in my crew. Dark skinned and sneaky, he was reliable. I didn't want any nosy neighbors calling the cops. Groggy stepped out the truck and quickly made his way into the backyard, disappearing into the dark. Biscuit, Tank, and myself waited for a few minutes. A short while later, Groggy appeared.

"What you got?" I asked.

"Shit is secured. He got bars on all the windows. The doors are reinforced. He got motion detectors set up in the back. And the crib is definitely rigged with an alarm system. We try and break-in, and the cops be on our ass. No telling what kind of heat he got up in there," Groggy explained.

"Muthafucka!" I said smiling. "This nigga."

"What's gonna be our move?" Biscuit asked.

"We gonna have to come at this nigga some other way," Tank said.

"I know nigga."

I stared at the house, trying to study every detail of the place, trying to find some flaw. But I knew we couldn't be parked outside too long without Tiny or one of his neighbors noticing my truck parked outside his crib suspiciously and warning five-O.

"Aihght, there's too much at risk. Right now let's fall back," I said.

Tank started the truck and we slowly drove off. But I didn't come up here to fail. I knew there was a way to get at that nigga. It was just going to take some time. Tiny was better than I thought. We got a room at the nearest motel, paying cash. I wanted no attention on the crew while in Yonkers. We had to be ghost. We stashed our guns in one duffle bag and brought them into the room with us and dumped them on the bed.

I was cooped up in this cheesy motel-room, my mind running like Bolt, trying to find a way to get at Tiny. I needed to know how many people he had in the house, and what his schedule was. I wanted to lay this muthafucka out real bad.

"Yo, what about that nigga's bitch, Mega?" Biscuit said.

"What you talking 'bout?"

"I mean, he gotta trust her somewhat. A nigga will always lose his guard around pussy from time to time. And he must feel safe wit' that ho up here, since he think no one knows his location," Biscuit offered.

"And?"

"We get at him through her."

I smiled. "Damn, Biscuit let me find out you a thinking man behind the gun, too. I like that," I said.

Biscuit was right Tiny's ho could be his kryptonite. It was the only way because I was determined Tiny would never see the streets of Queens again. I told Tank to drive back to the block and watch that nigga's crib like a hawk. If he saw anything, call me. Tiny couldn't be around that ho twenty-four seven. She was our opening. Tank left the room around four in the morning. I got some Z's waiting for him to call.

It was around noon when he called back.

"What up?" I answered.

"She on the move," Tank informed.

"Follow that bitch, Tank," I told him.

After his call, I woke up Biscuit and Groggy and told them to get ready. We checked the guns and made sure shit was right. I got another call from Tank twenty minutes later.

"Yeah?"

"She stopped at a nail salon in a shopping center on Morris Crescent. How you wanna play it?" Tank asked.

"How long you think she's gonna be?" I asked.

"Probably fo' a minute."

"Ahight, I'll call a cab. Just watch that bitch."

The cab arrived in ten minutes. We packed the guns in the duffle bag, and piled into the cab when it pulled up.

"Morris Crescent," I said to the cabbie.

We drove for about ten minutes. Getting out of the cab, I noticed Tank sitting in the Range Rover across the street. We quickly got in.

"Where she parked her car?" I asked him.

He pointed to a small parking lot. I wasn't trying to follow and watch this bitch all day. I needed to make my move now, and shrewd. Fifteen minutes later, Tiny's ho came walking out the nail salon looking like money. She was a dime piece for sure and strutted around knowing she was the shit. She headed for her ride. I hit Biscuit on his Nextel. He was positioned near her ride.

She reached into her purse rummaging for her keys as she walked, totally unaware of her surroundings. When she neared her car, Biscuit was near with his gun. Before she could turn around to know what was going on, Biscuit ran up on her, striking her and pushed that bitch into her own ride.

Her car windows were tinted, so that made the kidnapping discreet and so much easier. I stepped out the truck and casually made my way over to the Benz. I got in the backseat of her ride. She was in the passenger seat, crying, as Biscuit held her at gunpoint.

"Bitch, shut the fuck up!" I barked.

"What y'all want? I got money, just don't hurt me," she pleaded.

I put my Glock to her head and told Biscuit to drive off. He slowly moved out the small parking lot, and Tank followed behind us in the truck.

"Listen, and listen good. We don't want you. It's your man we want," I said to her.

"Tiny?"

"You fuckin' with that nigga, so you should know enough about him. Who else stay in the crib besides you and him?" I asked. "And don't fuckin' lie to me."

"It's just us, no one else," she answered.

"Ahight. Where is he now?"

"He had to make a run back to Queens. He left around two."

"And is he coming back?"

"Yes. Around nine or ten."

"He got any guns, drugs, or cash in there with him?" I asked.

"Just a few guns. He don't keep no drugs in there. About twenty thousand dollars is in the safe in our bedroom," she said.

"Okay, you're doing beautiful. Now, how important are you to him?"

"Why?"

I knocked her upside her head with the gat and said, "Just fuckin' answer me."

"I'm his son's mother."

"Ahight."

"Oh God, you're going to kill him," she cried out.

"Bitch, if you don't want your son to lose a mother, you best be chill," I warned.

She remained frozen in her seat as we made our way down Riverdale Avenue and made a left on Radford Street. A short moment later, we pulled up to her place. She had an automatic garage opener and we parked the Benz in the garage, being out of sight from the neighbors as we dragged her out the car.

Once we were inside her home, Biscuit and I made the bitch strip butt-naked and then we tied her to a chair. It was going to be a long day for her. Tank was parked at the end of the block watching the area like a hawk. We had to be patient for this to work.

Several hours passed as we took comfort in Tiny's home like it was our own. We raided the fridge, watched movies on their large plasma TV and lounged around on their plush leather sofa. Biscuit repeatedly stared over at her naked, excited by the display.

"Yo, what's your name…? Are those tits real?" Biscuit asked her.

She didn't answer. Her tears dried a while ago, as she sat mute and restless in her own home. Biscuit got up, looking upset. "Bitch, I'm fuckin' talkin' to you," he shouted.

She said nothing, diverting her attention to the wall. Biscuit stood over her. He cupped one of her breasts and fondled her as she squirmed, cursing.

"Don't fuckin' touch me, you bastard!"

"Bitch, I do what I want." Biscuit laughed.

Biscuit continued groping her. His hand moved freely around her body, as she screamed out, "No! Please, stop it… Stop!"

Her pleads fell on deaf ears. Biscuit moved his hand between her thighs forcing them open. She tried to fight, but Biscuit slapped her. Then he pushed his fingers into her, causing her to cry out, tears trickling down her face. Despite her resistance I watched as Biscuit finger-fucked her. She cried but Biscuit continually fondled between her legs.

"Yo Mega, her pussy kinda tight," he laughed. "But I think her tits are fake."

I chuckled watching Biscuit panting.

"I wanna fuck this bitch."

"No time for that," I said.

"C'mon Mega, that nigga ain't coming around till what nine or ten she said. Let me hit this bitch. I need a quickie, see what she's workin' wit."

"Nigga, I said no. Let the bitch be," I demanded.

"You lucky bitch," Biscuit said.

"Why? I have a son. We have a son. Oh God!"

I went over to her. Looking in her eyes, I said, "This ain't nothing personal, it's just business between me and your man. Unfortunately for you, he lives here. Casualties of war, baby. Now, are you sure he'll be home by ten?"

Frustrated by her silence, I walked to the fireplace and picked up a picture of her son. I went back to her with the picture in hand.

"You got a handsome kid here. You want him to become a casualty of war too? Because I'll gladly send a babysitter here for you," I warned.

She sobbed louder, staring at her son's picture. "He's only five, don't hurt him!" she exclaimed.

"All you gotta do is listen and cooperate, everything will be good," I assured. "Now, you sure he's coming back here?"

"Yes, he thinks no one knows about him out here," she said.

"Is he coming alone?" I asked.

"He usually have security with him."

"How many?"

"Only Jose'," she said.

We knew where the guns were in the house, but she didn't know the combination to the safe. We had to wait for Tiny. Around eight, her cell phone rang. It was an unknown number.

"This him?" I asked.

She nodded.

"Ahight, answer, and you better not try anything stupid, or it will get ugly," I warned. "No codes."

I pressed the accept call button and pushed the phone to her ear.

"Hey baby," she greeted. "I just got home a short while ago. You know I had to get my nails done and did a little shopping at the mall. Where are you? Oh okay... How did things go? Okay... See you in a bit, baby... Love you," she said.

I hung up the call and asked, "Where is he?"

"He's about twenty minutes away."

"Does he always call ahead?"

"Yes."

Even though there was nothing strange about the conversation, I still didn't trust her. It was twenty minutes after eight. I called Tank and told him to keep an eye out. I told him Tiny was on his way, and he might have company. I asked what her routine was during the evening. Does she usually park her car in the garage, how many lights were usually on? We tried to make her home look normal.

At nine, a Burgundy Escalade pulled into the driveway. It was Tiny. Jose was with him. He called the house again before he came inside. I made her answer.

"Hello... Oh, you are outside, why? Okay, let me throw something on, you know I never be decent when you come."

She hung up.

"What did he say?"

"He says he wants me to meet him outside, in the driveway," she informed.

Damn, this nigga! I thought. He didn't want to walk into a trap. He wanted her to come outside so he can send Jose to check the crib for intruders. This bitch probably knew all about his habits but failed to tell us.

Grabbing her arm tightly, I warned, "Bitch, if you wanna see your son again, do as I say. My two shooters are parked outside, if anything goes wrong, they'll drop you and Tiny. Just be cool, and bring him inside. You try anything funny, and I guarantee I'll kill your son."

She walked outside in her skirt, stilettos and red top. I watched from a distance as she ran up to Tiny and hugged and kissed him. He sent Jose to search the crib. I hid in a dark corner near the kitchen. Biscuit and Groggy were hiding. I clutched the 9mm tighter, ready for anything.

I saw his silhouette nearing. When he was close, I jumped out of the darkness and quickly pressed the gun to the back of his head.

"Nigga chill, and do as I say. Drop the gun before I drop you," I demanded sternly.

He was reluctant until I slapped my weapon against the back of his head. Jose' quickly got the message. He dropped the gun.

"You're a dead," he threatened.

His eyes widened when Groggy and Biscuit came into view.

"Call your boy in and let him know that everything is cool," I instructed. "If you don't, then you'll die where you stand. Ya heard me?"

I slowly walked him to the door, and stayed out of view. I let Tiny see Jose' in the doorway. I still had my gun trained on him.

"Tiny, everything's cool up in here," he assured reluctantly.

I peeped Tiny walking toward the entrance with his baby-mother by his side. Everything seemed to be going good, until I noticed the look on her face. She looked reluctant. She started pulling Tiny by his arm vigorously trying to move him away from the door.

"Baby, it's a trap, they're gonna kill you!" she shouted.

One shot blew Jose's brains out, dropping him. From the doorway my gun was aimed at Tiny who was reaching for his. I shot him twice in the leg. He dropped on the pavement.

"Fuck!" I shouted, knowing neighbors could be watching.

His bitch was screaming frantically. I punched her and pushed her into Tiny's Escalade. Biscuit and I dragged Tiny off the ground and shoved him into the truck with the quickness. I took his keys and we sped off.

"Fucking stupid-ass bitch!" I shouted. She was unconscious.

Tank was behind us in the Range Rover. Shit didn't go as smoothly as planned. Even though shit did get ugly, it was all fuckin good.

"Fuck you, Omega! Me cousin gawn fuck ya blood-claat ass up!" Tiny said, clutching his bleeding leg.

Crippled with two bullet wounds in his leg. Tiny knew he was at our mercy.

Hours later, I had Tiny and his bitch tied up in the truck with rope and duct-tape and poured gasoline all over them and the Escalade. They knew what was coming next. She was crying frantically.

"Please! No, don't do this... What about my son! My son! No!"

Her eyes were puffy and soaked with tears. She wouldn't stop screaming. We were in an isolated and wooded area in Connecticut. There was nobody around for miles.

"Omega just let she go... Please, fo' my son's sake, let her go," Tiny begged. "You got what ya wanted. You got me, let her the fuck go! Please."

Tiny was in tears.

"Nigga, everybody dies tonight. Fuck your son!" I exclaimed.

"Mi cousin is gawn fuck you up, you coldhearted bastard! Why it gawn be like this?" he shouted.

Ignoring his cries, I smiled at Tiny. His hands and wrists duct-tape to the steering wheel of the car, and his bitch bonded in the passenger seat. I was about to cover their mouths with duct-tape, but thought against it. I wanted to hear them scream in agony.

"You fucked with the wrong man, Tiny. I outsmarted you and I'm the new nigga round the way. Your cousin, he'll be joining you soon," I smiled.

"Please, please, please... Don't do this...my son, Keon...he has no one to care for him...please, don't do this!" She shrieked.

"I'll see ya in hell, muthafucka!" Tiny exclaimed with rage dripping.

"Fuck you and your bitch." I said then set the truck on fire.

I watched his bitch squirm and cry out, as she tried freeing herself. She felt the fire bringing her closer to her fate. Biscuit, Groggy, Tank and myself stood around and watched them burn to death in the truck. The screams were piercingly loud and their cries heavy as the fire became more intense. Their suffering was agonizingly short. The flames engulfed the truck quickly and strongly and soon it had gotten so hot that we had to step a few feet back.

The truck exploded. One down and one to go, I thought. If you wanted the power and the respect in life and on the streets, this was necessary. Your heart had to be cold as ice. My heart was the Antarctica. I was here to rule, and stopped death by any means necessary from knocking at my door.

23

Let's triple our riches...
Turning darkness to light.
The future is you and kids.
Listen to our heartbeats...
Keeping us together...

America

I lay still in the soothing warm tub, collecting my thoughts. This was the third month of my pregnancy. I listened to some smooth R&B and had my eyes closed, enjoying some alone time. I thought about my husband and my music career.

Omar was my heart, but we were having problems. He wasn't completely honest with me that night he came home with a small wound to his head. Knowing his past, I began having my doubts. I began wondering if he was back on the streets. I hadn't spoken to Mr. Jenkins in weeks. There was no way to know about Omar's employment status.

I couldn't live through the lies, and the deception of the streets again. Trying my best to make us work was a difficult thing for me, especially being pregnant. I prayed everyday. I saw less of Omar. When he wasn't at work, he was out somewhere else, doing God knows what. Omar was a grown man and I couldn't keep tabs on him twenty-four seven. I had enough to worry about, my baby, and my own issues.

The music thang had slowed down since my fallout with Kendal. Everyone knew I was pregnant, and I stopped trying to hide it. It couldn't be hidden anyway. I was starting to show. Summer was officially here and I could no longer wear sweaters and coats.

I had come too far to put my career on a hiatus. Still pressing on, I was in the studio recording, doing ad-libs, hooks, and chorus for rappers. I linked up with another producer, Imagine, who had his own independent record label. He produced some of the finest beats that I've ever heard, and managed a few well-known rappers.

Imagine was a hustler, a businessman, and a go-getter. He knew how to make money. He was handsome, tall, and from the streets. Imagine grew up in Bed-Stuy and was once an A&R at Jive Records. He had personality and intelligence, and had a way of making you feel important when he talked to you. He made me feel like I was the next Beyonce, even though I was three months pregnant.

"America, the richest country in the world, and that name fits. You're rich in beauty and talents, America," he said the first time we met. "So, when is the baby due?" he had asked.

"February twenty-first, my doctor said," I told him.

"By then, with my help, you'll be a superstar. And you will be able to give your child whatever he or she wants," he assured.

I liked how that sounded and began working with him. But I missed Kendal and his silly antics. It was several weeks since we last spoke, and I was wondering how he was doing. He helped jumpstart my career and I knew I owed him.

I was sitting in the tub and started going over songs in my head. I had a few that I knew could be hits. I thought I heard Omar walked in.

"Baby, is that you?" I called out.

"Yeah," he answered.

He came into the bathroom, looking fine in wife-beater, denim shorts, and Timberlands.

"What you up to, boo?" I asked.

"I had to make a run out to Brooklyn," he said.

It was Saturday afternoon and he was using my car to get around. He's been gone since early morning, and my doubts about him going back to his old ways were piling on.

"What you got planned for the day?" he asked me.

He moved closer to the tub and got down on his knees, placing his hands on my shoulders, and began giving me a gentle massage.

"I'm relaxing for the day, trying not to stress myself," I said.

His touch always felt good. It always made me want to love him. He pressed his fingers into my skin, moving them in a circular motion. His grip was strong and comforting.

"You taking care of my seed, right?" he asked lightheartedly.

"I'm taking care of us." I smiled.

I was getting horny. We haven't had sex in over a week, which was shocking to me. Lately, Omar had been busy with other things.

"Are you behaving yourself?"

"America, I love you and only you," Omar sighed.

He misunderstood my question. I was about to ask him something else, but he said to me, "I gotta go, baby. I'll be back around eight tonight."

He got up and left. I sighed, watching him leave. Truth was I wanted him to get in the tub with me so we could enjoy each other's company. But my husband seemed in a hurry to leave. I remained in the soothing tub for another fifteen minutes, then stepped out and wrapped myself in a large towel. It was a beautiful day out, and I was going to enjoy it by going for a short walk.

As I made my way into the bedroom, my cell phone rang. I rushed for it, picking up and answering, "Hello?"

"Baby girl?" I heard Imagine said.

"Imagine, how is it going?" I replied.

"You busy this afternoon?" he asked.

"Why?"

"Can you make it down to the studio? I have some people that I want you to meet."

"One problem, I don't have my car."

"That's not a problem. I'll be at your place in an hour to scoop you. I told you, I'm gonna make you better than Beyonce. You were born to be a star," he said then hung up.

I stood there, wet and curious. I rushed into my bedroom to get dress. My time was coming and I could feel it coursing through my blood. I loved doing music.

About forty minutes later, Imagine parked his Cadillac in front of my building. I strutted out the lobby looking cute in denim caprice jeans, denim jacket and D&G sandals. Imagine opened the door for me. I thanked him for being a gentleman and got in.

"You look really nice, baby girl," hc said complimenting me and using his nickname for me.

"Thanks."

"I'm glad you got time to spare this afternoon. You ever heard of this kid named, Kemistry?" he asked.

"Yeah, he's supposed to be the next Fifty Cent out the hood," I said.

"Good, because I want you to do a track with him today."

"Stop kidding me."

"I don't lie about business, baby girl. He's making some noise in the biz, and I figure why not put you on something… Show him and his peoples your skills."

"I don't know what to say."

"Just go into that studio and give 'em the vocals you're working with," he explained.

"I will."

"I know you won't let me down, baby girl."

In no time we were in Manhattan on our way to the Hit Factory. Everybody recorded there, from Jay-Z to Fifty. It was my first time, and I was nervous.

I followed Imagine into the studio, and was greeted by the crew. My stomach was in loops. Imagine greeted other rappers, singers, and engineers. Then he turned their attention to me. I stared into their famous faces.

"Everybody, this is America," Imagine announced.

"Hello everyone," I wave greeting.

They waved and I knew they saw my protruding belly. Some of them glanced down, but remained silent. Imagine helped me get familiar with the studio and the engineers, and other singers. I hit it off with another singer by the name of Lady Soul. She was cute, thick in the right places, and knew a lot more about the industry than me. She put out two independent albums on Imagine's label, sung back up for Ashanti, Heather Headly, and even R. Kelly.

I spent about an hour getting familiar with my surroundings. It was around four-thirty in the afternoon when Kemistry strolled in with his entourage. I never met him in person, but he looked the same to me as he did in his videos.

Dripping in ice and diamonds, dressed like a thug in baggy jeans, Timberlands, he sported fitted baseball cap worn to the side, and throwback jersey. He had a hot single out, and was getting some airplay on the major stations in New York. His demeanor was cocky and arrogant.

Imagine had a few words with him. He nodded as he listened. Then he looked over at me, and my heart dropped. I wondered what Imagine was saying. Kemistry came over, eyeing me like I was a groupie.

"Damn luv, you're cute, and I've been hearing that you can blow in the studio, that's what's up." He then glanced down at my stomach and made a disturbing remark, saying, "Oh shit, you're pregnant, luv. Damn, you couldn't wait for a brother."

"Excuse me?"

"I'm just playing, luv. You gotta have some sense of humor, right?"

"Not like that."

"And you got some attitude, I like that," he smiled.

His first impression made him look like a jerk. I just wanted to do my thang and get away from him. The producer started putting a few beats together, majority of them were hot and I couldn't wait to get into the booth and record. Kemistry went into the booth first to spit a few bars down on a party beat. The sound had everyone nodding to it. Kemistry put on the headphones, moved closer to the mike, fixated his eyes on me and started spitting a verse to a track.

"This is hip-hop sensation y'all…make it last to the beat y'all….Yo that's right girl work them hips and swing them tits, work the club floor, tear up the dance floor/ honey got rhythm on all fours/ loved the way she twist around and hit the dance floor/ seductive in all ways/ boo caught my eye since I stepped through the door way/ so yo I'm top villain & got you ill- in/ you say my game is nice/ then lets get a room for the night/ got you shivering in all that ice/ slip my tongue down your throat, put my hand up your skirt &/ make it feel like the sun's connecting toward the earth/ so work it girl, just don't hurt it girl/ know you've been checking me out all night/ so it's up to you how you want to get this party started right/ see my smile, feel like I'm over seas cause that L and Hennessey got me feeling so nice/ I'm high out my mind & a little booty is all I need to satisfy me fully for the night/ you and me/ just doing things right/ just a little is all I need/ lusting 4 u from night 2 night/ go in my little stash/ so I can purchase the right ass/ no telling how many positions we'll end up in one night/ so if you're real with it, then come feel on it/ just don't taunt me with little kisses like you can't deal with it."

After his verse he looked over at me and smiled. We spent about four hours in the studio, and I got in the booth and tore it up. Everyone loved me, I felt so flattered.

"Girl, you got a gift with that voice," Lady Soul said.

"Thank you," I replied.

"Baby girl, we on our way," Imagine smiled like a proud father.

"Yo love, we need to do more tracks together. You're gonna make a nigga go platinum with your voice," Kemistry said giving me props.

As the evening rounded out, I listened to everyone else, and we were all equally talented. Imagine brought through a good mix of people to come together on a song. I was sitting next to the engineer observing him doing his thang, when I noticed Omega walking through the door with a young looking thug. He spotted me and smiled.

"Oh shit, America…?" he said.

I rolled my eyes at him. He walked over to me and said, "Yo, where your husband at? I've been tryin' to get him for a minute, but he's being hardheaded and shit. What, Soul too good for a nigga now?"

I just looked at him, remaining silent.

"Damn, it's like that, America? We go way back, since high school? I don't even get a hello from you," he said.

"Hey," I returned halfheartedly.

"I see you ready to drop my nigga's seed and shit… Soul Jr. is soon on the way. Y'all making me Godfather, right?" he asked, and then started rubbing on my belly without my permission.

"C'mon, you know I'm gonna have to teach that youngin' how to survive," he continued.

Hearing him talk had my stomach in knots. I looked fiercely at him.

"You and your thugs stay the fuck away from me, my husband, and my baby!"

"Now you're gettin' disrespectful. I came up in here showin' you love, and you wanna scream on me like that, like I'm some off-brand nigga," he said.

Before anything else was said, Kemistry smiled and greeted Omega.

"What's good my nigga," he gave Omega dapped.

"Kemistry, what's good you workin' hard on those tracks right?" Omega asked.

"I'm knocking these tracks out like pussy. Tryin' to get paid like you, know what I'm sayin'," Kemistry boasted.

"Yeah, my nigga," Omega said to him, while giving me a cold stare.

I sighed and tried to ignore his trifling ass. Imagine soon walked up to us and gave Omega dap and a hug.

"Imagine, what's good my nigga," Omega said.

"Business, Mega? What brings you here?" Imagine asked.

"Came to see my boy, Kemistry," Omega said. "But you know, I feel I'm not wanted here at the moment, you know how some bitches be hating."

"Imagine, I'm ready to leave," I said.

"Is there a problem?" he asked.

"I'm tired," I answered.

"Ahight, let me get my things," he said.

"I'll wait for you in the hallway," I told him.

Omega glared at me as I walked by him with attitude. I wanted nothing to do with him. He was probably the reason why Omar came home with the small wound on his head a few nights back. I said nothing else and waited in the hallway.

Imagine dropped me home around nine that evening. He was a gentleman and walked me to the door, thanking me for coming out. I thanked him for the opportunity. I walked into my apartment and it was dark and quiet. Omar was not in, I wanted to talk to him, but my husband was ghost. Saturday night and I wanted to be in my husband's arms, having him comfort me. Seeing Omega again brought out the bitch in me, and I wanted some comfort. But I was alone. I went into the bedroom, got comfortable for bed, and watched television until the TV started watching me.

As the days progressed, I worked on my music more and more. For me, it was work, recording in the studio, and home writing more songs. Omar was in and out as usual. I tried not to let it bother me. I called and talked to Mr.

Jenkins, and he confirmed that Omar's been at work everyday since starting. That brought some relief. Now, if I knew what he was doing with the other half of his time, I would be totally at ease.

Writing songs and poetry brought me comfort. I'd sit in my bed, or the tub, or sit by an open window and create music from my heart. I wrote dozens of songs and poems in the past month. I had plenty more to put down.

Going into my second trimester, I had my first sonogram scheduled in one week. I was anxious to know if I was having a boy or girl. I was hoping for a boy for my first.

Besides my small quarrels with Omar, life seemed to be going good for me. I was happy, praying for a healthy baby, and a strong, lasting marriage. As always there will be bumps and obstacles in the road.

Thursday afternoon, I came home to a large manila package addressed to me. It was thin, so I thought it was a recording contract. I couldn't wait to see what it contained. Excited, I tore it open only to be shocked and appalled staring at seven large glossy photos of my husband fucking a bitch.

My breathing became so intense it made my eyes watery. I was seething. There was no date, just Omar raw and exposed and doing the unthinkable to another woman. The pictures were so graphic that I was able to see the pink of the woman's vagina. There was one photo of my husband going down on this bitch, with his tongue deep in her.

"Ohmygod!"

Tears trickled down my face and I felt the urge to vomit. I knew of his cheating in the past, but to see pictures brought out sickness in me. I ran to the bathroom and threw up. It didn't matter if the photos were old or fresh. I had proof of Omar's infidelity in my hands. I remained in the bathroom for about an hour, trying to get myself together. I was a mess. I love him, but after seeing the photos of him acting a fool with another woman, I didn't know what to think.

Several hours later, after the tears dried, and my anger somewhat subsided, I sat motionless on my bed. There was a lot of shit running through my head. I left the pictures sprawled across our bed for him to see when he walked in. I rubbed my belly, thinking of the father of my child.

A quarter past ten, Omar entered the apartment. I was sitting in the dark when I heard him.

"Baby, you home? Why is it so dark in here?"

I didn't answer him.

"America?" he called out. "America?"

He walked into the bedroom and turned on the lights. He saw me seated quietly on our bed. He looked down at the photos I spread out. He moved closer, curiosity getting the best of him and asked, "Where did you get those?"

"Does it fuckin' matter!" I barked. "And don't you dare deny them."

"That happened a long time ago, America. That ain't me anymore, you know this," he tried to explain.

"I don't know shit about you anymore! I love you, and this is how you repay me, with this bitch! And I always knew, but kept giving you the benefit of the doubt. To see this shit in my face, Omar... Your fuckin' face in a woman's nasty crotch, and then you come home and kiss me with that stench on your breath... Oh, how could you," I cried out.

"Baby, I don't know who sent you those fuckin' pictures, but I'm gonna find out," he said.

"I don't care who sent them," I shouted. "Look at them, look at you. Look at how filthy you look in all these damn pictures. You call this loving me...?" I picked up a handful of photos and threw them at him.

"I fucked up, but I deserve another chance. That's not me anymore. I've changed, you hear me? I ain't that anymore, I swear on my unborn child," he assured.

"Don't you dare bring our unborn child into this argument. This shit is about you, about what you've been doing to me behind my back, this is just dirty and plain disrespectful to me, Omar..."

My voice trailed as I broke down and fell to the floor. Omar came rushing over to me to help, but I snapped, pushed him away, and screamed, "Don't you touch me! Don't you ever fuckin' touch me again!"

"America, don't act like this. I've been bustin' my ass since I got out. I got a job, been faithful, and married you. What more do you want from me?"

"I gave you my virginity and four years of purity, Omar. I held you down while you were locked up. I've been by your side forever. Been through the good, the bad, and the ugly with you. I kept myself innocent for you. But to see the pictures of you, in an uncompromised position with some bitch, that's a smack in my face," I cried.

"It just happened."

"It just happened?" I shouted uncontrollably.

"America, I don't love her. I love you. I fucked up ahight? That's what you want to hear. I fucked up. But it won't happen again. I promise you that."

I was crying. I love him and wanted to believe him, but the photos stayed in my head, haunting me. To see photos of my husband sexing a bitch… Especially the one with him eating that bitch out, it just ate away at me.

"Just get the fuck out."

"What?"

"I said leave…! Get the fuck away from me!" I shrieked madly.

"I live here too," he boldly returned.

"I don't want you here right now," I said.

"We can work this out, America. I ain't goin' any fuckin' where."

"Oh, really," I replied.

Then I picked up the cordless phone and threw it at him. He tried to move, but too late. It smacked him across his head, causing blood to flow from his forehead.

"America, you need to chill the fuck out."

The alarm clock followed him. He quickly moved out the way, and charged at me. Throwing me against the wall, Omar had me pinned against my back, clutching my wrists tightly, with his breath panting in my face and glared at me with anger.

"You gonna hit me now?" I asked. "You gonna start beating on your pregnant wife now, and seal the deal?"

"Damn!" he exclaimed, releasing me and pushing his fist through the bedroom wall.

"Fuck this, I don't need this, ahight? I'm out," he shouted and left out the bedroom.

I burst into tears when I saw him leave. I dropped to the floor with my back against the wall and cried louder. Those pictures of him were too much for me. I kept thinking whether it happened in the past or now. It happened. He had fucked someone, and now his past finally came back.

Could I get over this and forgive Omar? I wanted to move on and put this behind me but right now I was hurting. I couldn't stop crying. The more I thought about his sexcapades, the harder it hurt.

24

Challenges make life interesting.
Overcoming them makes life meaningful...

ERICK S GRAY

Omar

I swear when you try and do better something invariably gets in the way to fuck things up. Since I came home, I've been faithful in my marriage and holding down this part-time gig. Now someone had the audacity to mail pictures of me sexing Alexis.

That shit made me furious. All I could do was think how did those pictures come about? I didn't remember taking them, but I knew it happened a few months before I was locked up.

It had to be Alexis who sent the photos. Her outrageous outburst in the club that night, and her jealousy made her do it. I was ready to murder that bitch. Because of her stupidity, I had to leave my place. I didn't want to hit America, and left before things got out of control.

I drove around in my cousin's Lexus, needing a place. This nigga was making so much money in the game, that he gave me his Lexus and stated that he'll buy another next week. Omega told me to keep the twenty-grand, said it was for saving his life.

I had a new car and the twenty-grand. I tried keeping it from America. The streets were calling me. When I saw how much money Greasy and Omega were making, I felt a deep-rooted urging to get a piece. I'd be contradicting myself. I truly had peace of mind, but with this bullshit happening, and me making less than two-hundred dollars a week at the center, something had to give.

Rahmel's advice came to mind. Rahmel would say to me that this was one of those challenges that I had to overcome. This first real challenge was kicking my ass. I took the twenty grand and invested some of it into marijuana. I brought four pounds of haze and hydro, sold it off to different clientele in Queens and Brooklyn.

I was on the move and was seeing less and less of my wife. But I needed to make some extra money on the side. I wanted to take my wife on an exotic trip, but knew I couldn't come out and pay in cash. That would've fueled her suspicions. Technically I was back in the game, but on some really off the radar, low-end shit.

I was waiting for the right time to give America the honeymoon she truly deserved. Then the photos came, and totally fucked everything up. I was at odds with myself. One side of me wanted to get that money, like Greasy and Omega. The other side thought about Rahmel, America, and Mr. Jenkins. That side was telling me, change the way you think. You're about to have a son—look at the mistake Rahmel made and where he ended up for a long time.

I didn't want to end up back in jail doing a longer bid. Since I been out, I've been on the sidelines just observing. The game done changed. Omega's crew was brutal and ruthless. They put fear on the streets.

I drove to my cousin's crib in Elmont. I always had a place to stay. I parked at the dark, quiet house. His new 2007 ivory pearl Infiniti G35 Sport was parked in the driveway. Getting out the car, I rang his cell phone. He picked up after the third ring.

"What up, nigga?" he answered, sounding drowsy.

"Open the front door," I said.

A short moment later, his door opened and Greasy stood in front of me in a white robe.

"Damn cuz, it's all late and shit... What happened, you got deported from America?" he joked.

"Greasy, I ain't in the fuckin' mood right now," I said, my face tight with anger.

"Damn nigga, be grateful or sump'n," he said, closing the door behind me.

I walked in and sat on his couch. I wanted to be home with my wife, but had to settle for my cousin's place.

"I got two extra bedrooms, Soul. Just pick one and crash," he offered.

"You got company?" I asked.

"Greasy always got company," he smiled.

"I don't mean to intrude—"

"You family. I got you, cuz, don't even sweat it," he said.

"Thanks, I appreciate this Greasy."

I got up, gave him dap and a hug. Then I went upstairs to get some sleep and try to clear my head. I was still upset about the pictures, but sooner or later, the truth will come out, and when it does, somebody was going to feel it for sure. I stripped down to my boxers and crashed out on top of the comforter. Fifteen minutes later, I was sleeping.

"Wake your bitch-ass up!"

I looked up and saw the 40 cal pointing at me. I jumped up.

"What the fuck!" I jumped in a panic.

It was Omega playing around. Greasy was behind him laughing.

"Mega, what the fuck is wrong?" I barked. "Don't be pointing that shit at me."

"You should've seen the look on your face, Soul. You probably pissed on yourself," Omega joked.

I was out the bed and ready to smack the shit out of them.

"Your ol' lady kicked you out, huh. What's good wit' that?" Omega asked.

"Nothing I can't handle," I answered still sleepy. I looked at the time and it was almost noon. I looked over at Greasy and asked, "Why you let me sleep so late?"

"Man, I just got up an hour ago."

I went into the bathroom.

"Soul, we'll be downstairs," Greasy said.

I jumped in the shower, and got dressed in some of my cousin's clothes. Half-hour later, I met with them in the living room. Greasy had some bitch cooking breakfast in the kitchen, clad in some tight ass shorts and a skimpy T-shirt.

"Soul, you want some breakfast?" he asked.

"Yeah, lemme get some eggs and toast," I said.

"That's it? Nigga, eat sump'n before you passed the fuck out tripping over your shorty. Bitch, make my nigga some French-toasts, scrambled eggs, sausages, and all that," Greasy ordered.

She looked at Greasy with a attitude responding, "Nigga, do I look like fuckin' I-Hop to you?"

"Yo, bitch you stayed the night right? Start burning and make my nigga sump'n to eat, ahight?" Greasy reprimanded.

The bitch sucked her teeth and went to work. Omega was on his cell phone discussing business. I took a seat on the couch and relaxed. Omega soon got off the phone and took a seat across from me.

"I hear you dabbling in weed sells now. Quite frankly, I'm insulted, Soul. You better than that nickel and dime BS... That's what you choose to do wit' the twenty G's I gave you?" he asked.

"Cuz, you selling weed now?" Greasy asked.

"Here I am giving you a position in my empire and you wanna peddle that shit for what...? You can make more money in a day fuckin' wit' us than you do in two months," Omega said.

"Mega, I'm tryin' to keep a low profile, that's all. Don't take it so personal."

"You know I always got you, Soul. How you makin' out wit' that twenty grand?" he asked.

"I got most of it stashed away for a rainy day."

"Rainy day? Nigga, what are you somebody's grandfather?" Omega asked. "There's more of that to go around ten times, my nigga."

"Cuz, we is doin' it lovely right now, ya heard?" Greasy chimed in.

"I see... That's what's up," I replied halfheartedly.

A short while later, the bitch set a plate of hot cooked breakfast down in front of me.

"Good looking out," I said to her.

"You welcome. At least somebody appreciate the shit I do around here," she said, staring directly at Greasy.

"Bitch, you need to be thanking me for dickin' you down at nights... Who's your daddy?" Greasy said.

"Yeah, nigga, whateva," she answered.

"Don't pay that bitch any attention, she was born wit' an attitude," Greasy laughed.

I started eating my breakfast, and watching TV. Omega was back on his cell phone, and Greasy was messing with the bitch in the kitchen. I ate and thought about America, wanting to call her, but knowing she was probably still upset with me.

Those pictures were still in my head, and I was trying to figure out who could've sent them. I tried to recall when and why I took photos like that while enjoying breakfast.

"Soul, don't make any plans for the night. We takin' you to the strip club to get you some pussy. Mega and I ain't takin' no for an answer. You coming nigga, we ain't never really got the chance to hang out," Greasy said.

I didn't argue about it. I was down, but I was going to chill and get my drink on. But the cheating on America, I wasn't all for that.

We arrived at this upscale strip club called, *The Pink Pony,* in midtown Manhattan. Omega and Greasy wanted to get out of the hood and party in the city. We rode in Omega's white 2007 Yukon. It was tricked out with TV's, chromed, and a navigation system.

The three of us walked into the place, clad in platinum and diamonds, Timberlands, Nikes, throwbacks, fitted Yankees cap. Each of us carried a wad full of cash, looking like thoroughbred hustlers.

The strip club was nude and had an assortment of exotic fine looking women from black, white, Asian, Russian that was there to please and tease. The music was urban, with a strobe light flashing over the stage and the place was crammed with regulars that were eager to have a good time with their pick of strippers. We paid the measly twenty dollars admission fee, got searched at the door, and went in to ball and have a good time.

The three of us walked up to the stage eyeing this Asian chick with a body like Whoa!

"That's what Greasy's talkin' about."

"Can I get you fellas something to drink?" A female waitress asked.

"Yeah, beautiful, how much for you?" Omega joked.

She smiled and replied with, "I'm priceless."

"Please, everything comes wit' a price," he countered.

"I have a boyfriend," she answered.

"What your boyfriend got to do with this?"

"Listen, you want a drink or not?" she asked.

"Lemme get a few bottles of your best stuff. Y'all serve Moet and Cristal in here?" Omega asked.

"We have everything, it will cost though," she informed.

"I look like I care?" Omega asked.

"Okay."

Omega passed her a c-note before she walked away.

"That's for you, spend it in good health." He smiled.

She smiled and was off. We took a seat near one of the stages and watched nude girls perform. Greasy already started tipping a voluptuous chick nothing but tens and twenties. A short while later, the same waitress came to our table with two bottles of Moet and one bottle of Cristal. Then she set down our drinking glasses. Omega pushed a thousand dollars on her and told her to keep the change.

"You sure I can't get your number wit' that?" he asked. She smiled at Omega, walking away.

"Shorty ahight, Soul. Word, I need to get at that," Omega said.

I poured myself a glass of Moet, and sat back and watched the performances.

The night went on, and we got tipsy. Drinking and tipping the girls with big bills, we put up with the deejay's wack-ass music selection. I spent over fifteen-hundred. I sat there in my seat, eyeing the stage, as the fog machine began filling the stage.

"Ahight, my dudes, coming to the stage, is ours truly and one of the most beautiful girls known… Here's Joanna," the deejay announced.

As the mist cleared, and the stage was visible, there was Joanna, America's best friend, sprawled out on stage in a blue mesh long robe with nothing else on underneath, and in clear seven-inch stilettos. Her tits were exposed, and her figure was thick and shapely. She was so beautiful up on the stage twirling, grinding, and moving seductively against the long pole in the middle of the platform. I looked on in awe, as did Greasy and Omega.

"How Greasy ain't know that bitch a stripper…?" Greasy looked baffled.

"Damn yo, that bitch Joanna got my dick hard for a muthafucka," Omega said.

Her performance was top notch. She danced to Prince, Michael Jackson, Jay-Z and Ciara. Wowing the three of us like damn! Joanna was on beat, grinding it out on stage, enticing niggas. A few had to get up and use the bathroom. Even when she saw the three of us staring at her, her performance didn't stop, she never looked shocked. Joanna continued doing her thing like she just didn't care.

Greasy got up to tip her, and dropped five-hundred dollars on her easily. It felt wrong for me watching America's best friend perform naked on stage, but I couldn't turn away. She got paid that night, getting so much attention that I thought she was gonna need a bodyguard soon. When her session was finished, she donned her blue mesh long robe, collected her earnings in a trash bag and walked off stage diva-like.

"I need to holla at that bitch," Omega said.

He got up, and I followed behind him. We met up with her near the entrance to the ladies dressing room.

"Joanna, damn girl, when you gonna let a nigga get at that, and take you out?" Omega said loudly.

"What the fuck brought y'all here?" she asked.

"We came out to have a good time, had to get the fuck out the hood for a minute, you know what I'm sayin," Omega said. "Shit, if I knew you were dancing up in here like that, I would a came through sooner."

"Omega, just step off…you know you ain't my type," she barked.

"What! I heard every nigga is your type if they ballin'. Why you tryin' to play me? You know I'm makin' ends. Doin' big things in the hood," Omega boasted.

"Too thuggish for my taste, Omega. I don't deal with no thugs," she said.

"Thug? Bitch, if I'm a thug, then what the fuck was your father, he was the most thuggish nigga round the way," Omega said.

"No nigga, my father was a gangsta, not some wannabe. There's a difference. My father had class. You'll never be like my father. You're just crazy and a fuckin hothead."

"Yo, Joanna, watch what you say to me, before I slap the white off your ass," Omega barked.

"You'll never change, just fuck off, nigga," she spat.

Omega stepped to her, but I pulled him back, saying, "Nigga, chill, we ain't come here for beef."

"See, no fuckin' class at all," she told him, before walking into the dressing room.

"Fuck that bitch!" Omega hissed. "And fuck her father, what that nigga gonna do to me. He locked up in the feds, doing life way out in Kentucky somewhere. He don't hold no weight around the way anymore. She lucky I just don't take the pussy, I done did it before."

"C'mon Mega, you're tipsy, let's go back to the table," I said.

I had to hold Omega back and pulled him to the table. He was heated by Joanna's remarks. He sat down in his seat, and within minutes, he had some new chick on his lap with her tits in his face, calming him down.

After I knew he was good, I went over to the bar and ordered a Corona. As I stood waiting for the bartender to bring me my drink, I felt somebody slap me upside my head. I was about to turn around and get ghetto, but it was Joanna, glaring at me.

"What the fuck is wrong with you? You trying to get locked back up?" she said.

"What the fuck?"

"And what's up with you and my girl, America. She called me last night so upset... Crying bout you being in some pictures with some stank ho."

"Look, I done told her, those photos were taken a while ago. I'm good to her now, Joanna. Since I've been home. I've been faithful to her," I explained.

"We need to talk," she said.

"Ahight let me get my drink first."

Beer in hand, Joanna and I took a seat in the back, near the backrooms, where it was less crowded. She was always real and to the point. That's why I liked her. She sat across from me.

"Soul, you fuckin' up, I'm gonna let you know. I had a long talk with America last night, and right now, she doesn't know what to do with you. She loves you, but she's thinking about divorcing you if you don't get your act together."

"Divorce?" I exclaimed, choking on the beer.

"Yes. But I know she didn't truly mean it. She was just upset and shit. But don't be fuckin' my girl over, nigga."

"Yo, I'm gettin' my shit right, why the fuck she trippin? I'm working, I ain't wit' the streets anymore. Yo, I'm tryin' to do me."

"You could've fooled me." Joanna chuckled.

"Fuck you talkin' about?"

"I see you up in here with Omega and Greasy, and I know what they're about—trouble. You got the shines on, pocket full of money, and you got my girl seeing less and less of you everyday. What's good with that, Soul? Now you say that you ain't fuckin' up, but how does she know that."

"Because I ain't. I love my wife, and will do anything for her and my unborn. I'm just in here having a good time, and I know America still upset, so I'm giving her time to blow over."

"You need to go see her."

"She kicked me out."

"So what? You need to go over there and have a serious talk with her, before things get more dramatic with you two. She's upset, but I know she wants you to come back home to her."

I sat there, thinking about the drama that was going on between my wife and I. It wasn't supposed to be like this.

"I know you love her, Soul. You're not like your friends. I think you've changed, Soul. You're talented I mean extremely talented with music. When you first got out, I had my doubts and warned my girl to be cautious. But you're married to her and now y'all having a child, you and America have something special. Don't fuckin' waste my girl's time if you gonna be like your friends over there."

"C'mon Joanna, you know—"

"No, in a few years, they'll be where my father is— doing life in a federal prison. They've got nothing going for them... Yeah, they've got money, cars, women, jewelry and all that materialistic shit. The truth is they're empty inside. You're better than that, Soul. You have someone who loves you and you have something to look forward to, a child. My father was a hustler, took care of me with money... But where he is now? He'll never be a free man again. Don't end up watching your kids grow up from a distance behind bars like him. You and America, with y'all talents... Y'all could be the next JayZ and Beyonce in music. Usually I mind my business, but America's my girl for life, and I don't wanna see her hurt, Soul."

"Did America ask you to come and talk to me?"

"No, she was against it, but I can't stand by and watch the two of you fuck things up."

I sat uneasy in the chair, thinking about what Joanna just said to me.

"Look, I gotta go, you need to think about shit and get on the fuckin' job and be a good husband to my girl, and a great father to my godchild," she said.

She got up and left and I remained seated. My family issues weighed heavy on my mind.

"Yo, what that bitch was over here talkin' to you about?" Omega asked.

"What?" I replied.

"You been over there for a minute. You tryin' a fuck her, Soul?" Omega asked.

"I'm ready to go," I said.

"What now? I'm tryin' to bring some bitches wit' me," Omega said.

"With or without you nigga, I'm out," I said.

I got up and walked by him. I belonged at home, working things out with my pregnant wife. I was growing and knew it could only get better for me. I done been through hell already.

Riding silently in the back of Omega's Yukon, I was peering out the window, thinking about my wife and my life as we drove on the Long Island Expressway. It was very quiet. Around three in the morning, we were in Queens. Omega wanted to stop by the club on Liberty Ave. I just wanted to go home, but he needed to take care of some business.

There were lots of people outside when we pulled up to the club. I was feeling upset about this move. Saying they'd be back in a few minutes, Omega and Greasy got out the truck. I remained seated in the backseat.

I waited patiently for fifteen minutes but was getting agitated by the seconds. It hurt me deeply to find out America was thinking of getting a divorce. Even though she was angry, just the thought of it crossing her mind made me upset.

Trying to get my mind right, I glanced out the truck and saw Alexis exit the club nestled under a nigga's arm. All of a sudden the pictures came back to mind. It had to be that bitch that played me foul. She was always jealous of America, and wanted to destroy my marriage.

Without thinking, I stepped out the truck and walked up to them, as they were strolling down the block like a loving couple.

"Alexis," I called out. "I need to holla at you."

She and her male friend turned around, looking at me. "Soul, what you want?" she asked with attitude.

"Lemme talk to you a second."

"About what? I'm not feelin' you right now, you keep dissin' me," she barked.

I walked up to her and grabbed her arm, saying, "Why you gotta play games for?"

"What, nigga step off, cause I ain't fuckin' wit' you no more. Fuck you and your wife!" she shouted.

"Don't go there," I snapped, tightening my grip around her arm.

"Get off me!" she shouted.

"Yo, chill nigga," her male companion intervened.

"This ain't got nothing to do with you, nigga, so step the fuck off," I shouted.

"Why you gotta send pictures to my wife and blow my spot up like that?" I continued.

"I don't know what the fuck you're talkin' about. Get the fuck off me!"

"Yo, nigga, she said get the fuck off her!" her friend shouted at me. He stepped up to me like he wanted to battle.

"Nigga, you better fall back before I drop you," I warned.

"Soul, stop. Get off me, get off me now!" she screamed.

This dude walked up to me, grabbing at me. I jerked my arm free from his grip, and shouted, "Don't fuckin' touch me, nigga!"

"What you gonna do!" he chided. He got up in my face, towering over me by a few inches. I was far from being intimidated.

I glared at him, and saw the butt of the gun peeking from his shirt.

"She said step off nigga."

"Fuck you!"

That muthafucka sucker-punched me in the face. I stumbled back but quickly regained my balance. I went berserk on the nigga, two piecing him swiftly. The first caught him in the left temple and the second blow caught his right jaw. He stumbled back, dazed. I kept on him with a ferocious force building in me and continued my brutal onslaught of punches and kicks to his body and face.

He was out of his element, caught off-guard by my hand skills. He tried to protect himself by swinging wildly. I had the upper hand and saw him trying to reach for his gun concealed under his shirt. I charged forward and he grabbed me viciously and we both fell on the hood of a parked car. We wrestled with each other and he kept trying to reach for his weapon. And I wasn't about to give up the advantage.

I tried to remove the weapon from his waistband myself. We struggled for the possession of his gun. Then the nigga unexpectedly head-butted me and I fell back, losing whatever reach I had on his gun. When I quickly came to, I saw the 45 in his hand aimed at me and knew I was dead.

From out of nowhere a champagne bottle smashed over the nigga's head. He fell forward from the blow and I had another chance of redemption. It was Greasy striking him, and before I knew it, Omega was on him too, both beating the man severely with bottles and a brick in the street.

It happened so fast—before I knew it, there was a rumble of violence in the street. About a dozen men came out. Each man was down with either of the two crews' fighting. My rival came with support and they had his back in the fight, so did my niggas.

I was being pulled into the whirlwind of the brawl and went in swinging, striking at whoever was unlucky to come against me. I knocked down two with the boxing hand-skills. Soon I was outnumbered and found myself falling on the pavement. I had to curl into the fetal position from being stomped harshly by about three pairs of Timberlands. It didn't take a rocket scientist to understand what would transpire next.

Baka! Baka! Baka! Baka!

Gunfire exploded and people quickly scattered for cover. I couldn't tell who was shooting, I just heard the shots lighting up the night. I hugged the cold concrete for my cover and kept my head low. I was badly bruised and beaten, and felt paralyzed in the fetal cold position under the blanket of violence.

After the crowd scattered, I didn't see Greasy or Omega and wondered if they had ran after hearing the shots. The sound of police sirens pierced the night. I knew that I had fucked up and could hardly move. I felt myself being roughly pulled off the pavement. My arms were twisted behind me and my wrists encased in handcuffs. I was quickly placed under arrest and detained.

My heart dropped, my eyes had shed agonizing tears, as I sighed heavily with my thoughts on America. This would devastate her. The police put me in the back of a marked car and I knew with my record that I would be seeing Riker's Island.

Several hours later, I was still at the 103rd pct. being charged with an assortment of charges. My freedom was looking bleak with every passing hour. There was no going home and my marriage was in jeopardy.

Reality was setting. I wanted to be mad at the world, blame others, but I only had myself to blame, for being so fucking stupid. I'd been doing better now I was wondering what happened? Where did I go wrong? Shit, I had a long time to think and contemplate. I was where I didn't want to be, back in a jail cell awaiting my fate.

25

Always accept the challenges.
Feel the exhilaration of victory...

America

I got the phone call about Omar being in jail and I was devastated. Joanna called me. I had to hang up. I couldn't stand it anymore. I cried long and hard that night and became sick. Nauseated, I spent an hour in the bathroom vomiting.

What went wrong between Omar and me? I contemplated with tears of hurt, betrayal, and anger trickling down my face. I was upset with myself for kicking him out. Maybe if he had stayed, he would've still been home and out of trouble.

"Oh God, what have I done?"

I was scheduled to take my first sonogram in a few days, but now I didn't have my husband by my side. It hurt me that Omar wouldn't be there. I just wanted to lock myself in the apartment for as long as I could. Joanna kept calling, but I wanted to be alone. I needed time to console myself. I felt so cursed.

A week passed, and I sat in my doctor's office, trying to hold my head up. I couldn't help but to notice a few other pregnant women in the waiting room with me. They had their husbands or mate looking happy and elated. I felt myself becoming emotional again. I was trying to be strong, but Omar was deep in my thoughts. One woman looked over at me and smiled. She was with her husband I assumed, and she looked about ten years older than me.

"Boy or girl?" she asked.

"Excuse me?" I replied.

"I was wondering if it's boy or girl?" she repeated.

"I'm sorry but I have no idea yet," I replied.

"You're carrying well. How many months are you?" she asked.

I looked at her for a moment, wishing she would stay out my business. I was becoming jealous of her. I wanted to be her. I wanted my husband sitting next to me, keeping me company and making me laugh.

"Four months," I said.

"Your first?"

"Baby, I'm gonna run across the street to the store, you want anything?" the guy she was sitting with asked.

"I'm okay, sweetheart."

"Be back in a minute."

I watched him leave and was thinking that should be me too, having Omar look out for me and catering to my needs.

"Is this your first?" she repeated.

I didn't answer her. My mind was miles away off in a zone, with my emotions soon to erupt. I needed to leave.

"I have to go," I uttered, stood up and bolted from the doctor's office.

Once outside, I walked as quickly as I could, trying to separate myself from the doctor's office as far as possible. I couldn't do it without Omar. We promised each other that we would know if it was a boy or girl together.

Strutting down the busy street, I found myself in tears. I didn't care who saw me. I just needed to be out. I couldn't walk any further, I was becoming winded and a serious wreck. I leaned against a brick wall, and fell to the floor.

As I lay there, I heard a female shouting, "Is she alright?"

A few good Samaritans tried to help me up, but I wasn't hurt, at least not physically anyway. I just wanted a normal, peaceful and loving life with my husband, and that was snatched away from me because of my stupidity.

Someone must have called 911. Because moments later, an ambulance pulled up. Paramedics were standing over me, asking if I was okay. They told me to nod. I nodded meekly, and soon they helped me to my feet. They put me into the ambulance and gave me some oxygen to help me breathe better. When everyone was sure that I wasn't giving birth, they relaxed but I couldn't.

I was taken to the hospital to undergo observation. I didn't resist. I wasn't in any rush to get home. I called Joanna and she met me at Marry Immaculate hospital. She stood by my side the whole time, comforting me. I didn't know what else I could do. I had to be strong and get through this difficult situation for my baby.

26

His heart grows cold.
As his days grows old.
The streets he calls home.
Ruthless until the day he dies.
His life is but a curse and a lie...

Omega

I felt bad for my dude, Soul. He caught a bad one that night. Greasy and I happened to escape before the police rolled up. I was looking for Soul, but couldn't find him in the mix. I didn't know who fired first. I shot back and hit some nigga in his chest. But my nigga Soul, he was back in the system. He needed a good lawyer. I couldn't do nothing right now, I was having my own problems on the block.

Since Tiny's departure, his territory was open market, and I was moving in to set up shop with that meth, so was every other crew that wanted in on his turf, and that brought more beef, and gunplay.

Tiny's death hadn't been confirmed yet, but other niggas caught the drift. He hadn't been seen in several days, and when a nigga is missing for that long, chances are, he ain't never coming back.

My name was definitely ringing and my reputation was on the rise. In the streets, I was the man to see for kilos of crank, coke, and guns. I was feared and got lots of pussy. Putting the murder game down with my fierce crew had my rep spreading like the virus.

With Tiny out the way, I only had to worry about his cousin Demetrius, and a few small up-and-coming crews that wanted to take over his turf. Those small crews had to be dealt with before they became a bigger headache for me.

Crystal Meth became the new drug in South Jamaica, Queens. Crack was still selling, but meth had every fiend hooked. My clientele ranged from the middle class blue collar working man, like sanitation and construction workers, cab drivers, college students, teachers, and every other drug fiend. Even doctors, cops, and lawyers were strung-out.

The drug was popular, it gave a high for up to eight hours or more, and stimulated the body—gave muthafuckas energy for work, overtime, sports, and sex. Taken orally, methamphetamine stimulated the brain cells, by increasing the release of dopamine, which in turn initially enhances mood. A meth user experienced increased wakefulness and physical activity, and decreased appetite.

Everybody wanted some, and I had the supply. With my Mexican connection, I released unlimited crank and meth into the streets making my money hand over fist. But with my vast richness came rival crews, haters, and more trouble. I wanted Tiny's turf to expand my operation and I was ready to lay down any nigga the hard way.

The corner of Foch Blvd and Guy R. Brewer became a hot spot. It was Tiny's old turf and with that area, you could make close to five-hundred thousand a week. I put Biscuit and Monk on it, told them to hold it down and drop any nigga that opposed us. We had the muscle and the guns. Biscuit worked with the SMG PK machine gun—that shit could air-out a corner quick. I was making so much money, that I had several money counting machines and was weighing thousands and thousands of bills in garbage bags on scales. I owned a 3400 square feet bricked home in New Jersey, with the master suite on the first floor, a vaulted ceiling in the family room, a gas fireplace, eat-in kitchen with a large dinette and breakfast area, bay windows and a two car garage. The neighborhood was quiet and far from Jamaica Queens.

I had six cars, including a red Ferrari 360 Modena spider and a silver Continental GT. I had it all, and was still climbing my way to the top.

The bitches, yeah, I was still fucking Judy, Jazmin, and my new bitch, Cindy, plus a few other bitches on the side. I took care of them and they all took care of me. I moved my ride-or-die bitch, Jazmin into my home in Jersey, and kept Cindy in a two-bedroom condo out in Queens. Judy did her and had her own little place. She was still my source down at the 113th.

Jazmin was a month pregnant by me, and I was cool with it. I wanted a son. I wanted to teach my son the streets and have him be my little prince. She was nervous telling me at first, because she didn't know my reaction. I needed a seed to carry on my legacy out on the streets when I'm gone. I wanted a new generation of me.

Despite a few set backs and bumps in the road, life was good. I was willing to bleed these streets red. Money was coming into my organization by the truckloads, and my relationship with the Mexicans was getting stronger on the daily. I was feeling untouchable.

Friday night, I was in the master suite lounging butt naked on my king size bed. Jazmin was sprawled on top, giving me the best blowjob ever. She had me hard like steel and grunting as I felt myself about to cum in her mouth.

The television was on, but I wasn't paying attention to it. I was in bliss, with my fingers tangled in Jazmin's hair and swelling in her mouth. I glanced at the news that was airing and the backdrop looked familiar to me. Suddenly the ten o clock news caught my attention as I stared at the charred Escalade in the wooden scene. It was Connecticut. I reached for the remote and turned it up.

"We're here in Connecticut, a few miles from New Haven where state troopers are investigating the remains of two charred bodies in this truck behind me," the female reporter broadcasted. *"As you can see, the area has been confined, as state troopers investigate the remains of what seems to be of a man and a woman burned alive in the wooded area. Now police believe that the couple may have been dead for a little over two weeks, and were found bound to the seats of the vehicle. They have not been identified yet, and a full investigation is underway."*

I was surprised it took that long to find Tiny and his girl. Jazmin stopped sucking me off, as she looked at the TV and then at me and asked, "Everything cool, baby?"

"Ah… Yeah. Ugh… Oh yeah don't fuckin' stop now," I said.

I continued to watch the news while Jazmin kept doing deep-throat. The police finding the bodies didn't bother me none. I wanted them to be found. Jazmin was sucking my dick good, but I wanted to know if they had any more information. The police were left without clues. I knew soon, that the streets would find out that it was Tiny and then word would get around, and Demetrius would know I ain't the one to fuck with.

Fall was on its way. That meant school was starting soon. And meth was being demanded everywhere on the campus and even in high school as athletes used the stuff to get pumped up before a game. Scholars used the stuff to stay up for studying and working. I was the king of Queens, and on my way to becoming the king of New York.

Word on the streets was that the remains found up in Connecticut belonged to Tiny and his baby mama. Both bodies were so badly burned and decomposed that it took medical examiners and state troopers days to identify the bodies. They ran the partial plate on the tuck and then neighbors pieced together what cops needed to hear—that a young couple had been missing for days.

Of course the speculations of his death were pointed to my crew, but no one tried to come against me. I had a few visits from some detectives about the homicide. They came around asking me questions about the murders. There was no hard evidence against me. So everyone speculated but they couldn't do a damn thing about it. I was sitting in the back office on the phone with Jazmin when Biscuit walked in.

"Yo, Mega…you got company," he said.

"Who?"

Before anything else was said, two plain clothes detectives walked into my back office without any permission. They walked in on me like they owned the joint. One was puffing on a cigar and glared at me like he dared me to ask him to put it out. They both were black, tall, clad in dark suits, and one wore a derby over his baldhead. I was familiar with the both of them, this wasn't the first time they came through harassing.

"Omega, how's my favorite thug doing this Friday night?" detective Grey asked nonchalantly. He was thin, with dark even skin, a thick mustache, and failing hair.

"Fuck y'all want!"

"Damn nigga, is that anyway to treat old friends," his partner Howard said. He was the same height as his partner, but was clean-shaven, and looked like he could be a pimp.

"Baby, let me call you back. I gotta handle something," I told Jazmin over the phone.

"Yeah, call that bitch back. You and I, we need to talk," detective Grey said.

"City needs to pay y'all more, and then maybe both of y'all wouldn't be such dicks. That's why y'all coming into my office tryin' to look hard, tryin' to look for some pussy to fuck. Well detectives, I ain't the one you need to try and fuck," I said eyeing both detectives coolly.

"You a smart-ass ain't you Omega?" Howard chided.

"Yeah he is, tryin' to be like his older brother," Grey stated. "You know I was the one that locked up his older brother... Rahmel right? And you know, I'm itching to put you behind bars."

"Y'all ain't got shit on me, so what's the point."

"Point is," Howard began, taking a seat on my desk, "we know what you're about. We know that you had something to do with Tiny's death. We know you're the one responsible for bringing meth into this community. You're a drug dealer, Omega... Getting rich off of other people misery. How do you live with yourself?"

"In my half a million dollar home, far away from you inner city pricks," I replied sarcastically.

"Nigga, you respect my partner, or I swear, I'll break your fuckin' legs right here in this office," Grey threatened.

I glared at Grey as he continued to puff on the fuckin' cigar, blowing smoke in my direction.

"Look here, you heartless muthafucka, I have a daughter, and a son, fifteen and seventeen and if anyone of my kids get hooked on anything you're pushing in these streets, mark my words, I will personally come back here and fuck you up before I shoot you down," Grey warned.

"Just teach your kids to 'Just say no'."

"You think I'm joking," Grey shouted, coming at me heatedly, but his partner held him back, a smart idea for the both of them.

Hearing the disturbance, Biscuit walked into my office, not fearing police. He glared at both men, itching to shoot them both down without having a second thought in his head.

"You think your little teenage body guard is going to have your back when the NYPD comes swarming down on your bitch ass?" Howard exclaimed.

"He's just being a witness right now, in case I need to bring up a lawsuit against y'all," I informed, mocking them.

"Listen here, you little shit face, one day, you're gonna fuck up and when you do, I'll be there with the Vaseline and put you where your brother is. You can't win, we will. When it's time to bring you down, I'll make sure you hit the concrete face first, maybe break something. Enjoy it for now, because sooner or later, everything comes to an end," detective Grey stated.

"Y'all done? I gotta get back to business," I said.

Both men gave me one hard stare and then casually walked out my office. I wasn't scared.

"What the fuck they wanted?" Biscuit asked.

"They're just bored, that's all."

"Fo' real, Mega, I can fuckin' give them something for their boredom," Biscuit mocked.

I smiled, admiring his heart. He truly didn't give a fuck.

"Nah, we good for now. Let them do their job, and I'll do mines," I said to him.

The night wore on and it seemed like everyone wanted a piece of beef with me. I was counting money in the office when the phone rang. I told Biscuit to get it. He picked up as I placed several hundred bills in the money counter.

"Mega, it's for you... That faggot-ass Demetrius," Biscuit informed, tossing me the phone.

I knew he would be calling soon. I put the phone to my ear and exclaimed, "What the fuck you want?"

"Yuh murder mi fuckin' cousin like that... Yuh blood-claat dead, mon, mi comin' fi yuh head... Yuh take mi fi joke?"

"Nigga, I told you, get in my way, and I'll put you the fuck down like a stray dog," I quickly retorted.

"Yuh dead... Yuh family dead!"

"Nigga, check this... Suck my muthafuckin' dick and get the fuck off my phone!" I shouted. "I ain't got time for games, you fuckin' faggot!"

I hung up, not giving a fuck. He wanted a war, I had the guns, and I had soldiers who would go all out.

A week later, Biscuit called me up and said that two of our meth labs had been hit and set on fire. I was furious. I lost four men in the blaze and now cops were investigating. I knew Demetrius had a hand in this.

I arranged a meeting with all my street enforcers and lieutenants to set up a strategy to get at this nigga before he fucked up my stores. Demetrius was unpredictable and could be at any place at anytime. According to my lieutenants, his boy, Jagged, had a familiar spot he liked to attend on a regular basis. We had to go through Jagged to get at Demetrius. The hit was given the green light. It'd be only be a matter of time. Greasy and I was rising to the top and there was not a damn thing stopping that.

That night, Greasy and I celebrated our success over booze, pussy, and watching Menace II Society on my 60" LCD flat screen. We had Judy and her partner Ivory keeping us company. We had them cop-bitches butt-ass naked, high as an antennae, and running around my spot acting the fool, sucking and fucking. Judy's titties were in my face and I finger-fucked her. Greasy was getting his dome bronzed by Ivory.

"We doin' it, Mega... This the life right here, money, pussy, power, and being untouchable," Greasy laughed with a glass of Cristal swirling in his hand and smiling.

"For all our hard work and for continue success... Salu my nigga," I toasted.

"I'm sorry about Soul, Greasy. He should be in this room right now, gettin' paper like you and me. You know that nigga is hard-headed," I said.

"Yo, Soul's like a rock. He can hold his own. Ooh yeah, girl... Greasy ain't sweating, Mega."

"I got him a good lawyer, Greasy. He'll be ahight."

Greasy nodded, focusing his attention on Ivory. "Bitch, you look so much better being out of that pig skin," he laughed.

"I do, huh," Ivory replied, pressing up against my boy, stroking his dick and kissing him passionately.

"Yeah, let Greasy get into all that pork chops."

Judy smiled over at them and then took another hit of crystal meth up her nostril.

"Fuck me, Omega. I want you inside of me now and handle your business like a stallion."

Meth made her go crazy sexually. She loved to fuck and I wasn't complaining. Her pussy felt so much better when she got high. It was no limits with her. She took it in the ass, down her throat, between her tits; she didn't care where the dick went. Judy took me by my hand and led me to the steaming ready Jacuzzi upstairs.

"Greasy, I'll see you tomorrow morning, my nigga," I said, following Judy's round ass up the steps.

It was early Thursday morning when I got the call. Biscuit was on the other end and told me I needed to come down to Greasy's place in Elmont. I knew what to expect, it wasn't a shock for me, this was the game, and this was life. You gonna lose niggas on your way to the top. But Greasy was like a brother to me. I put my emotions to the side and drove the hour-long ride to his home.

Police wasn't called to his place yet. I needed to see for myself. Biscuit and Monk met me when I arrived. Greasy's girl found the body and had called Biscuit.

"Shit ain't lovely Mega, for ' real. They did Greasy sump'n awful. Fo' real, fo' real," Biscuit said.

"Where she found him?" I asked.

"In the basement," Biscuit said. "They put in some work on him before they killed him."

I followed my crew into the home and walked down into the basement. The cellar was dimmed and still and I smelled death as I approached his carcass. I stood silently and observed Greasy's lifeless body swinging from the ceiling.

"Damn!" I uttered, hating what I was seeing.

He was naked, with a chain around his neck, cut the fuck up being butchered down the middle. His genitals was stuffed in his mouth and left a Colombian bowtie on him. Slicing his neck opened and pulling his tongue through it was a mark of disrespect. His hands and feet were bonded.

"Bring him down!" I demanded. I couldn't see my nigga hanging and looking like that.

I didn't want to look weak so I held back my tears. They tortured and disrespected my dude. I knew Greasy lost his life cruelly for the family. Monk and Biscuit slowly removed the chain that was tightened around his neck and brought him down from his suffering. His girl was upstairs in tears; she discovered the body and was truly fucked up. There was nothing I could do now, except carry out some brutal revenge in his name. I stared down at Greasy, shaking my head. His death would not be in vain.

"What now, Mega?" Monk asked.

"Leave him there and report it," I instructed. "Monk you stay behind with his bitch till the police gets here." My cell phone rang. "Who…? Alexis, what you want bitch. I ain't got the time to talk to you right now…I ain't got time to talk about no damn photos either, bitch… You ain't send 'em. I know who did. So what's new, bitch?" I said, hanging up on the bitch.

That nigga Soul just lost a thoroughbred, family member, but I shoulder that lost too. Greasy was my fam. I didn't want to fucking talk trivial bullshit about photos with that bitch. I glanced at Biscuit and saw his veins ready to explode. He wasn't trying to shed no tears, real gangsters don't cry. He wanted to spill blood. The nigga Soul, was on that love-Jones shit. Right now if he was putting fear in these niggas hearts out here, this might not have gone down like this. I got to think everything through now. It was time to pay Jagged that visit of death, peel that nigga's cap back.

Several days later, we got word that Jagged was hanging out at his usual spot in Harlem, a low-key bar off 145th street. It was around midnight when we got the call about his whereabouts. The crew was at the bar twenty minutes later.

I stepped out, with Biscuit, Monk, Tank, Whistle and Groggy behind me. We were well armed and ready. Jagged was about to feel my wrath. Shortly after, our source came walking out the bar smiling at us. Her name was Jennie, a bartender in Harlem for years, but lived in Jamaica Queens. She was about her money.

"He's in there now, right?" I asked.

"Been sitting at the bar drinking for the past hour. But he's got company with him," she informed.

"How many?" I asked.

"One, trying to be subtle by the back entrance nursing a beer. He's wearing a black T-shirt, braids, and a thick goatee."

"Ahight, how many customers inside right now?" I asked.

"Just Jagged, his protection, and this old dude that always comes around. It doesn't start getting crowed in here until after one."

"You did good, baby girl," I said. I passed her an envelope filled with hundreds. She smiled and took the money.

"This is what I want you to do, I'm gonna call the bar, you pick up and tell that old nigga it's for him. Have him take the call in the back. Then you let a few of my boys in from the back exit and be cool about it," I instructed.

She nodded and walked away. I called the bar ten minutes after. It rang and she followed the plan. Jagged was getting sloppy having a one-man security when there was a war going on. He used his reputation and size to intimidate his enemies and rival crews. I wasn't the one to fuck with and didn't give a damn about his rep.

Monk, Tank and Whistle went around the back, while Groggy, Biscuit and I planned on entering from the front entrance. I waited for a short moment and then entered the bar first. Jagged and his boy turned and saw me walking in and knew what time it was.

His security stood up rapidly, reaching for his weapon, but Monk crept up on him from the back and popped two in his head using the silencer dropping him dead. I had my gun trained on Jagged's head and ordered him not to move.

"What yuh gwine do wit' that? Yuh know yuh shouldn't point that shit at me."

His voice showed no signs of fear even though he was outgunned and outnumbered.

"What the fuck you say, nigga?"

"If yuh know what's best, yuh and yuh blood claat boys will turn around and walk out dat bumbo claat door and mi try and act like yuh didn't come in here and disrespect dis place of business like dis."

"You put your hands on Greasy, you fat-ass bastard?"

"We told yuh, behave and continue suckin' on our tits, and life fi yuh would be good. But yuh leave da nest, play house on ya own, and make up yuh own rules. Yuh misbehave and yuh get spanked, young blood."

I knew he was the one responsible for doing Greasy like that. It had his signature of brutality. Jagged was heartless, he tortured niggas for fun, and just thinking about what he did to Greasy had me fuming.

It took everything that I had in me, not to pull the trigger at that moment, because I wanted information on Demetrius. And I knew he had the goods. Jagged was ol' school, and like Greasy, he was loyal to Demetrius. It would be a bitch to get him to talk.

"Mi admire yuh heart, but what yuh came here for, it won' happen, not from mi or any of mi people—"

Before he could say anything else, I shot him, but he didn't go down.

"Bombo claat!" he shouted, charging me.

I let off on him again, but he didn't fall. He was fast and rushed at me. Knocking Biscuit and me down, the gun fell. My goons charged at him, but he became a raging bull and dropped two of my men to the floor like they were kids.

"Yuh blood claat batty-boy, mi come fi yuh and kill yuh wit' mi own two hands," Jagged said in a rage.

I got up and started punching him, but even with two upper gunshot wounds in his torso, he struggled with us. I jumped on his back trying to choke him, but he moved back quickly, smashing me against a mirror wall. It shattered I dropped and suffered a few cuts. Blood was everywhere. Jagged wasn't going out easily.

"Mi a Jamaican Don. Yuh a fuckin' batty boy. Mi don't fall, mi kill yuh hear? Mi gwine kill yuh all!" he shouted.

This nigga had to be on PCP, he was like an ox. Monk and Whistle went at him striking him across the back with a chair, but he turned and grabbed Monk viciously and snapped his neck like it was a twig. With Monk down, Whistle charged for Jagged and was immediately thrown across the bar like a rag doll.

"What the fuck!" I shouted.

Biscuit pulled out a huge blade and thrust at him, plunging the blade into Jagged's back. Jagged jerked forward and finally stumbled, but he didn't fall.

"Fuck yuh!" Jagged shouted, feeling the wounds slowing him down.

He tried to rush Biscuit with the knife still rooted in his back, but was sluggish and fell helplessly against the bar, clutching the railing for some dire support and stumbled against the barstools. I stood up and went for my gun.

"Omega, yuh will fall... Yuh fuckin' batty boy," Jagged said. "The Jamaican mafia will come fi yuh."

Biscuit walked up to the now weak and fading Jagged and began plunging the knife into his neck repeatedly. He must have hit an artery, because blood started gushing out like a fountain. Jagged clutched his neck desperately, trying to stop the uncontrollable blood flow spewing from his gash, but too much was spilling and he collapsed down on the floor, his breathing becoming sparse. I stood there and watched him die slow.

"That's for Greasy, you fuckin' bitch!" I said spitting on him.

Moments later he was dead. Jennie stood behind the bar frozen and with her eyes wide. She had blood on her.

"Yo, lock that fuckin' door, Jennie," I ordered.

She nodded, but she didn't look right in her mind. What she witnessed fucked her up. She locked the door and stood by it looking panicky.

"Jennie, you gonna be okay?" I asked.

She nodded. We had to clean up. I had blood on me, and so did

Biscuit, and Whistle. I looked at Monk's lifeless body crumpled to the floor and uttered, "Fuck!" We couldn't step out this bar looking like we just came from a feeding frenzy. Jennie showed us where we could clean up in a bathroom downstairs. I went first followed by the rest of my crew.

We had to get rid of Jagged and his bodyguard's bodies. There was one way of cleaning this shit up without leaving any evidence behind, burn down the bar with the bodies. Jennie thought I was crazy. Groggy and Whistle went to the truck to get the kerosene while Biscuit and I tried to set it up. Jennie was quietly sitting on one of the barstools and looked in a deep trance.

When Groggy came back with the kerosene we started dowsing the two bodies first, and then the rest of the bar. Biscuit and I held each other's gaze for a moment, thinking the same thing. He pulled out his gun, put it to Jennie's temple squeezing off three shots. We dowsed her, set the bodies on fire and the bar and exited the back where Whistle was waiting in the truck. The bar went up in flames.

I took Greasy's death personal and now one of the men responsible for his gruesome death was burning in hell. I would wear the crown and become the king of New York soon. I was gonna own this town through drugs and music. Kemistry was my young protégé on the rise and I would have money coming at me in every direction. I'd be Scar Face and Diddy rolled in one, having money, power, and respect. No one would stop me now.

27

Life's challenges shouldn't paralyze you.
They're to help you discover who you are...

Omar

They say everything occurs in three's. I truly believe that this was true and here was how the tri-factual manifested itself in my life. First, there was my re-incarceration after only being out for a little over five months. Next I get the news that Greasy was dead, the news really fucked me up. Thirdly, I was in Rikers' Island for the past three weeks. With my parole violation looming, I was looking at least eighteen months upstate.

I was fucked. I felt that I let everyone down, my wife, my unborn, and the folks who supported me. I thought about Rahmel and his struggles. I was just another statistic, a Black man returning to prison after a parole violation.

My emotions had taken over, and I did a very dumb thing, carrying out actions without thinking of the consequences. Now my freedom, maybe my marriage and witnessing the birth of my first-born were the privileges I had lost.

For the first time in a while, I felt alone and afraid. I feared the unknown, and losing everything that I had worked to attain. I sat in my cold jail cell, feeling the world go still, isolated and ugly. It was hard to remain positive when I was surrounded by so much negativity—the guards, the inmates, the bars, the tainted minds of men that wanted to see harm done. The system was bearing down on me with it laws and sentences.

I was alone in a cell when the C.O announced that I had a visitor. I stood up, clad in my gray jumpsuit, with the acronym **D.O.C.** imprinted in black on my back. I now belonged to them.

I followed the guard through the corridor, muting the shouts from numerous inmates caged behind bars. We were like wild animals in a zoo and I was used to this type of environment, I shouldn't be. I was on my way to becoming a family man, but now I was inmate number *00B46599*, in for violation of parole, plus other numerous charges.

An hour later, I walked into the sizeable visitor's room. I knew who had come to see me. I never thought that we would be seeing each other like this again, with me confined and restrained. There was a slight smile when I saw America seated by herself, looking angelic, beautiful, and was about to become the mother of my child in about a month.

She was wearing a loosely fitted gray Sean John sweat suit, with her hair styled into a long ponytail. She was dressed so simple, but still in my eyes she looked so radiant. She looked up at me and smiled. It was a smile of wonder and doubt. I saw it in her eyes. She came to me with news, good or bad, but she had something to say to me.

I thought of my child and our marriage, and couldn't help but wonder if it could still last while I did a second stint behind bars. I walked casually to America and she stood embracing me in a loving hug. Her belly had grown bigger and my child was maturing in her.

"I missed you," I said affectionately with a warm smile to match.

I tried to give her a kiss, but she pulled away. That hurt me. I was still her husband, but she pulled away from my kiss, something she never did.

"We need to talk," she said glumly.

We both took our seats across from each other, with a small synthetic table positioned between us. She held my hands in hers and gave me eye contact.

"Everything okay?" I asked.

A heavy sigh escaped her lips, and before she went on with anything else, she asked, "How are you holding up in here?"

"Trying to remain positive about things, but it's hard. I miss you America, and I know I fucked up. I hate myself for that. That night I left you I just lost it. I'm sorry about the pictures, my past, and what I put you through. But you know, I'm still trying and I love you, baby and I want us to be together."

"Omar, please, before I let you go on, there's something you need to know," she said.

I stared at her, my heart racing and my nerves on the edge.

"I can't do this with you anymore, Omar. I want a divorce," she said.

"A divorce…?" I shouted.

"Yes, Omar I tried with you, but if this is where you're gonna keep ending up, I just can't do it anymore. I just can't, Omar," she said gravely.

"America, it ain't gotta be like this. I've made a mistake. I fucked up. I deserve a second chance."

"I gave you many chances, Omar. I've stuck it out with you since the beginning, and you know it. But it's not fair for me and your son to be put through this endlessly," she said.

"My son…?"

"Yes, I'm having a boy," she informed me.

I knew it. I smiled inwardly thinking about my unborn son, but then the news of her wanting to divorce me crushed me.

"I took the sonogram and the doctor confirmed it."

"America, can't you see that I've changed. I just made one simple mistake and it now it's costing me my family, my freedom, and my marriage."

"Have you Omar or should I call you Soul. You changed Soul?" she replied with some doubt in her voice.

"Yes indeed. You've watched the change. I'm not trying to go back to my ol' ways. I'm trying to build a family the right way."

"Oh really Omar. You wouldn't lie to me about anything would you?"

"America, why would I lie, boo? You mean everything to me… All this was just some ol' bullshit."

"You wouldn't lie huh, Soul?"

"I'm telling you boo, I just got caught up in some bull—"

"Then tell me why I found fifteen thousand in cash, a pound of marijuana, and a loaded gun hidden in my apartment. Is it your shit, Omar?"

Damn, I thought. That was so stupid, stupid, fucking stupid of me. I cursed myself, it was mine, all mine. The gun I held from the shootout, knowing that I should have gotten rid of it. And the money and drugs, I couldn't explain to her. She caught me dirty.

"Where did you find it?" I asked.

"In my closet, under a lose floorboard. How could you, Omar? How can you just sit there and lie to me about everything. I trusted you and you just did me wrong. I told you, please don't put me through that hell again," she said.

Tears started trickling down her face as she looked at me with hurt in her eyes.

"I need a fresh start," she continued. "And if divorcing you and moving on can do that for me, then so be it. I will always love you and you will always be the father of my son. I won't keep you out of his life. I promise you that. But our marriage, the relationship we had together, it's dissolved and at this point in our life, there's no more mending. You just have to go on with your life."

I couldn't believe what I was hearing. I tried to hold back my emotions, and be strong despite my situation. Her words punctured something in me. How the fuck did it get to this point? I asked myself. I remember several months ago, the look on America's face when I stepped out of prison after four years, and the passion and love she showed me was priceless.

True hearts, it seemed like we would remain together forever. But now, the look and expression she gave and showed me, felt distant. This was a new woman seated in front of me. In my mind, I kept thinking, how did all this transpire? How did I let it get to this point between us?

She was the only woman that I truly loved. The thought of losing her was making me go crazy. I released my hands from hers before continuing.

"America, be for real wit' me, are you seeing somebody else?"

"Not right now, but to be honest, there is someone who has been looking out for me and has been there for me. I'm thinking about giving him a chance."

My blood was boiling. I hated to hear it, but in my position what could I do. I let her down once again. Of course this time around she was going to do her.

"We had our chance, Omar, now I feel it's time for me to move on and see what else is out there for me," she added.

I had no words for this. My heart pained and my mind was spinning too fast.

"I'll always love you, Omar. Be safe in here, and when you get out, remember that you still have a future for yourself and your son," she said, sounding like a counselor. She became teary eyed and held onto my hand, gazing into my pained soul, and said, "Give me this divorce, please. If you truly love me, let me break free and start over. And if we are meant to be in the future, then God will bring us together again. But for now, I can't do it with you anymore. I need for you to change and be a different man for our son and for yourself. For your, baby."

I couldn't hold back my tears anymore, and a river started flowing down my face. It upset me to look at her and know we wouldn't be together anymore and to see her move to another man was just unthinkable. I've been in her life for almost ten years and now it felt like a new chapter was opening up for the both of us. We were on different pages.

"Whatever, America, go ahead and do you. I didn't expect for you to wait for me after the shit I done put you through again. But I'm sorry, and I still do believe in us. And I will get my life right, baby. I promise you that, for our son and myself. I will get it right and the next time I walk out of this place, it will be for the last time."

"Thank you. I gotta go now; Kendal is waiting for me outside," she halfheartedly said.

Hearing her say his name, made my heart sink, I was drowning in my sorrow. I fucked up and this nigga came off the sideline into my starting position. I never felt so helpless in my life. America stood and so did I. We embraced and hugged each other for a long time. Then she gave me a kiss on my lips with tears streaming down her face and said to me, "Take care of yourself."

After that, I sat back down and the C.O. escorted her to the door. But before her exit, she turned to look at me with this sudden afterthought and our eyes studied each other and I still saw some deep-rooted compassion in her eyes for me. I knew our love was still there. I knew and felt that America still had that burning love in her heart for me. I nodded.

America disappeared behind the thick steal door and I started to reminisce about all the good times we had together. I shed a few more tears and then got myself together and was soon escorted back into lockup.

Two months later I was back upstate in Franklin Correctional facility in Malone, New York. It hurt me to be there again, but that was life. I fucked up, but I wanted to get it right this time. And with a son on a way, I had something to look forward to. It was motivation to raise my child right, so he won't have to go through what I went through in life. I wanted to be the father that my father wanted to be to me before he died of cancer.

28

The definition of a strong woman or man is someone who can weather many storms.

Without loss of goodness
in his or her character...

America

I walked out the visitor's room in tears, and I was so emotional, I almost fainted. Omar was my lover for life and I loved him still, but I couldn't bear putting myself through another incarceration. My heart and spirit told me to move on with my life. We needed to go our different ways.

Kendal came through for me. He was there for it all. I had his full support. He had called me one night to apologize for his actions. I broke down over the phone to him. I told him that I was sorry for misguiding him and what had happened between us. He explained to me that he wasn't sorry for the way he cared and felt about me, and confessed his love for me again.

I invited him over that night and he came knocking on my door one hour later. And over some Chinese food and a few glasses of wine, we talked almost all night and really got to know each other. Kendal was definitely a sweetheart and soon one thing led to another and we were together, but taking it one day at a time.

My wounds were still fresh and he understood my pain. He deserved a chance with me, and I couldn't keep my feelings for my Omar forever. It was strange having a new man in my life, but sometimes we have to play the cards we were dealt.

February 28th I gave birth to my son at three in the morning in Jamaica hospital. He was seven pounds and ten ounces. I named him Kahlil Omar Stanfield.

Kendal was right by my side holding my hand, giving me encouragement when I gave birth. He was so proud that you thought he was the father, and some of the nurses and doctors actually thought that he was. They congratulated him and welcomed him to fatherhood. Kendal ate it up.

Omar found out about the birth of his son that same week. He called me collect and I informed him about the birth. I told him the name I'd chosen, the weight and who he resembled. I could picture him smiling. I promised to send him a few pictures of Kahlil and he couldn't wait to see them.

Deep inside, I was upset that Omar wasn't there personally to witness his son's birth. He had a few months left upstate before he would be released again, and everyday I prayed for him, my son, and my new boyfriend. I prayed for everlasting life and happiness for all of us.

For the first time, with Kendal and my son around, I felt like a family. My music career was taking off. I was signed to an independent label and working on my first album, with the help of Kendal.

My life finally seemed to be in order and moving in the right direction. My divorce from Omar was finalized a few weeks before Christmas and we both were cool and talked from time to time.

I didn't know what the future held for me, but I became a born again Christian. I believed that everything in life happens for a reason. I wanted to live life right and do the things I loved doing, which was music, raising my son to be a respectable man, having a family and being loved—minus all the drama.

29

Life is too short to wake up with regrets.
Love those who treat you right.
Forget the ones who don't.

/ **Omar**

I was ecstatic about the birth of my son, Kahlil Omar. But saddened that I couldn't be there to see him born. I promised him that enough was enough and I was gonna change my ways for him.

I had a few months left on my bid and I felt blessed because I knew that I was getting out again and had a second chance. The extra charges against me were dropped and I was serving out the rest of my previous time.

Rahmel was, of course, upset to see me returned to lockup. He preached to me and said, sometimes a righteous man will fall many of times before he is able to stand on his own.

"A baby," he said. "Before they're able to stand tall and walk, they'll stumble and fall many of times before they are able to get it right and walk on their own without any support. You stumbled and fell a few times, but Soul, you will get your life right. Believe me, you will get it right. Just dust off the mistakes and pain, and keep it moving. Keep it moving my brother and think of your son, this is not the end for you, it's only the beginning for us, Soul... Only the beginning."

And he was right, I had to close one chapter of my life and open another. This was definitely not the end for me, only a minor set back in my life. I had to prepare myself for bigger things to come.

I sat on my cot and began writing America and my son a poem. I wanted to write them something meaningful and uplifting, and even though we were now divorced and my son was only a few months old, I wanted them to understand my journey— our journey.

Our Journey

We came a long way baby, and just to let you know that our journey is still not at an end. The miles that we will travel, I know our road will never end. Our life together has just begun, so I'm holding on to you for an eternity. Now that we're brought in this world a life, a part of our love, a child that the Lord blessed us from above. So every night I pray, asking him for guidance and protection, everlasting love and affection, let there be endless love past

Love & Gangsta

on from generation to generation.

So free us from wickedness and deception, our heavenly Father let us unite, create, and let us be born into a new nation. Give us all the strength in our hearts and let us all be stronger in our souls, and together, I know that my people will grow. The love will always flow. For faith will bring us unity and much health. That faith in thy self will bring a better change in this world today. That faith in thy self will create a better way for our younger generation someday. That faith in thy self will stop us from hating and envying each other, slaying negative thoughts toward each other.

Let my people know that we are all successful in different ways, that the Lord skilled us in many ways. Lets all care for each other and stop disrespecting and criticizing one another, being against each other will get us nowhere among each other. Praises to my newborn baby boy, let him know I will always be there for him till my dying day. And when I rest my spirit will be at his best. Bringing unequivocal thoughts into my world the day you were born. I rest my old ways and prepare for better days. Be prepared for the love in me. This is our journey, boo. Making right, just for the love of the both of you—mother and child. This is our journey, only the beginning….

To be continued...

Believe everything happens for a reason.
If you get a chance, take it. If it changes your
life, let it. Nobody said it would be easy
They just promised it would it be worth it

ERICK S GRAY

TOMORROW...

Tomorrow... how will I see my tomorrow, without me getting abstracted from the past? Man, I wish it was a joke, but I ain't in the mood to laugh. When I done see the death, seen the pain, seen the sorrow and mothers tremble from the grief that grabs them tight like a cold winter night. You can't cover that shit with no coat, cuz is seeps within, runs thick through their veins as they watch their child to lay….deceased to the gunplay or some other wicked way, and I keep thinkin' about my last days, keep thinkin' about my brothers last days, keep thinkin' about my man that was gunned down standing right next to me on that cold chillin' day. I done watched my pops bury three, so my family embrace close to me, cuz I'm like one of the last of his seeds—think if I cut myself will I'll bleed just as deep…yo I think about the love and I consider about the hate. I think about my life and I reflect on them unjust days. I say to myself, *what if?* When they killed my man and I pistol whipped one from inches from his life…I wanted to take it further and just squeeze, say fuck it—let him bleed. I had to watch his grandmother weep and cry out *"Oh Lord, why He"*….that hurt me, yo…watching a friend for fifteen years being buried so deep and his family looking so stricken with grief. Some nights I sit alone and think of murder one, slump back in a seat with my chest heaving with grieve, done dried my umpteenth tear, got the gun cocked and feeling such an anger presiding over me…feeling this cold freezing me in such a atrocious way, sayin' fuck this book shit, I'm ready to just kill shit…cuz common sense and humanity done been left me.

Tomorrow... how will I see my tomorrow with my mind enduring from thoughts of a bothered past? Yo I wish I could bring 'em all back—from brother to brother, Vincent, Corey, Keith…I write this verse, because I hate when the agony overcomes me, tryin' to separate me from a thing call sanity, there been plenty of nights when I done buckled down on my knees, eyes watery with both fear and care, cuz I admit, I was scared, and try to imagine being free from the adversity that swells through me, gotta reach for the heavens and grab back that sanity, man I remember I used to call out for Christ and cry for the heaven to make it better for me—I lost one in the prison Attica the day before his release, and the first brother perished in a fire and the next I found dead in his sleep. I called out for my moms and watched her go wild, clutching for her dead son, crying out, *"No, not my baby, no…"* It took three to hold her back, cuz it hurts to see a mother curved over her baby's casket, screaming out *"Lord, please bring him back to me!"* I couldn't understand it, *why this family*? I knew that death doesn't discriminate…it even came for my younger cousin at the age of fifteen, shot down three times by gang violence on Christmas Eve…damn, I thought, why the devil want to see my family fall, tryin to see us gravel and crawl. But I stood tall, and watched them bury Pashad the day after I was born and then four months later, we put his mother to rest. She was just too heartbroken over her son's violent death.

Tomorrow... there were times when I never had any thoughts of tomorrow, lived for right now, cuz I walked around untouchable and ran with the best of them, wilding and fighting like the rest of 'em...I remember that December night when we put four cops in distressed, cuz they rolled up on our block, disrespected and put my right hand in cuffs. I was only nineteen with a smirk, as we threatened four officers that we surrounded locked in their wagon and had screaming out that 10-13...tried to live life like a rush, ran through women and money faster than Carl Lewis. Yo I thought who could touch me, at age twenty-one I was sitting on fifty to eighty thousand cash, nobody couldn't say shit to me. My walk said P.I.M.P, and my mouth ran slick. Yeah I thought about God, but had no time for Christ, I was the one running my life, I even brought a gun to school when I just only fifteen...I had to ask myself, why my dude snitched on me, and had me running from security, but it was cool, cuz I still did me.

Tomorrow... shit, the way my timeline went, man I knew one day my mother was goin' to bury me, went to my first strip club at thirteen, and got stabbed at fourteen, almost got caught with that .45 at fifteen...at sixteen, I got caught up in a hold up on the green line where niggahs ran up on the bus and popped off shots, and takin' that fast buck...and my fingers were quick, cuz I used to steal, just walk in the store, never hesitate...shoplifting should be subtle and quick, and if the manager try to flip, you just punch him in the mouth and dip. I had guns pushed in my face, been shot at and me and my dudes done jumped on niggahs faces, even went through a high speed chase on one chill Halloween night. I done seen thugs cry, shots fly, and cops lie...sat through court cases and got pushed through central bookings, even got a few cousins on the run...I remember back then, it was hard for me to pray, man faith, that shit seemed so far away cuz I felt that God was just so many miles away from me.

Tomorrow... I used to be scared of tomorrow and wanted to live back on yesterday, cuz I know what happened yesterday, wanted to rewind time and kill that line... cuz I felt my family done been through enough .I would shake from the pains and cry when there were so many rainy days and wondered when that sun gonna come our way. Who could break down on shit like that... the shit we done been through, but kept my grief concealed and ask myself what kind of world we live in when my niece at sixteen finds her moms murdered, chain around her neck and swinging from a basement pipe, cops suspected drugs or conspiracy...no teen should witness any shit like that, no family should experience evil like that...and then see my aunt murdered by the man she gave birth too...caught him creeping through her purse on a late night craving for cash for that devil's candy, the confrontation left my aunt dead with multiple blunt force trauma from a hammer to her head...and I ask God how can I forgive my cousin for that....an animal that committed such a heinous act. I say *Fuck him* and let that bastard rot where he at....

Tomorrow... so much to say about tomorrow...where will I be tomorrow? I done love and lust...got drunk and fucked...I was wild like that, me and my niggahs got bugged like traps, ran through women like cash...had a bitch every different day of the week... even got caught with an STD, woke up that sunny morning to go pee and it felt like hell was burning between my knees, pain like that will make any man collapse down to his knees, make you cry out, *"Oh God please!"*...shit, lost count of how many times I got checked for HIV, doc would tell me you all clear, and then my dumb ass would go back out and do the same shit all over again it....Yeah, I protected myself, slide that latex back...but in the end, I know only abstinence or marital it's the only two best ways to protect your health.

Tomorrow... sometimes I frown on tomorrow...my story is far from fiction, me and my family we done been through it all...and I'm learning day by day, when I get stressed or really fuckin' upset, I'm able to suppress my rage by pressing my thoughts, emotions and attitudes down on sheet with the pen...for me, literature and writing is healing within. I say to myself, what made me write this letter and express my pain, hurt, deaths and struggles to all y'all...I could never really talk about it, so say, let me just write about it...had to let y'all know what was going on with me....and why this is me. I'm changing and growing, becoming more educated and more knowing and I try to read a verse before I spit a curse. I love all y'all and say keep God close. I learned to be quick to forgive and use hard times to develop a better stepping stone in you—hard times should produce better results in you.

Tomorrow... I look forward to tomorrow...cuz thinkin of yesterday keeps me humble, and lookin' forward to a bright, better and more productive future keeps me going, along with my daughter being born. I now look forward for tomorrow...day by day, I watch her grow, watch us grow...tomorrow y'all....let's look toward tomorrow... OBAMA 2008....

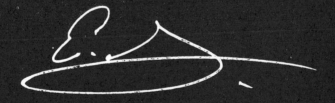

WHERE
HIP-HOP
LITERATURE
BEGINS...

**AUGUSTUS
PUBLISHING**

Augustus Publishing was created to unify minds with
entertaining, hard-hitting tales from a hood near you.
Hip Hop literature interprets contemporary times and
connects to readers through shared language, culture
and artistic expression. From street tales and erotica to
coming-of age sagas, our stories are endearing, filled
with drama, imagination and laced with a Hip Hop steez.

GHETTO GIRLS IV
Young Luv
ESSENCE BESTSELLING AUTHOR
ANTHONY WHYTE

...etto Girls IV Young Luv
.95 // 9780979281662

Ghetto Girls
$14.95 // 0975945319

Ghetto Girls Too
$14.95 // 0975945300

Ghetto Girls 3 Soo Hood
$14.95 // 0975945351

THE BEST OF THE STREET CHRONICLES TODAY, THE **GHETTO GIRLS SERIES** IS A WONDERFULLY HYPNOTIC ADVENTURE THAT DELVES INTO THE CONVOLUTED MINDS OF CRIMINALS AND THE DARK WORLD OF POLICE CORRUPTION. YET, THERE IS SOMETHING THRILLING AND SURPRISINGLY TENDER ABOUT THIS ONGOING YOUNG-ADULT SAGA FILLED WITH MAD FLAVA.

Love and a Gangsta
author // **ERICK S GRAY**

This explosive sequel to **Crave All Lose All**. Soul and America were together ten years 'til Soul's incarceration for drugs. Faithfully, she waited four years for his return. Once home they find life ain't so easy anymore. America believes in holding her man down and expects Soul to be as committed. His lust for fast money rears its ugly head at the same time America's music career takes off. From shootouts, to hustling and thugging life, Soul and his man, Omega, have done it. Omega is on the come-up in the drug-game of South Jamaica, Queens. Using ties to a Mexican drug cartel, Omega has Queens in his grip. His older brother, Rahmel, was Soul's cellmate in an upstate prison. Rahmel, a man of God, tries to counsel Soul. Omega introduces New York to crystal meth. Misery loves company and on the road to the riches and spoils of the game, Omega wants the only man he can trust, Soul, with him. Love between Soul and America is tested by an unforgivable greed that leads quickly to deception and murder.

$14.95 // 9780979281648

A POWERFUL UNFORGIVING STORY
CREATED BY HIP HOP LITERATURE'S BESTSELLING AUTHORS

THIS THREE-VOLUME KILLER STORY FEATURING FOREWORDS FROM
SHANNON HOLMES, K'WAN & TREASURE BLUE

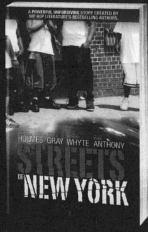  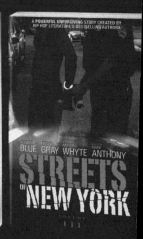

Streets of New York vol. 1
$14.95 // 9780979281679

Streets of New York vol. 2
$14.95 // 9780979281662

Streets of New York vol. 3
$14.95 // 9780979281662

AN EXCITING, ENCHANTING... A FUNNY, THRILLING AND EXHILARATING
RIDE THROUGH THE ROUGH NEIGHBORHOODS OF THE GRITTY CITY. THE MOST FUN YOU
CAN LEGALLY HAVE WITHOUT ACTUALLY LIVING ON THE STREETS OF NEW YORK. READ
THE STORY FROM HIP HOP LITERATURE TOP AUTHORS:

ERICK S. GRAY, MARK ANTHONY & ANTHONY WHYTE

Lipstick Diaries Part 2
A Provocative Look into the Female Perspective
Foreword by **WAHIDA CLARK**

Lipstick Diaries II is the second coming together of some of the most
unique, talented female writers of Hip Hop Literature. Featuring a
feast of short stories from today's top authors. **Genieva Borne, Cam
Endy, Brooke Green, Kineisha Gayle, the queen of hip hop lit; Caro
McGill, Vanessa Martir, Princess Madison, Keisha Seignious**, and a
blistering foreword served up by the queen of thug love; Ms. **Wahida
Clark**. Lipstick Diaries II pulls no punches, there are no bars hold
leaves no metaphor unturned. The anthology delivers a knockout w
stories of pain and passion, love and virtue, profit and gain, ... all to
with flair from the women's perspective. Lipstick Diaries II is a
must-read for all.

$14.95 // 9780979281655

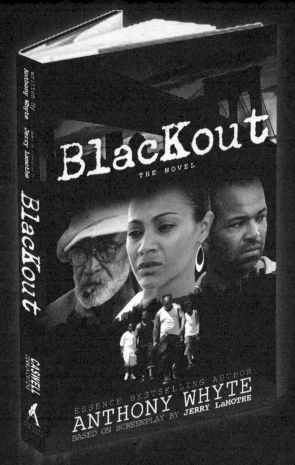

The lights went out
and the
mayhem began.

t's gritty in the city but hotter in Brooklyn where a small community
n east Flatbush must come to grips with its greatest threat, self-
estruction. August 14 and 15, 2003, the eastern section of the
nited States is crippled by a major shortage of electrical power,
he worst in US history. Blackout, the spellbinding novel is based on
he epic motion picture, directed by Jerry Lamothe. A thoroughly
veting story with delectable details of families caught in a harsh
hours of random violent acts, exploding in deadly conflict.
here's a message in everything… even the bullet. The author vividly
aces characters on the stage of life and like pieces on a chess-
ard, expertly moves them to a tumultuous end. Voila! Checkmate, a
terary triumph. Blackout is a masterpiece. This heart-stopping,
ge-turning drama is moving fast. Blackout is destined to become an
erican classic.

ASED ON SCREENPLAY BY **JERRY LaMOTHE**

spired by true events

US $14.95 CAN $20.95
ISBN 978-0-9820653-0-3

CASWELL
COMMUNICATIONS

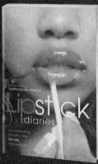